THE DARKEST HOUR

AMY CASE

Scripture is taken from the King James Version and the Christian Standard Version of the Bible.

ISBN   979-8-6161-8238-8

To Koisha, you are a true blessing from God.
My love is always with you.

"...weeping may endure for a night, but joy cometh in the morning."
~Psalm 30:5

"It is said that the darkest hour of the night comes just before the dawn."
~Thomas Fuller

CHAPTER 1

❦

*"Can a woman forget her nursing child, or lack
compassion for the child of her womb? Even if these
forget, yet I will not forget you."*
Isaiah 49:15

"Leah, waar kom je?" Abigail yelled as she
came rushing through the back door of the
Zook farmhouse.

Leah answered from the kitchen as she
heard the back screen door slam shut. "I'm right
here, Abigail Schrock. Why in all the world are
you yelling? Is everything gut?"

Half out of breath, Abigail replied. "It is
more than gut, for sure and for certain. I
practically ran all the way over here to tell you
that I have the most wunderbaar gut news for
you. Adam Beiler has asked many questions
concerning you. According to his sister-in-law,

Katie, he is for sure smitten with you. She has overheard him talking about you a few times now. She said Adam refuses to discuss it with her. But, she knows he wishes to court you." Abigail was out of breath as she tried to continue. "I'm telling you, Leah, it's true, for sure and for certain. Katie told me this herself. It turns out; Adam has loved you for many years. She can't understand the buwe at all. Katie has tried many times to get him to talk to you about his feelings. But he now refuses to discuss any of it with her."

Astounded, Leah took a deep breath before responding to the recent turn of events. "Ach Abigail, please tell me you are serious and not simply teasing me. Indeed, you are aware of my feelings for him. He used to ask Lyddie Fisher about me all the time. That was when we were much younger, of course. Over the past year, he hasn't shown much interest whatsoever. I figured what little attention he did give me was to help Aaron Stauffer get closer to me."

Abigail was known for always putting her hand on her hip when she was somewhat annoyed, and that moment was no different. Scolding Leah as if she was a child, "Leah Zook, I know how you feel and trust me when I say, I would never tease you with this! I may harass you about a lot of things, but I would never hurt your feelings about something which you have desired for so long now. I'm not Miriam Stoltzfus, you know."

Leah giggled. Whenever a conversation held a sour note, Miriam Stoltzfus' name was almost always a part of it. "Vergeef me, Abigail, you know

I do not think you are anything like Miriam Stoltzfus."

Leah's mind trailed off thinking about Adam Beiler. She had been in love with him for many years. As a matter of fact, she fell in love with Adam when they were kids. Back then, she had thought he liked her too. He and Aaron Stauffer paid particular attention to her during their school's recess time. And, the softball and volleyball games they always took part in after the Sunday preaching. Perhaps it was because she was the best girl to have on their team when it came to either sport. Leah excelled at sports. But that was a long time ago, and things had a way of changing. A heart could also change. And that was true for some, but for Leah's heart, it would never change. Adam Beiler was still the only boy who could completely capture Leah's heart. No one knew of her feelings except her two closest friends, Lyddie and Abigail.

She missed her dearest friend, Lyddie. Leah was thankful Bishop Miller hadn't forced the People to shun Lyddie's family when they left the Amish Faith. The bishop was an understanding man who had a kind heart. He took into account all the Fisher family had endured with their previous bishop, Samuel Stoltzfus, and truly understood why they felt the need to break away from the district. It was because of Bishop Miller's decision against enforcing Meidung on the Fisher's, which caused the division in the church. Much of it confused Leah. She understood that a small number of the People wanted to remain under the strict Old Order while others desired to break free from some of the harsher rulings the

Old Order followed. She may not have understood a lot of their rules growing up, but there was one thing she did know. Meidung was the harshest of all punishments. It was something she never wanted to experience. Knowing the bishop would not hold Lyddie's family to it overjoyed her. It meant they could remain good friends. Leah shuttered to think of what her life would be like if she didn't have Lyddie Fisher to lean on.

During their school days, Lyddie helped her friend in many ways. Leah was shy and didn't make friends easily. She only interacted with the others when it came to sports. Leah struggled with her lessons and found the English language hard to master. It was Lyddie who encouraged her throughout those awkward years, always assuring Leah she was no different from anyone else. Lyddie helped Leah understand that not everyone learned on the same level, nor did they mature at the same time. Lyddie scolded Leah often for looking down on herself. She continuously reminded her how she made things harder than they were. Leah wondered why that was, but didn't know how to overcome it. Later in her teenage years, Leah grew out of many of those self-doubting ways. She was still plenty confused at times, but she learned it was because she struggled with the differences in God's Word and the ways of the People. Lyddie always reminded Leah how she "Overcomplicated things," and Leah guessed she still did to some degree. Like Lyddie, Leah didn't mature as fast as some of the girls, which made her feel out-of-place at times. She was short, skinny, and considered herself quite unattractive. Miriam Stoltzfus was the first to confirm Leah's observations of herself, and she often reminded Leah of her homeliness throughout their childhood and far into their Rumspringa.

Miriam Stoltzfus may have taunted Leah with her opinion on Leah's looks; however, Leah blossomed into a beautiful girl. Perhaps Leah didn't gain much height, but the rest of her body caught up with the other girls her age. Her hair was a buttery blonde color, and her eyes were deep sapphire blue, which stood out against her pale skin. She had a mole on the right side of her neck. She considered it a curse until one of the boys told her it was a beauty mark put there by God to make her stand out from all the others. She would always be grateful to Benjamin Lapp for telling her such a tale. He was the first boy to tell Leah she was beautiful, and it made her feel better about herself.

Even though Lyddie and Leah had remained close friends, Lyddie didn't have much time for her as she once did. Nevertheless, Leah was confident their friendship was as strong as it had always been. Anytime Leah needed her or had some exciting news to share, Lyddie always made the time for her friend. As busy as Lyddie's new life kept her, the girls did enjoy lunch together now and then at the one-room schoolhouse where Lyddie taught. For this, Leah was thankful. She couldn't wait until their next lunch together so she could tell Lyddie all about her news on Adam Beiler.

Leah wondered if Adam had any interest in her. And if he did, why hadn't he ever approached her? They never talked together without Aaron

Stauffer right there beside them. If Adam headed toward Leah for any reason, Aaron was close on his heels. Many of the girls thought Aaron wished to court Leah; however, he had never made a move toward courtship either. Was it possible these boys were taking part in the same old game some of them enjoyed playing? She thought back to the time her friend Sara had gotten her heart crushed when the boy who asked for her hand in marriage, up and wed another. He gave absolutely no thought of what it would do to Sara sitting in Sunday preaching hearing Deacon King announcing him published to another girl. He wasn't the only boy who ever played this game. Some of them only thought about themselves. As difficult as it was to believe, pregnancy before marriage was a reality in the Amish community, albeit not often. But, not all boys were like that, and Leah wanted to believe Adam Beiler was one of the exceptions. After all, Naomi Stoltzfus had been sweet on him for some time now. She even went so far as to ask him to marry her, but Adam never seemed to pay her much attention.

Leah's mind continued to dream of becoming Adam's girlfriend. She couldn't think of anything more amazing than becoming his wife. The next singing was still over a week away. She didn't know how she would ever be able to wait that long to find out what Adam Beiler had up his sleeve. She hadn't attended the singings for the last couple of months, because she was almost two years older than most of the girls attending and was starting to get somewhat embarrassed at the fact she still hadn't found a mate. Over the years, there were a few boys who asked to drive her home after the singings, but she almost always turned them down. Eventually, they quit asking.

Once upon a time, Simon Glick and Leah became close, but when she thought about spending the rest of her life with him, it saddened her. She knew she had already lost her heart to Adam Beiler. Reuben Mast had also shown an interest for a while. Still, she couldn't forget Adam. Both of these boys were kind to her. They had the makings for a wonderful husband, just not for Leah.

Then there was Benjamin Lapp. He was also interested in her. Although he had never come right out and asked her to marry him, he did talk about a union between them often. He was more favorable than them all with his kind spirit and gentle smile. He was the most handsome boy in their entire district, although he was oblivious to that fact. He stood out among the others with his tall, muscular figure. His dark, black hair brought out his intense blue eyes. Although Leah believed the curls which hung from under his hat were his most attractive feature. Benjamin never used his looks to draw in a girl's attention. He was anything but vain. It still didn't keep some of the younger girls from paying particular attention to him, though.

Leah was sure Benjamin would make an exceptional husband, and she wondered if she could eventually fall in love with him. However, she didn't feel there was enough room in her heart to love two men, for she would never get over loving Adam Beiler.

Benjamin deserved a wife who would love him deeply, and Leah couldn't promise him her whole heart. When Leah finally felt comfortable enough to discuss her feelings with Benjamin, he was heartbroken. It was Benjamin's sister, Ella, who told Leah she was a fool not to fall in love with a man like her brother. Leah felt Ella was probably right. By turning away Benjamin Lapp, she may have ruined her chances of becoming a wife and mother. But only time would tell what Leah's fate was.

Leah felt terrible for hurting Benjamin. But it was still Adam Beiler's attention she desperately wanted to attract. Leah had held out for so long, hoping and praying Adam would take an interest in her. When it didn't look as though he would ever ask her to court him, Leah gave up and stopped attending the singings. The last thing she wanted was for the younger girls to wag their tongues, accusing her of being desperate to latch on to a husband.

After Leah and Benjamin went their separate ways, Leah watched Ella Lapp push her brother toward Annie Glick. Leah was happy for Benjamin, but somewhat confused when he and Annie married so quickly. For him to take a wife so soon after he and Leah stopped courting, she felt his feelings for her couldn't have been sincere.

Abigail spoke with frustration in her voice, and her hand placed upon her hip as usual. "Leah Zook, if you are going to continue to ignore me, then I may as well leave. What are you so deep in thought about anyway?"

The tone of her voice brought Leah back to their conversation. "Ach, I'm ever so sorry,

Abigail. I was just wondering if Adam Beiler was playing games. I have loved him for so long. I am afraid of getting my heart broke if he is out for some fun. Why do you suppose he is becoming more vocal now? Ach, Abigail, please tell me, do you think he is playing games? I have been in Rumspringa for two years now, and he has never once made a move toward me. I believe he is afraid to be seen alone with me. Every time he comes around, he brings Aaron Stauffer with him."

"I do not believe he is out to hurt you. You know how shy he is, and could it be he too is afraid of being hurt. Adam could have gotten married a long time ago if he wished to. He could have settled for Naomi Stoltzfus over a year ago. You know how she has chased him. Unlike you, she hasn't hidden her feelings from him or anyone else for that matter. But, he hasn't paid any mind to her at all. Nee, I am confident he is not a game player. You have known him long enough to know that, Leah. I have no clue why he acts the way he does. I'm going to tell you something, but you must promise not to get angry with me. Nearly a week ago, I tried talking to Adam about you, but Aaron Stauffer interrupted us. I was going to talk to him again, but I never got the opportunity to do so. Please say you are not upset with me."

"I'm not upset with you. I like Aaron Stauffer. He's a nice buwe, most of the time. But, it frustrates me how he is always in the way. I know I shouldn't feel ill toward him, but lately, he is like an irritating mosquito the way he buzzes around me."

The girls both laughed. Abigail was right, Leah did know Adam quite well, and he had never seemed the type to play those despicable games. Leah was sure Naomi felt about Adam Beiler the same way she did. She couldn't get him out of her heart, and she supposed Naomi couldn't either. Leah felt sorry for her. The pain of loving someone while they were oblivious to your existence cut deep within the heart. Leah knew this pain and felt Naomi did as well.

Naomi Stoltzfus was a sweet soul who wore her heart on her sleeve, especially when it came to her feelings for Adam Beiler. She was the opposite of her cousin, Miriam Stoltzfus. Naomi had a kind spirit, and everyone enjoyed having her in their circle of friends. She loved helping out with everyone's children. She would make a wonderful wife and mother. Leah always prayed it wouldn't be with Adam, though. She had set her mind to helping Naomi find another boy. After all, Naomi deserved happiness the same as Leah and Abigail.

Unlike Naomi, Miriam despised children. She desperately sought after a husband but wanted nothing to do with being a mother. She was so much like her mother, Adele Stoltzfus. After Miriam was born, Adele had no more babies, which proved a blessing. It puzzled Leah how anyone could despise a gift from God. Unfortunately, Adele raised Miriam in the likeness of herself. They were both miserable souls.

Miriam Stoltzfus wasn't the least bit finicky when it came to picking out a husband. She was desperate, for lack of a better word. All Miriam wanted was a man, and her mother wanted one for her as well. Together they scared off half the young boys in the district. They even tried finding her a husband from the nearby communities. As wrong as it was, the boys found much humor in cracking jokes about Miriam Stoltzfus. And, Leah's brother Luke was no different. He joined in on what the boys called *"The horror stories of Miriam, the wretched maedel."* It wasn't just her lack of affection for children, which turned the boys away. It was also her disgruntled personality. Keeping company with her was extremely hard. That was the general opinion anyway. She had tried her best to latch on to Leah's brother, Luke. Adele even went as far as to beg their mother to have Luke spend time with Miriam. Luke wanted nothing to do with it but went to have an evening meal with her as a favor to his mother. That was the only time Luke kept company with Miriam Stoltzfus.

Abigail stood back from the counter, put her hand on her hip, cocked her head to one side, and said, "You know Leah, the way Aaron Stauffer hangs on you, it is no wonder Adam Beiler hasn't made a move. They're best friends, so if Aaron is smitten with you, it would only be natural for Adam Beiler to keep his distance. It puzzles me ever so much trying to figure out what those two are up to, though. Since Adam hasn't made a move toward you, it must mean Aaron wishes to court you. How I wish Aaron Stauffer would finally realize you are not interested in him, and he would turn to his attention toward me. But, alas, he has never given me the time of day."

"I wish that too, my friend. If Aaron Stauffer only realized what a wunderbaar gut maedel you are. I wish that almost as much as I wish for

Adam Beiler to want me for his aldi. Ach, Abigail, I know how you have felt about Aaron Stauffer for some time now. Why must things always be so complicated for us? Maybe I should give up on Adam Beiler." She quickly added. "But, I still wish to have nothing to do with Aaron Stauffer, even if you weren't pining after him."

Abigail's forehead wrinkled as she tilted her head and spoke. "Ach, Leah, maybe you should have kept Benjamin Lapp when you had him. He was ever so crazy about you. If Adam Beiler didn't exist, you would have fallen in love with Benjamin Lapp, jah?"

"Abigail Schrock, it is not fair of you to ask me such a question. Besides, he is now married to Annie."

"Come on, Leah, tell me. You know I won't say anything to anyone else. It is just me here, so please tell me; do you think you could have fallen in love with Benjamin Lapp?"

Leah hesitated before Abigail pushed for an answer. Frustrated, Leah answered her. "All right, jah, I suppose I could have. It would have taken some time, I imagine." She smiled as she remembered the good times she and Benjamin Lapp shared. "He is such a wunderbaar gut man. But my heart belongs to Adam Beiler, and it always has. It is a love I fear I will never get the opportunity to share with him. At the same time, it is a love that I know will burn in my heart for all of my days. No matter how Adam feels about me, I will always be in love with him. Ach, Abigail, each time I get my hopes up over Adam Beiler and I being together, my heart breaks a little more when it never comes to pass. What am I going to do?"

Abigail's expression quickly turned from a sympathetic one to that of determination. "I'll tell you what you are going to do, nothing. If Adam Beiler does not make a move toward you at the next preaching, I am going to talk with him. I will find out what that boy is up to, for sure, and for certain. I promise I won't embarrass you or anything like that. If I have to pretend I'm interested in him myself to get some answers, then that is what I will do. No worries, Leah, I will take care of this once and for all. You will have some answers come next preaching day, I promise."

The girls continued to talk while making their cookies. Leah had been working with Abigail on her cooking and baking skills for many months. Abigail was hoping to learn something to help her with her way around the kitchen. Amish men expected their mates to possess excellent kitchen skills. Abigail was afraid she would never marry because of her shortcomings in this department. As sad as it was, Abigail most definitely was the worse cook in their Amish district, for sure and for certain. She had trouble making the simplest dishes. Hard as she tried, it wasn't a talent she possessed.

In all fairness to Abigail, it wasn't her fault. Her mother, Zelda, had a stroke immediately after giving birth to Abigail. It left her paralyzed on one side and very weak on the other. It also left her with somewhat of a mean spirit. The neighbors had taken over the kitchen duties and the care of Zelda Schrock. Leah felt sorry for her friend.

Abigail had a difficult time dealing with the ill-treatment and lack of love she had received from her mother throughout her life.

Zelda Schrock blamed Abigail for her condition. She refused to have much to do with her daughter unless it was to belittle her in some way. When Abigail's father, Noah, suggested they let their neighbor, Mollie Fisher, raise their Abigail, but Zelda wouldn't hear of it. She told her husband. "I can hear the People wagging their tongues about me giving away my only boppli. Nee, I won't hear of it. You can bring someone here to take care of me and the boppli." Noah was at a loss, he loved his wife, but he knew his daughter needed more than his Zelda was able to give her. It was a blessing having Mollie come each day. Mollie was such a wonderful substitute mother to his Abigail. Mollie Fisher had cared for both Zelda and Abigail since the stroke, and she continued up until her mother had taken ill. So after four years, Noah had to find help elsewhere. Zelda insisted Abigail was now old enough to work in the kitchen, and the need to hire someone else to care for them full-time was unnecessary. Noah did what he could; he knew their four-year-old daughter should not have so much responsibility placed upon her. It was hard on an adult taking care of his wife, and for a child, it would be an impossible chore. He tried hiring a few women to come and help out part-time, but Zelda always ended up chasing them off.

It didn't take Noah long to realize the verbal abuse his Abigail endured from her mother. Because of Zelda's attitude toward their daughter, Noah kept her away from his wife as much as possible. Abigail grew up working on the farm with her dad. Although she could take care of the animals and do many of the farm chores, it left no time to learn the skills of baking, and how to prepare a hearty meal. Now, with her grown up and ready to wed, Abigail wondered what man would want to marry a woman who couldn't feed him. Zelda Schrock didn't help matters by continually drilling that notion into her daughter's head. She pointed out many times over, as a woman Abigail was a complete and utter failure. She often asked Abigail how she ever expected to get a husband if she couldn't feed him. Zelda Schrock always had a way of making her daughter feel unworthy, and because of this, Abigail felt sure she would never attract attention from a man.

Abigail was two years Leah's senior, and all the girls her age were already married. Most of them already had a baby with more on the way. Even though Leah had promised to work with her in the kitchen until she caught on, Abigail felt it would never happen. She became very discouraged at times, and with good reason, she couldn't seem to catch on to baking and cooking meals in general.

It was most likely an issue with low self-esteem, rather than not being able to cook. Leah was, after all, no stranger to feeling a lack of self-worth. Even though she had parents who loved her and cared for her, she still felt unworthy as a younger girl.

CHAPTER 2

❧❧

*"So Jacob served seven years to get Rachel, but they
seemed like only a few days to him because of his love
for her."*
Genesis 29:20

The time passed slowly, and Leah found herself
wishing it was not an off Sunday. She was
looking forward to the next singing. Unfortunately, the singings only took place on preaching
Sunday. And, in the Amish district, the
preaching's were held every other Sunday. They
had no fancy church buildings like the Englishers
did. The services took place in the homes or barns
of the People. Each family in their district took
turns at hosting the Sunday meeting. The same
evening, the teenagers enjoying their Rumspringa
would hold their singings in the barn of the
hosting family. During the time of Rumspringa,

most teenagers found the one they wished to marry. Adam Beiler's parents would host the next preaching service at their home.

A thought occurred to Leah. *"Maybe, just maybe, this was why Adam had started to make his intentions known."* She would be sure to show up at the next singing. If nothing came of her and Adam this time, she would give up on her notion of ever becoming his wife. After all, enough was enough. She had already wasted too many years waiting on Adam Beiler to make a move toward her.

When Sunday morning arrived, Leah's nerves were on edge. She had trouble concentrating on the preacher's sermon. During the second sermon, Abigail kept nudging Leah to pay attention to her Grossdaadi Zook while he preached. Leah also needed a constant reminder to stop staring at the section where Adam Beiler sat. As often as Leah looked across the room, Adam never looked back in her direction. She refused to look over at Adam Beiler again. Leah was not only making a fool of herself, but a stern warning from the bishop was sure to follow the services. Either Abigail misunderstood Adam's sister-in-law or Katie didn't know her brother-in-law as well as she thought. Whatever the case may have been, Leah wasn't going to get caught up in these childish antics any longer. She had let herself get overly hopeful, and now here she was facing disappointment over Adam Beiler once again. She scolded herself for being so foolish.

After the sermons, Leah informed Abigail her mother wanted her to help the other women serve the meal. "Nee, Leah, not today of all days, you must come with me and play volleyball. Please tell your Mamm anything, just come with me. Adam Beiler asked if you were going to join in on the game today, and I told him you would."

Without even thinking, Leah let her guard down, and her hopes soared yet again. "He asked you that personally, for sure and for certain?"

"Jah, Leah, he did, for sure and for certain. His exact words he spoke were, *'Is Leah going to join us in the game today?'* I told him you would for sure be joining us. He gave the biggest smile. So, tell your Mamm you wish to join us today."

"Ach, Abigail, who are we kidding? They most likely need me, so they stand a chance at winning the game. The other team slaughtered them at the last game, and Aaron Stauffer said it was because I wasn't on their team. You know how those boys hate to lose."

"Nee, it wasn't like that. Leah, you didn't see the look on Adam's face. I'm serious; he was ever so excited. He wants to spend the time with you. He didn't ask for you to play on his team, he asked if you would come and join them."

Finding it hard to contain her excitement, Leah whispered to her friend. "I will join in as quickly as I can." She then touched Abigail's arm. "Danki, for telling me Abigail, please make sure he knows I'll be there as soon as I can break free."

As the women prepared for the meal, Leah thought to herself how long the preparations seemed to take that afternoon. All she wanted was to join the others playing volleyball. Her mother was aware of Leah's distraction and urged her daughter to have some fun and join the other teenagers. After hugging and thanking her mother, Leah quickly took off in search of the volleyball game.

"Ach, that hurts." From out of nowhere, someone grabbed hold of Leah's arm. She spun around to see who had just about yanked her arm out of its socket. She wasn't surprised in the least to see Aaron Stauffer standing there in front of her. For many months he had pestered Leah. Even though he never asked her, his behavior led her to believe he wanted to court her. Leah questioned him many times about his behavior. He always changed the subject. Aaron hung around Leah every chance he got, even during the singings, which was another reason she stopped attending them. As much as she told him she was not attracted to him, he never acted as though he cared. Leah thought it was strange the way he continued to single her out despite knowing she wasn't interested in him. He seemed happy to hang around her. His behavior puzzled Leah, and she was at her wits' end with the boy.

In some ways, Aaron was different from the other boys. He was very handy in the barn, behind the plow, and with a hammer. What made him different was the fact he liked to cook. Most believed it was due to his parents not having any girls and him being the youngest of nine boys. At a young age, he learned to help his mother in the kitchen, and he enjoyed it. He didn't want anything to do with the household chores, but he loved to cook. Because of it, he got teased quite often while growing up. But he never seemed to let it get to him. He had a witty comeback for the harassing he received. He often reminded the others he would always be able to take care of himself, without the help of his mother. They all knew, if they wished to eat well, they would be at the mercy of a woman for the rest of their lives. Leah believed Aaron Stauffer had gained a little more respect from the boys over this. However, it didn't sit well with his father. It was not natural for an Amish man to cook his meals and take care of himself.

Aaron was a kind and gentle soul and would make any woman a good husband, just not Leah. Knowing this gave her the courage to push him toward Abigail. If Leah could get Aaron interested in Abigail, it would save her from turning him away. Before she could even act on it, Aaron mentioned Abigail's name.

"Leah, I know you have always thought it was you who held my interest and rightly so with my actions. Despite that, it is Abigail Schrock I wish to get close to." It relieved Leah to hear this. Aaron continued. "I know Abigail is almost two years older than me, and wouldn't think of courting me. But tell me, has she ever talked about me at all?"

"Does Adam Beiler know you're interested in Abigail Schrock?"

"I don't think so. Adam thinks it is you I wish to court. What's that got to do with Abigail, though?" The smile, which seemed a permanent fixture on Aaron's face, was now gone. Leah had never seen him look so sad. "Ach nee, is she smitten with him?" He quickly added. "Ach Leah, please tell me, are they courting?"

"Aaron Stauffer, you and Adam are best friends, I would think you would know before anyone who Adam Beiler wishes to court."

Aaron seemed stumped at Leah's words. "He's never mentioned Abigail Schrock to me, so I don't think he has his eye on her. But, then again, Adam Beiler isn't the type to tell even his best friend what's going through his mind about the girls, especially if he is smitten with one. Whenever I try to get him to talk about a maedel he would consider courting, he says he isn't interested in courting. He turns the conversation back to me. Leah, you are the only maedel we ever discuss."

"Me? Why would you waste your time talking about me?"

"He thinks you're a great maedel and will make me a wunderbaar fraa. You see, Leah, for some time now, I have let him believe it is you I wish to court. You know how much taunting I get from the others about my liking to cook and hang out in the kitchen. The teasing doesn't bother me in the least, but if they were to make fun of my liking Abigail or her liking me, I'm not sure I could hold my temper."

"Aaron Stauffer, you are both free to choose a courting partner. Why would anyone make fun of you and Abigail Schrock if you were to court?"

"You know—" He hesitated. When Leah didn't respond, he continued with a hint of irritation. "Because—" He hesitated yet again before he finally blurted out, "She's two years older than me."

Trying her hardest to hold back the sarcasm in her voice, she asked. "Please say you are joking with me. Surely you do not think you're the only buwe who has fallen for an older maedel, do you?"

Aaron shrugged his shoulders. "I guess I never really thought about anybody else. Tell me, Leah, do you think she would consider courting me? Does she ever talk about me? Please tell me, has Abigail Schrock ever seemed to have shown an interest in me?"

"To be honest, Aaron Stauffer, Abigail has spoken of you many times." Playfully slapping him on the arm, Leah scolded him. "Ach Aaron Stauffer, why have you waited so long? You have wasted so much time for us all. Why have you acted so silly all these years?"

He interrupted Leah. "What do you mean by that?"

"I mean, you could have courted Abigail long ago had you not been prideful about your age difference. You and she could already be starting a family instead of you continuing to play your silly game. You have messed up a lot of things by pretending you were smitten with me. And—" Leah stopped abruptly. She didn't want to let her feelings for Adam spill out.

"And what? Go ahead, say what's on your mind, Leah, I can take it."

Leah had to think fast. "Because of your silly games, Abigail thinks you wish to court me. She has given up on courting and feels she will become an old maid."

"Why is that? She's easy to look at, she's kind, and I have noticed how gut she is with the kinner. So, tell me, why has she not married yet?"

Giggling at Aaron's way with words, Leah replied. "Well, for starters, please do not ever tell her or any other maedel they are easy to look at. Use the word pretty or beautiful, but never easy to look at. I can assure you this; you will get a much nicer response. Abigail Schrock indeed is all you say she is and much more. She does not feel she will make a gut fraa because of the skills she lacks in the kitchen. She seems to do gut when she is helping me, but when left alone to cook, she fails miserably. You had better never repeat what I just told you, Aaron Stauffer, do you hear me? I would never wish to embarrass or hurt one of my dearest friends."

"Will you help me, Leah? Help me get close to Abigail. When I hang around you, she pays me no mind, for sure and for certain."

"Ach Aaron, believe me, she notices you. She also notices, it is me you always come after. You have made her think you are only interested in me. Tell me something, have you ever told any of this to Adam?"

"Nee. I told you, Adam thinks it is you I wish to court."

"Jah, like I said, you have made Adam Beiler and everyone else, for that matter, believe you are only interested in me. It is most likely why none of the other boys wish to court me. You have, for sure and for certain, been convincing of your intentions toward me. Will you kindly tell Adam Beiler it is Abigail Schrock you wish to court? I will bring Abigail to the singing tonight, and you can explain all of your brainless actions to her. But first, you must tell Adam your interest is in her and not me. He is your best friend, after all."

Leah hoped their conversation would encourage Aaron to come clean with Adam and Abigail. The Amish bonds of friendship are strong, loyal, and respectful. Therefore, it would only stand to reason Adam Beiler would not betray his friend by going after Leah. If Adam had any interest in Leah whatsoever, it would come to light at the singing. This day Leah would either start courting Adam or walk away from her dream of ever becoming his wife.

It had been a while since Leah had spent time with her aunt, and Abby Miller begged her to come back to the Ethridge district. She would take her aunt up on her invitation for an extended visit to Ethridge. If Adam wasn't interested in a future with Leah, then maybe Leah's future was in Ethridge, Tennessee.

By the time Aaron Stauffer and Leah had finished talking, it was time to eat. She felt thrilled at the thought of Abigail and Aaron getting together, at the same time, Leah was sorely disappointed she hadn't gotten the chance to play volleyball with Adam. The game was worth missing if Aaron Stauffer told Adam he had no intention of courting Leah Zook.

That evening when Leah and Abigail entered the barn of Adam Beiler's parents, Adam and Aaron Stauffer were nowhere in sight. The girls looked at each other with disappointment on their faces. They went and sat with a couple of the other girls who hadn't paired off with their intended mates yet. Leah forced herself to relax and have a good time with Sara's telling. She had the funniest tellings of all the girls. She had a way of making everything sound so mysterious. They were all engrossed in the story when Miriam Stoltzfus walked up to the table. Silence fell over the group. Miriam made her usual snide remarks to Sara. With a curled lip and a turned-up nose, she looked to Leah, "Ach, Leah Zook, I thought you gave up on finding a buwe long ago. So, tell me, why are you here tonight? Do you think one of the younger boys will come after you and ask your permission to court?"

Leah was as cool and calm as she could muster. "Nee, Miriam, unlike you, I did not come here this evening for a buwe. I only came here to spend some time with my friends before I make a trip to Tennessee to visit my aenti there in Ethridge."

Abigail Schrock shocked Leah when she spoke on her behalf. "Jah, Miriam, Leah is not like you. She is a confident maedel who doesn't feel the need to have a buwe swooning over her, unlike you. So, why not go try to find a buwe to keep company with so we can get back to Sara's telling."

Miriam turned, threw her head back, and walked away in a huff. The girls giggled out of control. When Sara gained her composure, she commented on Abigail's remarks to Miriam. "Ach, Abigail Schrock, not one of my tellings holds a candle to what you said to Miriam Stoltzfus. I don't think Miriam will be back to annoy us again." The girls laughed and carried on until Aaron Stauffer came and interrupted them.

"Leah, can I talk with you for a minute?"

Leah frowned as she got up from the table. Aaron pulled her away from the others. Once they were out of earshot, Leah scolded him. "What in all the world are you doing, Aaron Stauffer? Are you a dumm kopp or what? If you do not wish for the others to think you and I are courting, why would you pull me away in private like that? You have worn my patience thin, for sure and for certain."

Aaron looked to the floor. "Please, don't be upset with me, Leah. I only wished to ask you if you talked to Abigail for me. And if so, what she said. Do you think she will permit me to take her home tonight?"

"Jah, Aaron Stauffer, I talked to her. But you had better stop rattling on and get over there to make your intentions known. Do it before someone else comes and snatches her away from you." Leah looked over in Abigail's direction. "Did you tell Adam about wishing to court Abigail?"

"Nee, I did not. I never got the chance. His Daed sent him on an errand, and I haven't seen him since the noon meal."

Leah's voice held a note of displeasure. "Well then, it serves you right, Aaron Stauffer." She pointed over to the table where Abigail sat with Adam. "Take a look, Adam Beiler is over there with Abigail now. He is most likely asking permission to take her home tonight. All because you can't fess up and tell her how you feel about her. Are you going to go do something about it, or walk away like a wounded animal?"

"But Leah, he's my best friend. If he wishes to court Abigail Schrock, then I can't do anything about it."

Leah was ever so upset with Aaron Stauffer, and she let him know it. "Ach, Aaron, please leave me alone. I have had enough. I am going to tell Abigail I'm going home. Either you go with me and make your wishes known to Abigail and Adam, or else don't come to me again with your troubles. I mean it, Aaron. I have had enough, for sure and for certain."

As the two of them walked over to Adam and Abigail, Leah looked to Abigail and spoke. "I think I will head home early. I have a lot to do with my upcoming trip and all."

Abigail stood to her feet, grabbed Leah's arm, and pulled her aside. "You can't go now. Adam was asking about you, and I told him you have never been interested in Aaron Stauffer and had no intention of courting him. I didn't tell him anything about how you feel, but he did ask me if I thought you would permit him to take you home tonight. I never got to answer him, because it was at the moment you came and interrupted us."

When Leah looked back to the table, Adam was gone. Leah looked around, but Adam was nowhere in sight. The girls quickly returned to the table. Abigail snapped, "Where did Adam Beiler go?"

Aaron stood and answered. "He said he was going up to the house. Can we talk, Abigail?"

"Jah, for sure, we can. But you must wait for a moment."

Abigail turned to Leah and said, "Go after him." Raising her eyebrows, she gave Leah a gentle push and repeated herself. "Go after him. Now!"

Leah promptly walked toward the barn doors. No sooner than she exited through the doors, she saw Miriam Stoltzfus with her arm interlocked in Adam's. She started to head toward the road but thought better of it. She turned back and rushed over to Adam and Miriam. "Adam,

Abigail Schrock said you wished to speak with me. It is true, jah?"

Miriam quickly chided, "Leah Zook, you are ever so rude. We were in the middle of a conversation. Now, leave us be."

Pulling away from Miriam, Adam answered. "Jah, Leah Zook, I do wish to talk with you." He looked back at Miriam and said. "It is ever so important I speak with Leah. It would be gut if you went back to the barn and joined the others, Miriam Stoltzfus."

Miriam stormed off in a huff. With half a smile on his face, Adam looked back at Leah. "Danki, for rescuing me from the likes of Miriam Stoltzfus. I thought for sure she was going to follow me right into the outhouse. She sure doesn't take a hint, does she? I'm ever so glad there are not many like her in our district. Ach, listen to me, now I am the rude one."

Leah chuckled. "Ach, Adam Beiler, you are for sure not the first buwe to ever say such a thing about Miriam Stoltzfus. Tell me, has your Mamm ever made you take an evening meal with her and her mudder?"

"Adele Stoltzfus tried to get my Mamm to make me take a meal with them, but my mudder refused to push me into doing so."

"Well, let me tell you, my bruder Luke wasn't so lucky. Mamm asked him to do her the one favor of going to share a meal with Miriam, and my bruder did it. It was the only time he shared a meal with her. He told Mamm he would have to think twice before he ever did her another favor."

The two of them stood laughing until Leah remembered Adam was on his way to the outhouse. "Ach, vergeef me, Adam Beiler, I have kept you from doing what it was you had come out here to do."

"Nee, you haven't really. I only told Miriam Stoltzfus, I was on my way to the outhouse, thinking she would turn back to the barn. When it didn't work, I wasn't sure what I was going to do. Danki, Leah Zook, you really did save me from her."

"Well, Adam Beiler, it was my pleasure. But, isn't the buwe supposed to do the saving?"

"I promise to save you from something,— sometime." He stumbled with his words. "—How's that sound?"

Leah felt sorry for him. She knew it was hard trying to get your words to come out correctly. She had been in that same place many times. "It is nice to know I will have someone looking out to save me." She quickly added. "You know, from something."

"Leah, umm, he hesitated before continuing. Why did you come out here?"

"I was going to walk home."

"Ach, you wish to leave so soon?"

"I could ask you the same question. If you were not coming out to use the outhouse, then why were you out here?"

"You caught me. I was going to the haus for the night."

"Were you not having a gut time at the singing?"

"Nee, Leah, I was not. I only wanted to come out here to see if you were here. I asked Abigail

Schrock earlier today if you were coming to the singing, and she said you would be here. But she also said you would join us in the volleyball game and you didn't. Leah, Abigail says you are not interested in Aaron Stauffer, and you two have never courted, this is true, jah?"

"Jah, it is true. I can't believe you two have never talked about this. You are best friends, after all. Do boys not talk about such matters? It seems it is all we girls talk about when we are together."

"Some boys do, but the way Aaron has always acted around you, I assumed the two of you were secretly courting, and he didn't wish to talk about it with me. I asked some of the others, and they also figured you two were courting. I have never been able to get near you without him coming to your side, so it seemed I was right in my thinking."

Leah's face turned red as she confessed. "To be honest with you; I told Abigail your friend Aaron was like a pesky mosquito. Come to find out he was using me to get close to her. He said he was going to tell you everything before the singing tonight. The only reason I came here tonight was to find out just what it is you are up to. Katie Beiler told Abigail she knew you were smitten with me, but you refused to talk about it. Then today, Abigail said you had asked her about me. I figured it was because you didn't want to lose another volleyball game, but Abigail insisted there was much more to it. When I heard you were hoping I would be here tonight, I thought I would come and find out what sort of game you and Aaron Stauffer are playing. When Abigail told me you had asked her if she thought I would permit you to take me home, I was going to come and talk to you about it. But you disappeared. I wasn't planning to head for home until I saw you with Miriam. What I really came out here for, was to say I would, for sure and for certain, like for you to take me home tonight."

Adam smiled and asked Leah to join him back inside the barn with the others. As they stepped inside, they spotted Abigail and Aaron still sitting at the same table talking to one another. Adam nudged Leah's elbow and asked if they should go to join the two or leave them alone. Before Leah could answer him, Aaron was waving them over to the table. The four of them sat and talked and laughed about Aaron and his foolish ways over wishing to get close to Abigail.

Together they made plans to visit different places. Leah asked if they would all like to go to an outdoor concert on a Saturday afternoon. She explained how Lyddie's church held them in the warmer months. And, she would like to hear Lyddie sing about God. They all approved of going, but only one time. They agreed that nothing good would come of them getting into the music of the Englishers. It was Aaron Stauffer who said they would all go to hear their friend Lyddie sing, but Leah should pick another fun activity to do.

Leah thought for a moment. "Ach, I know. How about we all go bowling together? I have heard it is right gut fun." They decided they would all like to try a game or two of bowling. "Now, it is your turn Abigail, where would you like for us all to go?"

Abigail hesitated. With some prodding from Aaron, she finally blurted out, "Ever since Sara told me about her trip to Manheim, I have wanted to go. So I would like for us all to go and eat at the restaurant and play some miniature golf. Does that sound wunderbaar gut or what?"

Aaron laughed. "If it includes food, I'm there. Everyone knows how much I love to eat."

Abigail's face turned sorrowful. Aaron leaned in. "Abigail, what is it?"

With her head down, she spoke quietly. "You may as well know before you take me home tonight. And after I tell you, if you choose not to take me home, I'll understand, for sure and for certain."

"I don't think there is anything you could say that would change my mind."

"Ach, but the fact of the matter is, I can't cook." She quickly added, "I've tried. Honestly, I have. Leah has helped me, and I can't seem to get the knack of it. You may love to eat, but I won't be able to feed you."

Aaron reached and squeezed her hand. "Then I guess I'll do the cooking for us."

Abigail smiled and squeezed his hand a little tighter before releasing her grip. "Now then, Aaron Stauffer, it is your turn to pick a place for us to go."

"I know what I wish to do, but I doubt very much you girls will go for it. I want to go over to Lancaster one night and go on a ghost tour they have there. Simon Glick says it is the thing to do. I, for sure and for certain, want to go, but only if you all agree to come with me." They shook their heads in agreement. "So that settles it, we will go see what this ghost business is all about. Well, Adam, that leaves only you to come up with something to do before our Rumspringa ends."

Adam reached up and rubbed the back of his neck. "What I wish to do is too far away. How would we explain it to our families if we all disappeared for a couple of days? Rumspringa or not, I don't think we would ever be able to pull it off."

Leah looked at him with a curious smile. "How far away is this place you wish to take us? I am sure it is something special if you want to travel for a few days. You have, for sure, piqued my interest."

Abigail spoke up, "Mine too, and my mudder wouldn't know, much less care if I disappeared for a few days. Tell us, Adam, where would you like to take us?"

Adam quickly blurted out. "Niagara Falls." He lowered his head and spoke again. Ach, it's just a silly dream."

It was Leah who reached out to Adam and placed her hand on his shoulder. "Our dreams are never silly. I would love to see Niagara Falls too. Lyddie has shown me pictures, and it is such an awesome sight. I will agree to go if we get permission from the bishop, but I bet it is ever so expensive."

"I'm sure we would never be able to pull off a trip to the falls. I guess I'll pick the amusement park."

They agreed the amusement park was a sure deal. It would be fun to go over to Hershey and spend the day on the roller coasters. It would be the first place they would all go together. They made plans to go the following Saturday.

That evening for the first time, Abigail had the hope of being a wife and having a family of her own. It was also a special night for Leah. Adam Beiler did indeed take her home, and she permitted him to hold her hand along the way.

CHAPTER 3

❧

"A man's heart deviseth his way; but the LORD
directeth his steps."
Psalm 16:9

Adam and Leah had an incredible courtship
throughout the spring and summer months,
spending most of their time talking about their
future together. They took their baptism
instruction, the bishop baptized them, and they
joined the church. Leah never thought she would
become a wife. Now, here she was finally planning
her future with the man she had loved for so
many years. In the fall, they became published
and married.

Leah was eager to start a family. Everyone
else her age was expecting or already had at least
one baby. She reminded herself, she wasn't
everyone else, and her time would come. She and

Adam had so much work they wish to accomplish and decided it would be best if a baby didn't arrive right away.

Ever since that night in the barn, Leah kept Adam's dream of seeing Niagara Falls close to her heart. When he was a little boy, he had seen a picture of the falls with the ice everywhere. It became his greatest desire to see Niagara Falls during the winter months, and if she had it her way, her husband's dream would be coming true in another week. Leah counted the money she had saved from selling her baked goods to the local English bakery. She had more than enough to make the trip. She decided to hire a driver to take them on the long journey. Lyddie helped Leah make the arrangements, and they booked a room for a night near the falls. Lyddie explained they would need a passport to go into Canada. It would be hard enough for an Amish couple to obtain one, but it would be impossible for them to acquire one in such a short amount of time.

When Leah approached Adam with the details of the trip she had planned for them, it was hard for her husband to contain his excitement. He picked Leah up into his arms and spun her around. "I can't believe you have done this for me. Ich liebe dich, my fraa." When Leah finally got her husband to put her down, they sat at the table to discuss the plans of the trip.

Adam was sorely disappointed when Leah told him they would each need a document allowing them to cross over between the two countries. These passports would be the only way they would get to see the falls from the Canadian side. When Lyddie and Blake suggested they go ahead and travel to New York to see the American side of the falls, Leah persuaded Adam to take the trip. Leah convinced him they would enjoy the winter's beauty along the way. Blake assured Adam. "Believe me, Adam; you will be anything but dissatisfied with seeing the falls from the American side. I'll tell you what I'll do. If you are not completely satisfied with the view, I'll give Leah back every penny it took to get you both there. Lyddie readily agreed. Adam admitted he would like nothing more than to see the vast expanse of water in the winter.

Adam Beiler was like a child on Christmas morning, waiting to open his gift. He had trouble sleeping the night before they were to leave because of his excitement. Leah suggested a cup of hot cocoa might do the trick. Adam had only slept a couple of hours before it was time to get ready to leave. He assured her he would nap during the six hours it would take to get to the falls.

Adam and Leah sat waiting at the kitchen table for their ride to come. The driver was running late, and the snow and freezing rain were beginning to make Adam somewhat anxious. When the SUV finally pulled up to the house, the man apologized for his tardiness. He reached out to shake Adam's hand and introduced himself as Parker Carson. He turned and presented his wife, Melanie. After loading their bags in the back of the SUV, Parker told Adam the inclement weather sweeping across the area would make the drive time somewhat longer than he expected. Some of the roads were already slick from the freezing rain, which fell during the night. The driver assured them once they reached the interstate, in Williamsport, they would have better road conditions. Leah was a nervous wreck and hoped the driver was right. She had already suggested they cancel the trip, and now she was sure they should have turned back. They had planned to spend the night near the falls, so it didn't matter if they were running a little behind schedule.

Approximately ten miles outside of Lancaster, the roads became very icy in places. When the SUV slid on a patch of ice, Leah panicked. She urged the driver once again to turn back, but the driver insisted it would be fine to continue. Leah had a feeling the trip would become a nightmare.

The huge semi-truck gave no caution as he flew passed them, throwing ice and snow over the windshield blinding the driver. Adam held tight to Leah's hand, giving her comfort as they continued their trek across the snow-covered highway.

Once they got off the heavily traveled interstate, the roads were even slicker. Leah begged for the driver to turn back. Parker cautioned Adam it would not be a wise decision as most of the bad weather was behind them. If they were to around now, they would head straight back into the heavy snow and freezing rain. Adam suggested they search for a motel and continue with their trip the next morning. The driver and his wife agreed it would be wise to postpone the trip until the following day. It seemed like they had looked for a motel for hours with no luck at all. As the search continued, the snow turned back to freezing rain.

Without warning, the SUV jerked to the left and crossed over into the opposite lane of traffic. Another driver swerved to avoid hitting them. Parker tried bringing his SUV under control; however, it was as though it had a mind of its own. They hit the curb and spun back across the street. Their vehicle was not only in the proper lane of traffic again, but it also faced in the correct direction. After making sure no one received injuries in the mishap, Parker apologized. He offered to pay for Adam and Leah's room for the night since it was his persistence that brought them to the quaint little town.

They settled in their motel room, and Leah breathed out a heavy sigh as she sat on the edge of the bed. She felt the tension from her head to her toes. She looked to Adam, who was taking off his boots. "I believe I will go fill that tub in there with some hot water and try to relax."

"Go ahead, my fraa. You deserve it after the ordeal we have been through today. I'm sorry you felt the need to make this trip for me. I love you ever so much for planning it, but I should have insisted we wait for warmer weather."

"Ach, not so, we would never get to see the water iced over if we waited. Besides, tomorrow we will forget all about our unpleasant road trip and take in the beauty of Niagara Falls."

"How is it that you are always right?" He pulled his wife to her feet hugged and kissed her and told her to take as long as she wished in the tub.

The bed proved so comfortable neither of them wanted to crawl out when the light came shining through the window. Adam rolled over and held his wife. "The sun is shining this morning. Maybe the rest of our trip will be a gut one."

"I hope so. I'm not sure I can take another day like yesterday."

A knock at their door interrupted their conversation. Adam hurried to pull on his pants, as he called out. "I'm coming."

Adam stepped out into the hallway to give Leah her privacy while Parker explained he was going to have the SUV checked over to make sure there was no damage to it after hitting the curb with so much force. Once he was sure it was safe to continue, they would be on their way once again.

A few hours later, they were back out on the highway. Leah was thankful the roads were in better condition. Soon, Adam's dream would come true. They would see the very falls Adam had longed to see ever since he had heard about them as a child.

As they stood gazing over the falls, they both agreed the view was magnificent. The snow and ice only added to its beauty. As cold as the air was, both Adam and Leah enjoyed the experience. The fireworks display over the falls was spectacular. A winter light show covered the entire area. Neither of them had ever seen so many lights, and the colorful displays captivated their attention. Leah was sure she would never witness such beauty again. The time they spent at the falls was so enjoyable they decided to spend another night before heading back home. Parker and Melanie were happy to stay another night. He used his cell phone to call Lyddie and Blake and have them deliver the message to Leah and Adam's families of their intentions to spend another night in New York.

The roads were clear and dry the morning they headed for Pennsylvania. The trip back home didn't seem to take as long and was uneventful. Melanie and Parker kept the conversation lively. It was exciting to hear about the many trips they had taken all over the world. They both agreed, of all the places they had visited, Pennsylvania would always be home to them. Adam and Leah were happy they were back home safely tucked inside in their warm home before the next round of snowfall hit Somerton. It was now time for them to settle into married life.

Generally, in the first year of marriage, the couple lives with various family members. Whatever the Amish traditions may have been, neither Adam nor Leah was happy with the thought of this. Adam was ready to make the dream of having a large farm come to life. According to Amish custom, Adam, being the youngest son, would take over his parent's house and farm. However, his parent's farm was not big enough for what Adam needed. Adam and his oldest brother, Joel, discussed Adam's plans for a cattle farm. Adam explained how their parent's land wasn't nearly large enough to suit the needs of raising and selling beef. Joel's farm, on the other hand, consisted of eighty acres, of which he was only using about fifteen or so acres. Joel offered Adam the opportunity to buy a piece of his unused farmland. Still, Adam did not wish to live in one place and work the land in another area of the district. It was his duty to take care of his father's chores and household, once the time came that his father could no longer care for it on his own.

One night over the evening meal, Adam discussed his dilemma. It was Leah who casually mentioned it was too bad the brothers couldn't swap the farms out. Adam jumped to his feet, took his wife's hand, pulled her to her feet, and hugged her hard. "That is the perfect plan, Leah. Why should all that land of Joel's go unused? He has no intention of ever using it himself." Adam turned to his father, apologized for his behavior, and asked, "What do you think, Daed? Would you be opposed to Joel and Adeline taking over the farm here? They could live in the daadi haus until you and Mamm are ready to move into it. It is big enough for all of them, especially since they only have three kinner left at home now. And, it would give Joel the excuse he has tried to come up with for so long now, not to build a daadi haus on their property. Leah and I can have a daadi haus built when we start having our kinner."

Thomas Beiler ran his hand down the length of his beard before replying to all of his son's questions. "I suppose it would be a gut solution for both of my sons. Joel's bum leg keeps him from doing many of the things he has wanted to do over the years, so if you and your bruder agree to swap the parcels of land and farmhouses, I am gut with the decision."

Adam sat back at the table and quickly finished his supper. "Mamm, I wish for Leah to go with me over to Joel's if you don't mind her skipping out on the chores this evening."

"Nee, I do not mind, your Leah here is very organized in the kitchen, she has the knack of cleaning as she works. It makes for much less clean up after the meal. I mean to take lessons from her. It is ever so nice to have the extra time after the meal when all that is left to do is the dishes you see here on the table. You both go and talk to your bruder. I will miss Leah's skills when she leaves, for sure and for certain."

Together they quickly harnessed the horse and were on their way. It was a good half-hour ride to Joel's house, which meant they would either spend the night there or chance traveling back in the dark.

Adam helped Leah from the, buggy. He pulled her into his arms and held her tight. "I pray Joel goes for this idea of yours. It would be gut for us to make a life here on our own, jah?"

"Jah, I would like to live here all alone with you. She pulled back, smiled at her husband, and said, "We will never have the opportunity though if we do not go in there and discuss it with your bruder and his fraa."

They entered the kitchen just as Joel was getting up from the table. He grabbed his cane and motioned for Adam to follow him to the living room. Adam took Leah's hand and started to follow after his bruder. "Adam, why do you not go in and visit with Joel while I help Adeline here in the kitchen?"

As much as Adam wanted his wife to sit in on the conversation, he understood the ways of Amish women. They always helped each other with kitchen chores. He smiled at her, and said. "As you wish."

Leah pushed up her sleeves, placed the hot water from the stove into the sink, and asked, "I'll wash, and you can dry, jah?"

Smiling, Adeline replied. "Jah, that will be wunderbaar gut. So, what brings you and Adam out here so late in the evening?"

Leah told Adeline what Adam wished to propose to his bruder. "What do you think of the idea, Adeline?"

"I think it is the best idea ever, for sure and for certain. This place is too much for my Joel. He works too hard, and it takes a lot out of him. His body lets him know it, too. He is in pain with his leg most of the time. I believe Gott has put this idea in your heart for all the right reasons. I love all of my girls ever so much, but it has been hard on Joel not having a buwe in his younger years. Our Job has come along so late in life. By the time he is old enough and strong enough to help his Daed out around here my Joel won't be much help. Jah, this place is making an old man out of my ehemann, for sure and for certain. I do not think your Adam will have any problem talking Joel into parting with this farm."

"My Adam will be ever so pleased. He has such big plans, sometimes it scares me."

Looking out the window, Adeline asked. "You and Adam will spend the night with us, jah?"

"I will permit my ehemann to make that decision. It will turn dark soon, and I do not like being out on the road at night. So if he plans to go, we will need to leave soon."

No sooner than the words left Leah's lips, the men returned to the kitchen. Adam was smiling ear to ear, as was his brother. Adeline commented. "I take it those smiles mean gut news for us all."

Joel came and stood beside Adeline. "It is if you wish to leave here and live in my parent's daadi haus until they are ready to move into it."

Adeline reached and kissed his cheek. "It is an answer to prayer, my ehemann."

They went back into the living room and talked among themselves, while the girls played checkers and Job played with his wooden blocks. The men decided to make the shift in property within the next week. After finalizing all of their plans, they all headed for bed. As excited as Adam and Leah were, they were also extremely exhausted. It was the first of many nights they would sleep in their new home.

Transitioning into the new house went as smoothly as they expected it would. By Christmas, Adam and Leah were all settled into their new home. As they sat in front of the warm fire, they talked of all their plans. Of course, there was not much they could do in the fields during the cold weather. But, he could do some of the house repairs during the colder months. Adam promised Leah they would bring her dogs to the new place as soon as he fixed beds for them out in the barn. He couldn't wait to get started on all the projects he and Leah had planned.

Christmas morning, Adam stood on the back porch looking out over the field, between their farm and the next farm over. He wasn't sure he liked the idea of the Lapp's being their new neighbors. He knew how Benjamin felt about Leah at one time, and most likely still harbored feelings for her to this day. Even though Adam was aware it was Leah who stopped the courting between the two of them, he knew Benjamin was a broken man when it happened. It was one of the reasons Adam didn't pursue Leah at the time. He could kick himself now and his best friend too, their foolishness cost him so many years with Leah.

Leah always held a special place in Adam's heart, even as a kid. But it was hard to get close to her when they were in school. She kept to herself most of the time unless there was a good game of softball or volleyball going on. She may have been a small girl, but she was a giant when it came to sports.

There was enough land between the two farms to keep the distance between his wife and their neighbor. Adam scolded himself for trying to borrow trouble. Benjamin married Annie Glick a couple of years ago, and they appeared devoted to one another. Adam knew Leah loved him with all her heart. After all, he was the reason Leah stopped courting Benjamin Lapp in the first place. Of course, Adam didn't find that fact out until just before he and Leah started courting. It was Katie, his sister-in-law, who got Adam to realize Leah had been smitten with him all those years.

The Somerton Amish district set Christmas day aside for prayer and fasting, as did most Amish communities. Leah listened as Adam read from the second chapter of Luke. She loved to hear the story of the Christ Child's birth. Second Christmas took place on the twenty-sixth of December, and was a day of celebration with family and gift exchange. Leah had baked so many cookies, cakes, and loaves of bread they could feed the entire district. Adam brought Widow Beiler, his great-aunt, to eat with them. Leah's parents, her brother Luke, and his wife, Sarah, came to share the meal with them. Leah's mother had made her and Adam a beautiful quilt. She also made one for Luke and Sarah. Adam and Leah gave Widow Beiler, Leah's parents, and her brother's family each a beautifully handcrafted birdhouse. Even though Lyddie's parents left the Amish Faith, her father still had many Amish customers buying from his shop. After everyone left, Adam and Leah sat by the fire as they exchanged their gifts. Leah opened her gift and found a wooden box inside. Made from cedar, it had a beautiful carving of praying hands. On the back of the box, carved into the wood, were the words, *Leah's earthly treasures*. Adam told her it was to hold the money she made from selling her baked goods and her dogs. He urged her to look inside the box. She pulled a note from inside the box. As she read it, she became more excited. A new bedroom set, made by Isaac Fisher and his son-in-law Levi, would be delivered later that evening. Adam's gift was a large wooden box holding many hand tools he would need for building fences and other projects he wished to build. Leah asked Adam to follow her to the back porch, where he found several tools laying on the porch. "You will need these for all the work you will do on our farm." She reached and kissed his cheek.

He pulled her into his arms, kissed her, and whispered. "Danki, Leah. I will put them to good use, I promise."

Their first winter together passed quickly. They were so much in love, and a deep bond had grown between them. Leah and Adam were not the typical Amish couple. They helped each other with almost every chore there was, inside and outside the house. That would all come to a halt once Leah started having babies. For now, they would enjoy the time spent together. They kept busy with all the projects they were working on around their new farm. Leah was sure Adam felt disappointed she hadn't given him a son yet. But, he continuously assured her they had plenty of time to start a family. Adam convinced Leah God's timing was always right, and there was no reason they should not enjoy the freedom to work together on their many projects. Things would change soon enough, once the babies started coming along.

Adam had recently started building onto the barn. When he finished with that chore, they would start on, what they called, *Leah's project.* She wished to raise chickens and collect their eggs, so she would need a chicken coop to house them in. The demands from the English bakery had Leah using more eggs than she cared to purchase from the Stauffer's.

Abigail and Aaron were also married during the same service as Leah and Adam. She confided in Leah, after the last Sunday preaching, she was expecting a baby in late summer or early fall. They were both extremely excited about the news.

Aaron continued to work with Abigail on her cooking skills since their marriage last fall. He admitted Abigail had made tremendous improvements and now cooked delicious meals all on her own.

Everything was going wonderful, Leah felt so blessed, and she couldn't imagine it being any better than it was at that very moment.

Adam and some of the other men finished the work on the barn, and Adam purchased a dozen cattle and two more horses.

Adam was exceptionally supportive of Leah. She wanted to continue breeding and selling her dogs like she had done since she was twelve years old. The Englishers seemed to grab them up just as soon as the mother had weaned them. Leah thought she would have gotten used to giving them up after all these years, but it was still hard to let each one go. Adam surprised Leah with a room in the corner of the barn for the dogs. It had several smaller partitions within the room to separate the breeds. He had constructed doors so the dogs could go into an outside, fenced-in area on their own. He knew how particular his wife was about her dogs. It devastated Leah a few years ago when an Englisher hit and killed one of her puppies with their automobile. She vowed never to let them run free again at a young age. Most of the People frowned on the way Leah doted on them. After all, they were just animals. But, to her, they were so much more. The older women would scold her for treating the puppies as if they were human. They assured Leah, her feelings about the dogs would change once she started having babies of her own. Leah secretly wished they would keep their noses out of her concerns.

The temperatures dropped down below freezing the last few nights. Leah piled several

extra quilts on their bed. She teasingly com-
plained about Adam sliding his cold feet against
her legs. She just knew there was not another
man alive with feet as cold as her husband's. As
they snuggled up tight together, they discussed
the tongue-lashing the women had given her
earlier over her dogs. As Adam held his wife close,
he began confessing to her. "Leah, do you
remember how I used to come to your parent's
farm each time there was a new batch of
puppies?"

Giggling, she replied. "Jah, after the third
time you came and picked out yet another puppy,
I had to tell you, you couldn't have any more of
them."

"It never stopped me from coming back the
next time you had a new batch, did it?"

"Nee, how could I forget? I wanted you to
ask me to court you so badly, but you only ever
talked about my puppies."

"Leah, I liked you back when we were kids.
But I fell in love with you as I watched how
careful and loving you were with your pups. It
was like I saw a glimpse of what you were truly all
about. I knew if you put that much love and care
into an animal, you would make a wunderbaar
gut fraa and mudder. I used to tell myself. *If I
could get her to love me half as much as she loved
those pups, I would be a happy man.* My heart
broke when I thought you and Benjamin Lapp
were going to marry, and then, I realized my best
friend wanted you for himself. To this day, I could
kick Aaron Stauffer. We could have started our
life together so much sooner if it hadn't been for
his foolish antics."

"We are together now, and that is all that matters. Ach, Adam, I have loved you with all of my heart since we were kinner. You have made me ever so happy, for sure and for certain." They fell into a fitful sleep, holding each other tightly.

Adam and Leah made plans to start building the chicken coop as soon as they purchased the needed supplies. The snow was now gone, the days were getting longer, and they were spending more and more time outdoors. Leah's chicken coop would be their last big project to make the farm complete. Her brother, Luke, offered to help Adam raise the coop, but it had been Leah's wish to have chickens. And it was her wish to build the coop with her husband. Once she started having babies, her working on such projects would come to an end.

Leah watched as Adam was finishing up in the barn. He was nailing on the last of the boards in the dog's area. He had gotten overheated in his heavy coat and now worked only in his shirt. She realized how much his body had changed. He was much too thin when they first married, and in just a few short months, his arms had become much more muscular, as did the rest of his body. She attributed it to all the work he had done around the new farm. The love Leah felt for her husband began building up within her heart all over again. She never thought she would become Adam's wife, let alone hold so much more love for him than she did before they married.

Adam read the Bible each night. Leah noticed immediately how different his prayers were from those of the preachers during the Sunday sermons. He tried to teach Leah on the precepts of God, but it left her confused and discouraged. Her husband was patient, but Leah couldn't seem to grasp his teachings. They were somewhat different from the doctrine of the People. Every morning and night, Adam prayed for his wife. He asked God to open her heart to His teachings. Leah convinced herself she needed to try harder and prayed God would help her understand what is was her husband was trying to get through her dull-witted brain. Adam prayed the way Leah had heard her father pray in secret. She never understood him either. Adam always told her not to worry; God would open it all up to her in His time. She didn't quite understand that either.

CHAPTER 4

❦

"Blessed are they that mourn: for they shall be comforted."
Matthew 5:4

L eah had no way of knowing her world was on the verge of crashing down around her. That dreadful day continually played over and over in her mind. It consumed her days, and it replayed so vividly in her dreams each night. She was afraid her question of how something so horrible could happen, would remain forever unanswered.

The day didn't start in the usual way, Leah and Adam had never stayed in bed late into the morning. They were always up before dawn. But that particular morning, Adam wanted to stay in bed a little longer. He assured Leah they were deserving of a lazy morning just this once. He held to her tightly and told her how much he loved her. Leah wondered why Adam showed more affection than usual that morning. Not that her husband wasn't a loving man, they just never took the time in the morning to hold each other. There was always so much work to do. Instead of questioning her husband's motives any more, she decided to enjoy their time together. When the couple finally crawled out from under the quilt, they got dressed and headed out to the kitchen for some hot coffee. Leah started breakfast while Adam went to care for the animals, promising her, as he went out the door, he would be sure to feed her dogs as well. After they finished eating the delicious breakfast, Adam helped clean up the kitchen. He kissed her cheek and told her he was sorry for getting such a late start on the day. Leah hugged him and assured him it was a welcomed change, and she wouldn't have wanted the day to start any other way.

Their morning laziness had set them back an entire day. Today they were going to start the building of the chicken coop after they purchased the lumber and other needed supplies. They went out to the barn and together harnessed the horses and hooked up the wagon. It was nearly noon before they were finally on their way to pick up the lumber for the chicken house.

Out on the road, the couple talked. Leah was feeling guilty about staying in bed so late. Adam tried to convince her they did nothing wrong. Then a scripture from the Book of Deuteronomy came to mind. "You know, Leah. In Old Testament times, a husband would devote the first year of the marriage to making his wife happy. Even though we are no longer living under the law of the old covenant, I believe there is much wisdom in that practice. It will make for a strong marriage, for sure and for certain."

Leah teased her husband. "Ach, Adam Beiler, a strong marriage is a wunderbaar gut thing, indeed. However, being as lazy as we were this morning is far from gut. Maybe we should pick the evenings for our laziness, when there is no light to do our chores."

Adam shot Leah a sideways glance. "Are you saying you did not enjoy our morning? Have you grown tired of me already?"

She tucked her arm under his and hugged tightly against him. "Nee, I will never tire of you. I think I could easily get used to more mornings like this one. I merely thought we should repeat our laziness this evening too."

"I like the way my fraa thinks."

They met another Amish couple while at the lumber store and talked longer than they had intended, and for the second time that day, the couple had let time slip away from them. They rushed to get the lumber picked out and some tools Adam needed. With the lumber now loaded on the wagon, they hurried to get home before the darkness overtook them. As they were talking, they realized they had forgotten the hinges, the handle, and the door latch for the coop. Adam assured Leah they had time before those items would be needed, and they could purchase them later. He had just reached over and kissed her and declared how grateful he was to have Leah for his wife and went on to say he was looking forward to working together on the chicken house. Leah tucked her arm in his as a chill ran through her and reminded him she was the blessed one to have such a loving, kind, and gentle husband.

The car, which raced up behind them so quickly, startled the couple. Without warning, it swerved over into the opposite lane, pulled up beside them, and forced their buggy off the road. A young man got out and walked over to them. At first, the tone of his voice was friendly. Then suddenly, his facial expression changed, and he pulled a pistol from under his jacket. He demanded that Adam climb down from the wagon. Adam assured him he didn't need the gun as he would fully cooperate. The man asked Adam how much money he had and before Adam could answer, he yelled at Adam to hand all the cash over to him. The man tucked the bills into his pocket. He looked to Leah and asked if she had any money in the tote which hung from her wrist. Leah quickly handed the cloth tote to him. He pulled out the money she had tucked inside it and threw the purse to the ground, before pushing the rest of the bills into his pocket.

The man's face held the strangest look as he tried to provoke Adam to a fight. His anger intensified when Adam refused to fight him. Then without warning, the man swung and hit Adam across the side of the head with the pistol, immediately knocking him to the ground. Leah quickly jumped from the buggy and ran to Adam. He was obviously in tremendous pain and bleeding profusely from the wound on his head. As she knelt to help him, she felt the man's hand on her shoulder. He pulled the prayer kapp from her head. She cried out in pain as he took a fist full of her bun. He pulled her away while knocking her off her knees and to the ground. He raised his gun and pointed it at Adam. Screaming, Leah jumped to her feet. Shielding Adam, she begged and pleaded him not to harm her husband. Once again, the man pushed Leah hard to the side, making her lose her foothold. She stumbled and fell, hitting her head. As she tried crawling to her husband, the man fired the gun into Adam's chest. Leah tried to get close to her husband. The man grabbed her, pulled her to her feet, and dragged her toward his car.

The Amish are pacifists. They believe violence is inexcusable. At that moment, Leah didn't care what the People's beliefs were. She was fighting for her life and wanted to get back to her husband.

She repeatedly kicked and hit the man. It wasn't until the sound of an approaching vehicle that the man released his grip on her. He quickly climbed into his car and sped away. Leah struggled to her feet. The pain in her neck and head intensified. She rushed back to Adam's side, sat next to him, and gathered him in her arms. She begged him not to leave her. She knew her husband's condition was critical. The blood continued to flow from Adam's wounded chest and head. As her tears mixed with her husband's blood, she began to panic. Adam talked soothingly to his wife. He assured her he was going to a place where he would be healed and never feel pain again. Although she heard what her husband was saying, she couldn't understand his logic. She urged Adam to save his strength. She needed to get help, but how? She pleaded with him to hang on. She tried to lift him to get him on to the flat buggy. He whispered, telling her she had to let him go. Leah argued she would not leave him to die.

The car passed by slowly, without stopping. Leah screamed out as loudly as she could. All at once, the car skidded to a stop and quickly backed up. She began yelling in German. Realizing the Englishers could not understand her, she repeated her plea in English. "Please help me. It's my husband. He needs help quickly. Please hurry." While the man used his cell phone, the woman knelt beside Adam. She prayed a quick prayer and then asked Adam if he had accepted Jesus Christ as his personal Savior. He slowly nodded, signaling he had. She reminded him he had no worries. Soon he would be with Jesus, and Heaven would be his eternal home. Leah couldn't understand why there was a look of peace on his face. She felt helpless and confused. Leah had no idea what the woman was talking about with Adam. How could this woman know he would make Heaven? Leah didn't want to hear a stranger telling her husband he was going to die. Adam looked deep into Leah's eyes. Squeezing her hand, he affectionately told her he loved her and asked that she stay strong for him. Adam talked about things Leah couldn't comprehend. He then asked her to promise him she would finish their chicken house project. Leah sobbed. She begged Adam to stay and help build the coop. She reminded him nothing about the farm meant anything to her if she didn't have him beside her. Leah reached down and kissed Adam's lips. She told him how much she loved and needed him. He moaned as he struggled to talk. Once again, he whispered he loved her, before closing his eyes for the last time. Leah held him tightly and rocked him while begging God to open Adam's eyes again.

The sirens in the background grew louder. Leah felt as though her head would explode from the piercing sounds the vehicles made as they came closer. She now knew God was not going to answer her request and bring Adam back to her. The Englishers took Adam from her arms. She begged and pleaded with them not to take him. The woman held Leah and prayed over her. Once the Englishers left with Adam, the woman told Leah her name was Colleen and offered to drive Leah home. Leah remembered thanking Colleen and telling her she wanted to have some time alone. Colleen reached and took Leah's hand and started praying over her yet again. Leah didn't much want her prayers. At the moment, she didn't want anything other than to have Adam back with her. Leah broke loose of the hold Colleen had on her hand. She climbed into the buggy, slapped the reins, and the horses headed toward home.

Once home, Leah unhitched the buggy, removed the horse's harnesses, fed them, and made sure they had water before heading to the house. It wasn't long before Bishop Miller brought an Englisher into the kitchen where Leah sat at the table. The same table she and Adam had shared their late breakfast at just hours earlier. The bishop introduced Detective Darcy Andrews. They came and sat at the table. The detective asked many questions about what had happened to Adam. Leah wasn't sure she was even answering the questions. All she knew was, she wished for it all to go away. She hopelessly wanted to wake up from the nightmare she was sure she was experiencing.

The bishop stayed behind after Detective Andrews told him she would wait outside. Bishop Miller had always been a kind man. However, at the moment, Leah thought he was anything but kind. He rattled on about God's will, His reasoning, and the Amish way. Leah remembered asking him to please give her time to process what had happened to her husband. Unlike the People, Leah would, for sure and for certain, never believe or accept it was God's will for her husband to die in such a violent way. But if it had been the will of God, then she wanted nothing to do with a God who would permit such wickedness to happen to those who chose to follow Him.

Adam had never brought harm to anyone or anything, and he certainly did not deserve what happened to him, and Leah didn't know what it was she had done to deserve it either.

The next few days, Leah's house was overly busy. She was not permitted to spend time alone, which angered her. She felt trapped in her own home, and no one understood. The bishop reminded her she could not change God's will. He instructed Leah to pull herself together and move on. Leah wanted so desperately to scream. She merely wished to have time alone and wanted everyone out of her house. Not one of them could begin to understand what she was feeling. No public display of grief or show of emotion would be permitted. It was an Amish custom and left many hard in the heart.

The funeral service seemed to take forever, when in reality, it only lasted two hours, and much like a Sunday preaching. The People sang hymns, the deacon prayed, and Bishop Miller preached a sermon. Leah couldn't believe they were all standing there worshiping a God who would allow such horrible things to happen. The bishop, staying true to their customs, never mentioned Adam's name during the preaching and funeral service. Bishop Miller eventually spoke Adam's name, his birth date, and his death date, but only after the services ended. It was over, Adam was gone, and Leah was to show no emotion. *"How was she supposed to obey such a rule? The man she loved with all of her heart no longer shared her life. And, the People expected her to go on as if he never existed at all. She vowed to keep him alive, if only in her memories."*

After everyone left the gravesite, they went back to Leah's house for the communal meal. It took hours to feed the hundreds of people present. Once they all had finished eating, the women cleaned the kitchen, and the men put all the furniture back in its place. The crowd started to thin out. Finally, the only ones left inside the house with Leah were Lyddie and her English husband, Blake Talbert.

As busy as Lyddie was, she always made time for her friend Leah. Lyddie understood Leah's confusion. Growing up, Lyddie struggled with the customs of the Amish People. Leah realized if it had not been for Lyddie's support and encouragement through those last few days, she would have made a displeasing scene, screaming and throwing a fit for everyone to get out of her house and leave her alone. Lyddie asked Leah to stay with her and Blake for a while. When Leah refused her offer, Lyddie hugged her and told Leah she understood her need for some time alone. "Leah, I want to help you in any way I can. If you need anything at all, please don't hesitate to call on me."

"Danki Lyddie, all I need is time alone and no one seems to understand that."

"I can't pretend to grasp what you are going through, but I do understand you need to have some time to yourself. So my friend, on that note, we are leaving. I'll check in on you in a day or so if I don't hear from you." She hugged Leah again before she and Blake disappeared through the door.

At last, Leah was alone to grieve the loss of her husband. The nighttime temperatures were still down close to the freezing point, and a chill raced through her body. Leah was thankful Blake brought some wood in and started a fire before he and Lyddie left. Leah went into the living room, sat by the fire, and let her tears fall. It may have been unacceptable behavior, but she had fought them all day and couldn't have held them back any longer if she had tried. She cried and slept and cried and slept some more. Leah did this throughout the rest of the evening and all through the night. She held tight to Adam's pillow, wishing he was the one she had her arms wrapped around. She hurt deeply and thought she would go out of her mind with grief.

The morning came all too soon. With it came more tears, questions, confusion, anger, and pain. "Why would you take Adam away from me, Gott? We will never be together again. We will never have any kinner. I will never again feel his kiss on my lips, his arms holding me, his cold feet under our quilts on the cold winter nights. I will never see his face or hear his voice again. How could you do this to us, Gott? What did I do that was so wrong to deserve the punishment of living without Adam for the rest of my days?"

Leah thought about ending her life. It would put an end to all the pain she felt. *"But would she be with Adam again if she did take her life?"* Leah wasn't so sure. Had she done enough good works in her lifetime to cover the sin of taking her life?

She cried again and again. She cried for Adam, for all the babies they would never have. But she especially cried for herself. She was angry with God for taking Adam so soon after they had married. They needed to raise a family in the big house they purchased, and where they were to grow old together. Leah had no idea where her life would take her now. What would she do, and how would she make it alone? She raised her voice and cried out to God for the answers she was sure would never come. Leah wept until she had nothing left in her, and sleep overtook her yet again.

When she opened her eyes the following morning, all the pain rushed over her once more. Leah begged God to allow Adam to walk through the door. She wished it was a horrible nightmare, and she would wake up safe in Adam's arms. It wasn't a dream though, Adam was gone, and he would never come through their door again. She was in danger of strict discipline for not behaving according to the People's instruction. Their teachings included accepting God's will and moving on. However, she couldn't imagine moving on in life without Adam Beiler by her side.

Leah sat up from the bed she had made on the floor in front of the fireplace. She heard footsteps. She put her hands to her chest, hoping it was Adam. It was her sister-in-law, Katie Beiler. She went to Leah, knelt beside her, and hugged her. Katie asked Leah to come home with her, but she refused. Katie tried to get her to eat something, but again she refused. Katie meant well. Nevertheless, Leah wasn't interested in food. She wanted some time alone and made her wishes known. "Why is it so hard for you to understand, Katie Beiler? I wish to have time to myself. I don't need anyone here watching over me. Please go away."

Katie now spoke in a firmer tone. "Leah, it is not our way to grieve so. Gott has spoken. He has made His will known. You need to get yourself together and get past this. Life is for the living, not the dead. You need to care for yourself, your animals, and this farm. You must figure out what it is you plan to do with this place now that Adam is—"

Leah abruptly cut her off. She was angry now, and the tone of her voice let Katie know it. "How can you, and the People, be so hard in the heart over things? How can you sit here and tell me it was Gott's will for a man to shoot my ehemann? How is it that a loving Gott can be this cruel? He took Adam from us, and in such a violent way, too. And you and everyone else seem gut with it like it is no big deal. Well, I'm not gut with it, and it is a big deal for me. I need time to think on my own. I don't need anyone telling me how to feel, and how to handle the senseless death of my ehemann. Just go away and leave me be. If I need you, I will send for you."

Katie started to speak. Leah sharply cut her off. "Katie Beiler, I promise you, I will never speak to you again if you do not get out of my house this very second." Leah was thankful she left. It wouldn't be the end of it though, Katie would go for the bishop, and they would be returning soon enough for him to speak to Leah or better yet, to discipline her over her anger and her actions.

As soon as Katie was out the door, Leah grabbed a pen and paper to scribble a note explaining she was going away to guarantee some privacy. She wrote Katie's name on the envelope and left it on the kitchen table where Katie would be sure to find it.

She rushed to her room and began stuffing clothes into a bag. The apron she wore the night of the incident peeked out from under her bed. Leah bent down and picked up the garment. Adam's blood still covered much of the fabric. At first, she held the apron close to her chest, and then she started ripping at the material and continued attacking it until it was nearly shredded. She hadn't realized how much anger had built up within her. She tossed the tattered garment to the floor and trampled it underfoot. Once her fit of rage ended, she stuffed more items into the bag as she wondered where she would go. She could always hire an English driver to take her to her Aunt Abby Miller's home down in Ethridge, Tennessee. When Leah went to visit Abby for a few weeks as a young teenager, her aunt invited her to come and live in their Ethridge district.

Abby left Lancaster County after her husband, Ezekiel, died from a massive heart attack at the age of twenty. Like Leah, she also had the desire to run away. Abby hired a driver and went to visit a friend in Ethridge, Tennessee, and never returned. Leah was sure her aunt would understand how she felt. Abby remarried a widower with four small children. She seemed quite happy in the letters she often wrote. Leah wondered how her aunt got over the death of the man she loved ever so much. It was never a secret Abby's husband, Ezekiel, was born with a heart defect. The doctors warned him it was only a matter of time before it shut down completely. Even with the years of warnings, it still crushed Abby when she lost Ezekiel.

Leah guessed she was a lot like her aunt. She wanted to run away from all those people telling her how she should handle Adam's death. Leah quickly finished filling the bag with everything she thought she needed. She rushed back to the kitchen and reached for her treasure box sitting high on the shelf. She gripped the money she had hidden inside. Pulling it out, she slid it into her apron pocket.

Leah's heart raced so fast it made her chest hurt. Her head still hurt from all the congestion caused by her endless crying. She reached and grabbed Adam's pillow from the bed she had made on the floor, the day of his funeral, and quickly headed out toward the barn to harness the horse. She surely would not have to deal with her brother at this hour. He would be back home by now taking care of his chores there.

Inside the barn, she looked everywhere for her horse's harness. She wondered why Luke would move it, and where he could have put it. She didn't have time to go on a scavenger hunt. As big and bulky as it was, it would be nearly impossible to hide. She was about to give up and leave when she heard her female terrier crying from the back of the barn.

She hadn't seen her dogs in days. Leah felt bad for neglecting them. She made her way to the back of the barn and opened the door. The dog was immediately at her feet. Leah bent down and hugged her. "Sorry girl, I have to go away for a while, Luke will take gut care of you though, I promise. If I could take you with me, I would. But, I don't even know where I am going. You must get back in your pen now." Leah kissed the dog's head. "You be a gut girl for me."

Leah went back to the front of the barn and searched for the harness some more. She didn't understand what could have happened to it. She decided she may as well head back to the house and face the wrath of Bishop Miller.

As she was nearing the house, she heard a car coming close. Leah thought to herself how she wished it would be her friend Lyddie. She stopped and watched the car pull into the driveway. Leah felt a sense of panic come over her. She ran toward Lyddie's car and swung open the door, climbing into the front seat, she rattled on so fast Lyddie couldn't understand her rambling.

Lyddie reached over and put her hand on Leah's shoulder. "Slow down, Leah. I can't understand anything you are saying. Take a deep breath and slowly repeat what you just said."

"Please, Lyddie, get me away from here and do it fast. I need to get out of here before the bishop comes."

Lyddie spoke in a soft tone. "Leah, you must calm down. We will go wherever you want to go. But first, tell me what happened. Why are you afraid of Bishop Miller coming to visit?"

"Can I please stay with you and Blake until I can arrange for a driver to take me to Ethridge, Tennessee, to my Aenti Abby's haus?"

"Of course you can. You can stay for as long as you need, you know that." Lyddie reached again and touched Leah's hand as she continued to speak. "I'll do whatever I can to help you through this."

"Danki Lyddie."

"Tell me what happened. And why are you expecting a visit from the bishop?"

"I need to get away from here before Katie Beiler comes back and brings Bishop Miller with her." Leah took a deep breath and slowly let it out. "Katie came to see me this morning. I felt like she was—like she was smothering me. She told me I was not behaving in line with our teachings, and I needed to get over Adam's death." A tear fell from Leah's eye.

Lyddie told her to take her time and finish when she was ready. After a moment, Leah continued. "She repeatedly told me what happened to Adam was Gott's will, and I must accept it. She then said I needed to decide what I wished to do with the farm. Ach, Lyddie, I wasn't the least bit nice to her. I yelled and told her to get out of my haus. I'm afraid I told her she was no longer welcome there. I'm ashamed of the way I treated her. But Lyddie, you didn't hear her go on the way she did. I know that is no excuse for yelling at her. Please, can we go? I don't think I can take another visit from Katie, and I do not wish to deal with the bishop, for sure and for certain."

Lyddie turned the car around and headed out of the driveway. They drove in silence for a while before Lyddie spoke. "Leah, I know you are hurting—."

Leah cut her off. "Ach, please, Lyddie, not you too."

"No, Leah, I was going to say, I know you're hurting, and when you are ready to talk, I'm here to listen. I'm not going to push you, and I am certainly not going to tell you how to grieve over your loss."

Leah whispered, "I'm ever so sorry, Lyddie. Danki so much, for being my friend and for understanding I'm having a hard time saying goodbye to my ehemann."

Lyddie reached over and gave Leah's hand a gentle squeeze but didn't speak. Leah was grateful Lyddie was still a part of her life. Even though Lyddie believed different from the Old Order Amish, she never tried to draw Leah away from their Amish roots. Lyddie never lectured Leah, nor did she pressure Leah to believe as she did.

When Leah asked questions about Lyddie's beliefs, and why she believed the way she did, her reply was always the same. "I can only tell of my own experiences with the Lord." And, "This is what the Bible says." She always made the

Scriptures interesting for Leah. Between Lyddie's account of the Bible and their strict Amish rules, Leah wasn't sure what to believe. Her father talked on the same line as Lyddie. But, he seemed nervous when he spoke of Jesus. Leah figured it was easier to follow the rules of their Ordnung. As much as she loved her friend, she still did not understand Lyddie's reasons for not joining the church, and for leaving their Faith. She finally quit asking questions because Leah was not only afraid of the wrath of the bishop, but the thought of being shunned terrified her.

CHAPTER 5
૭∽૨

"But I would not have you to be ignorant brethren,
concerning them which are asleep, that ye sorrow not,
even as others which have no hope."
I Thessalonians 4:13

Leah held tight to the bag she had brought with her, while Lyddie and Blake showed her to the room where she would be staying. They invited her to come to the kitchen when she was ready. They both hugged Leah and left her to her privacy. As Leah sat on the bed, she pulled Adam's pillow from the bag. Hugging it tight, the thought of taking her own life came flooding over her again. She yearned for the pain she felt to go away, and she desperately wished to see Adam one more time. Leah wondered if her aunt felt the same way after losing her husband. If she had, she never acted on it. Leah convinced herself, her aunt's loss was different from hers. Her aunt's husband didn't die from a senseless act of violence. There was no way it could have been as painful for her aunt. At that moment, Leah decided she would take her own life, but she didn't know how? The tears welled up in her eyes, and she heard her voice shouting. "If you want me to die, tell me how to do it!" No sooner than the words left her lips, she heard a knock on the door.

Lyddie came in, sat on the edge of the bed, and put her arm around Leah's shoulder. "Oh, Leah, please talk to me. I know you are in grave pain, but you mustn't think about taking your own life. It would crush Adam to know you are feeling so desperate that you would contemplate suicide."

"Ach, Lyddie, my heart holds so much pain. I cannot bear the thought of going on without my Adam. I need him here with me. I know the Amish believe everything which happens is Gott's will, and my grieving is unacceptable. But Lyddie, I don't much care how they expect me to feel and act. My Adam is gone, my heart's crushed, and I wish ever so much the Englisher had taken my life that day as well. I don't understand why he didn't just shoot me too."

"I can't begin to understand the mind of someone so tormented. And Leah, I cannot begin to know how broken-hearted, angry, and confused you are at this time. I can tell you my heart was heavy with pain when both my grandparents passed away."

Leah interrupted her. "But Lyddie, this is different, they didn't –."

Lyddie's voice was soft when she, in turn, interrupted Leah. "Shh, please listen to what I have to say. I am hoping what I tell you will bring you some comfort. I remember being so angry with God when He took Grossmudder Fisher. Grossdaadi Fisher explained so much to me after her death. The anger I had toward God was wrong, and you are wrong too. Grossdaadi explained to me the Bible tells us not to grieve as one with no hope. Leah, it is natural for us to grieve over the death of our loved ones. However, the Lord tells us we shouldn't mourn as if we have no hope."

Leah's voice held a tone of frustration. "I don't understand you, Lyddie. What does that even mean?"

"The day before Adam's funeral, you told me about the woman praying with him, and Adam had said he accepted Christ as his Savior years ago. Adam has made Heaven his home. He is with Jesus, and knowing this should comfort you."

"Well, I'm not comforted by any means. I am hurt, confused, and ever so angry. If I go back home, I will have to hear how wrong I am to feel the way I do. Katie kept telling me my actions are a sin against God. If I hear one more time, it was Gott's will for Adam to die this way, I'll—I'll scream!"

"You don't have to go home. You are welcome to stay here with us for as long as you want. I am here for you, Leah. If you wish to talk, I'll listen. Or if you need me to sit with you, I will. But for now, Blake has fixed us a delicious meal. Do you think you can eat a little something?"

"Lyddie, thank you for asking me if I wished to eat instead of demanding that I eat. Ever since the days before the funeral, everyone has ordered me to do things. They kept shoving food in front of me, saying how much better I would feel if I ate. As if the food would somehow make me forget my grief over Adam. Danki, for always being so kind and understanding with me. I can't remember how many days it's been since I have eaten. The thought of food made me sick to my stomach. But now, I believe I should try to eat something."

Lyddie showed Leah to the bathroom. After explaining how the shower worked, she told Leah to take her time and enjoy the benefits a hot shower offered. Leah didn't realize how much she had neglected her body since Adam's death. The hot water felt refreshing as it ran down over her head. She felt the tension in her body washing away, as well as the sweat and dirt. She thought she might like to stay under the water indefinitely. It felt good being clean again. Leah slipped into her mourning dress. It was customary to wear a black dress for one year after losing a spouse. As she combed out her wet hair, she thought how strange it was to wear a black dress to show sorrow, but yet any public display of grief was unacceptable. Maybe it was out of rebellion, but she chose not to pin her apron on, and she refused to pull her hair up tight under the prayer kapp. She didn't plan on going out in public, so she felt her black stockings were also unnecessary. She noticed the headache she had experienced since Adam's death wasn't as intense now. She peered into the large oval mirror hanging on the wall before leaving to find Lyddie.

Leah walked into the kitchen half expecting to get scolded for her appearance. Instead, both Lyddie and Blake smiled at her. Blake said. "Ah, Leah, there you are. You're just in time to see what a wonderful cook I am. I bet you had no idea I could whip up a meal fit for a king."

Leah scowled at him. Sitting down, she replied. "We shall see if you have a right to brag."

The food was as good as Blake promised. Or maybe it was because Leah had suddenly realized how hungry she was. It was not only pleasing to her stomach, but it also seemed to help strengthen her mind as well. She surprised herself by getting through the meal joking with them both instead of shedding more tears. Lyddie and Blake kept the conversation light during the meal, which was a big help to her. Lyddie told Leah she would let Bishop Miller and her parents know she would be visiting with them for a while. She would also ask Leah's bruder, Luke, to continue caring for the animals until Leah was able to return home.

The next couple of days, Leah talked and ate very little. She slept a lot, and neither Blake nor Lyddie scolded her for it. They seemed to support Leah's actions. She was never left alone, though. Leah knew it was because of her outburst of wanting to take her own life. Lyddie asked Ruth Stoltzfus Yoder to take over her lessons at the Amish school, while she spent time with Leah. After three days of this pattern, Leah started to feel almost normal again. She asked Lyddie why they had allowed this type of behavior. Lyddie explained to her it was part of the grieving and healing process, and it was something she had to come to terms with on her own. Leah was somewhat shocked when they gave her so much time to take care of herself. She felt a certain degree of guilt over it and told Lyddie so.

Leah knew she would never forget the words Lyddie spoke so sweetly to her. "Leah, you have been through a tremendous tragedy. You needed time to deal with your loss on your own. And, now that you are feeling some guilt, it means you are starting to heal. You are starting to get past the initial grief. You will always have a certain amount of hurt over your loss, but you will be able to move past it and live your life again. I'm not telling you it will be easy, but you're becoming strong enough to go home and start taking care of your farm."

"Please, Lyddie, do not send me away yet. There are things I wish to discuss with you. Things which are for sure confusing to me, nevertheless, they are things I need to know about."

"Oh Leah, don't fret, I'm not going to send you away. I told you, you are welcome to stay for as long as you need. You know you can talk to me about anything, right?"

"Jah, I know. Lyddie, I'm sorry I didn't tell you everything Adam said to me before he died. I don't know why I kept it hidden. Probably because I thought he was talking narrish. You see, he told me to follow Jesus, to forget about the teachings of the People, and accept that Jesus is the only way to Heaven. He told me he would be waiting in Heaven for me, but I needed to stop believing good works alone would get me there." Leah's eyes filled with tears, but they weren't for

Adam this time, it was because she wanted so desperately to know what he meant by his words. She wanted to know she would be with him again when it was her turn to leave this life. "Lyddie, why do you suppose this happened to Adam? Why do you think Gott permitted it? Why do you suppose Adam was telling me to stop believing in works alone? What did he mean? Ach, please, forgive me, I'm asking too many questions. I'm just ever so confused over it. I want to understand it all. I have heard my Daed's tellings over the years, and yours too, but they have always left me more confused. So, I would put them out of my mind and do my best to follow the Ordnung."

"I'm sorry I have left you feeling so perplexed. It was never my intention. I'm sure I can also say the same for your Daed. Let's see if I can answer some of your questions without leaving you with more confusion."

"Ach, I would be ever so grateful. I truly do wish to understand. I have been afraid to ask questions for fear of sounding like a dumm kopp."

"Never be afraid to ask questions." Lyddie suddenly giggled and continued. "You must have thought I was the biggest dumm kopp there was growing up. Especially with the multitude of questions I always asked." They both laughed, and it felt good.

"Leah, I'm sorry I cannot tell you why this happened to Adam. I can tell you the Bible says rain will fall on the just and the unjust alike. What that means is, bad things will happen to those who choose to follow Christ as well as those who do not. It's not a perfect world. God never meant for His creation to behave the way we have today. He gave us the ability to make our own choices. Unfortunately, our choices are not always the right ones. We, as humans, have messed everything up with our sinful and selfish desires. This man's evil nature and his bad choices are what caused Adam's death. It was not anything Adam did, and before you say it, it wasn't anything you did either. It was purely the evil within this young man's heart. I learned many years ago we will never have all the answers we desire. Nor will we ever have complete understanding while we are in this world. But, we do have the Bible, and it has all the answers we need for our time here. It is why it's so important to read and study it daily."

"This is one reason I get confused. The People's teachings are so different from what you believe. They say, in order for us to save our mind from confusion, only the head of the household, the bishop, and the preachers should read the Bible and recite the prayers."

"I understand what you are saying. I spent years torn between the teachings of the Ordnung and what the Bible says. They are very different in some ways. You know, it's like two different sets of rules. I do not wish to belittle the Ordnung to you. The Amish have the Ordnung, just as the Englishers have their laws. And, even though we must obey those laws, they are a list of man's rules. The rules God gives us are the rules which should concern us the most. These are the rules to follow, and we can find them in the Bible. I came to believe the rules of the Ordnung supported by God's Word needed following. We need to cast aside the rules which go against the teachings of God."

"Lyddie, please, can you make it simple for me? Like, tell me what Adam meant by not believing in works alone? Good works are what gives us our hope of making Heaven. But while Adam was dying in my arms, he knew, for sure and for certain, he was going to Heaven. He said he knew, without a doubt, he would be with the Lord. He wasn't relying on the hope which the People teach so strictly on."

"First, I'll start by telling you what my Grossdaadi Fisher always told me, *Works do not save you. You get saved to work.* Basically, this is what Adam told you. You see, doing good works will not get you into Heaven. I know this is the most common belief of the People. Nevertheless, it is one of those rules which doesn't line up with God's Word. It's like a half-truth. God's Word tells us Jesus is the only way. We must acknowledge we are sinners. We must believe in Jesus, believe He died on the cross for our sins, and believe God raised Him from the dead. We must trust He can take away our sins. Then we must ask Him to come into our hearts and cleanse us from our sins. We must make Him Lord over our life. Only then are we assured of an eternal home in Heaven. Good works will get us rewards in Heaven, but they can't save us, and get us into Heaven. Only by grace through faith in Jesus Christ will we make it there. It is a choice each one of us must make for ourselves. Adam made that choice. And, Leah, here is where the comfort comes in on our grieving. Adam didn't die with the hope of making Heaven. He died knowing he would make Heaven. It is why he had the peaceful look on his face. He knew he would be with our Lord Jesus Christ when he closed his eyes in death."

"But I do believe in Jesus. So what you're saying is because I believe in Him I will, for sure and for certain, go to Heaven when I die?"

"Not so, even the devil believes in Jesus Christ. He knows Jesus is the real deal. You must—"

"Ach, I am ever so confused again. Please tell me in a way that even my simple mind can understand it all. Adam was sure he was going to Heaven, and I want the assurance as well. How can I be sure?"

"It is not enough to believe. You must confess Him with your mouth, invite Christ into your heart, and allow Him to rule over your life. Ask Him to cleanse you of all unrighteousness. You must follow God's commands and let Him direct your path in life."

Leah's facial expression told Lyddie she did not understand a word Lyddie had just said. Lyddie apologized and continued. "Give yourself to the Lord. You know, like how the bishop instructed us to give authority to the church. I know it's confusing because of the teachings of the People. It is hard to forget something the People taught you your entire life, but it's pretty much what you will have to do to get rid of your confusion. Or at least, separate the two. I will try to simplify it for you. Do you remember how you vowed to give the church authority over your life? Well, instead, give the Lord the authority. We must submit to Him and always follow His ways."

"Lyddie, you taught the young kinner for so long now. You have been able to make them understand complicated lessons. Can you not explain this to me the way you would to one of them? Make it as simple as you can. I know I'm making it harder than it most likely is, but I can't seem to grasp it."

"Many people are walking around out there in the world lost because they make salvation more complicated than it is. Not all that long ago, a pastor came to the church to lead a class about witnessing. A simplified way to lead others to the saving knowledge of Jesus Christ was among his teachings. Pastor Herbert used what he called the A, B, C method. A—Admit, B—Believe, and C—Confess. We must admit we are sinners and cannot save ourselves. We must believe Jesus is God's Son, and He died on the cross to pay the debt for our sins. We must confess our sins and ask Jesus into our hearts. We must give Him authority over our life. There is no other way to Heaven except through Jesus Christ. This is what Adam was trying to tell you the night he died. Leah, accepting Christ as our Savior will not make our journey in life easy. But, we can have confidence knowing the Lord will be right there with us each step of the way. He will guide and direct our path in life. And, He will strengthen us along the way, to overcome the trials we all must face as His children. He will give you the strength to overcome this terrible ordeal you are facing now. I'll help you understand the Bible if you would like to start reading it for yourself. All of the scriptures I have written here for you will back up the steps of salvation. I know your Daed will also help you if you asked. The best place to start is with the Book of John. Read and memorize John 3:16. *For God so loved the world, that He gave His only begotten Son, that whosoever believeth in Him should not perish, but have everlasting life.* This verse is so important in helping us understand the love God has for each of us."

Leah reached and hugged Lyddie. The smile on her face told Lyddie, Leah was beginning to grasp the knowledge of Jesus Christ. "Danki, Lyddie. It means ever so much to have your friendship, support, and encouragement. I am starting to understand what Adam has tried so hard to teach me. He didn't have the way of explaining it to me so I could understand it all. So, it is true we must confess our wrongful deeds to the Lord and not to the bishop? Adam tried to tell me this, but I just warned him about being careful no one else heard him saying such things, as it could bring him much trouble."

"It is true. If you bring your sins before the Lord and ask for forgiveness, you will, without a doubt, receive forgiveness. He is the only One with the authority to forgive our sins. Asking the bishop to forgive you will give you right standing in the church. However, the bishop himself cannot give you right standing with God. That is between you and God alone."

It was as if something clicked in Leah's head. She now understood what Adam had tried to teach her all along, and what Lyddie was now explaining. Leah likened it to a gas lantern. When extinguished, she was in total darkness, stumbling and lost. While she stumbled around in the dark, she had no understanding of the Lord. But, when she lit that same gas lantern, and the light was brightly shining, she no longer stumbled. She could easily find her way. Leah now got it, Jesus was that Light.

"Ach Lyddie, I have been such a dumm kopp, for sure and for certain. I understand so much more already. I can't believe it has taken me this long to grasp salvation's plan. One of the reasons I tried to stay detached from this way of teaching was because I saw the friction it caused within our church. I didn't wish to take part in the controversy. I've heard some talk of a separation coming to our district. It frightened me ever so much, so I chose not to think about it. Some of the People did not approve of the way your Grossdaadi ruled over the community. They say Bishop Miller is much too lenient, even more so than your Grossdaadi was. They wish to follow the Old Order. There is, however, more who like the way things are now. More of the People talk of Jesus Christ and the assurance, but I couldn't understand what that assurance was they were speaking of."

"I can't say I'm surprised by this news. I remember when Grossdaadi Fisher passed away. Many of the members were hoping for a bishop who would enforce a stricter set of rules. Oh Leah, if only they realized many of the rules they are following do not even begin to line up with God's Word."

"What do you mean when you say they do not line up with Gott's Word?"

"I mean some of the rules of the People go against what God says. Like I said earlier, there are two different sets of rules, the Ordnung and God's Word. Obeying the Ordnung will keep you from receiving discipline. But, it will not get you into Heaven, for sure and for certain. You must obey God's Word, and His Word tells us there is only one way to Heaven, and that way is Jesus Christ."

Lyddie continued to explain the things Leah needed to know to make Heaven her home when her life on this earth ended. Lyddie took the Bible from the bedside table and opened it. She turned the pages and read Scripture from the books of Romans, Ephesians, Acts, and John. She finished reading with the verse from John 14:6. It amazed Leah, and those words filled her with such peace. For the first time since Adam's death, she felt she had real hope.

Leah contemplated taking her own life, not all that long ago. Now she sat there filled with such hope, peace, and joy. Leah accepted Jesus Christ into her heart and made Him Lord over her life that afternoon. It was remarkable how much she learned and came to understand in the few short hours Lyddie read and explained the scriptures to her. Leah did not understand every scripture Lyddie read. But she was confident God would help her, as would her father and Lyddie. Once Lyddie got through to Leah that she indeed was making it more difficult than it was, Leah came to the Lord with simple faith.

As the months passed, Leah grew in the Lord by "leaps and bounds" as Lyddie put it. Leah's dad guided her in their Bible studies, teaching her so much more than Leah ever imagined her stubborn mind would comprehend. But, the Lord opened up Leah's understanding.

It took Leah time to realize that although the loss of her husband left her with an empty feeling inside, through her time of grief, the Lord had filled the emptiness with the peace and hope she had never known beforehand.

CHAPTER 6

"...weeping may endure for a night, but joy cometh in the morning."
Psalm 30:5

Nearly a year has passed since Leah lost her husband. Her heart still aches for him. The difference is she no longer grieves as one with no hope. She holds firm to her belief that the day the Lord calls her from this life, not only will she be with Jesus, but she will have a glorious reunion with Adam as well.

There are many days Satan fights his hardest to beat Leah down, and there are those days when she feels she'll lose her mind. At times, Leah is still confused between the ways of the People and God's way. God is ever faithful, however. When Leah is at a low point, God brings Lyddie's words back to Leah's remembrance.

"Don't get stuck in this world. We are merely passing through it. Keep your focus on God and the heavenly home He has prepared for those who trust in Him. Remember, our salvation is in our Savior, Jesus Christ. He paid it all for us, and our future is with Him in that glorious home where we will never be separated from Him again. Keep your eyes on Him and the rewards He has promised His faithful servants."

When Leah left Lyddie's house a few months earlier, she and Lyddie talked about Leah facing her empty house alone. Lyddie took a moment to encourage her. "Leah, remember, the Lord does not promise us an easy journey in this life. However, we do have His promise that He will be with us in every trial we must endure." Lyddie hugged her and continued. "If you start to dwell on your pain or get discouraged in any way, go find a neighbor in need. It is hard to focus on your problems when you are working on helping others during their trials." Leah promised her friend she would do just that.

The past several weeks, Leah spent her time adjusting to a full house. Caring for her neighbor's children became a full-time job. Lyddie was right. Leah had no time to think about much of anything, much less her problems. Her house was busy with three energetic toddlers from morning till night. She invited the children and their father, Benjamin Lapp, to stay with her in her and Adam's house.

A terrible storm came through the area one evening, and lightning struck the Lapp's house. It burnt to the ground very quickly. For some unknown reason, Benjamin Lapp's wife, Annie, ran back into the burning building. Benjamin told Leah once they were all safely outside, Annie kept yelling their dead baby's name. When he had bent down to help their three-year-old daughter, who had fallen, his wife ran back into the burning building. Benjamin felt she got confused and thought the baby they had lost the previous month was still inside the house. She ran back into the flames to save him. Benjamin did everything he could to get to her before she disappeared inside the house, but it was of no use. The following day, they found her remains in the rubble. Better than anyone, Leah could understand the pain in Benjamin Lapp's heart over losing his wife in the fire.

He acted extremely grateful, in the beginning, for her allowing him and his children to come live in her house. It wasn't long, though, before he started treating her as if she was the one who took his wife's life. He refused to spend much time inside Leah's house with her and his three children. He also refused to sleep inside the house. Some nights, he chose to sleep in the barn, other nights, Leah had no clue where he slept.

Benjamin Lapp began helping Leah's brother, Luke, out around the farm. Having the extra help freed up some of Luke's time. Luke had worked hard trying to keep up with both his and Leah's farms, since the death of Adam. Leah did her best to help Luke, the added work and stress was taking its toll on her brother. He had his own growing family to care for as well as his farm. He was also employed three days a week at the tackle shop. Leah felt guilty as she watched her brother work so hard to keep things on their farm running as smoothly as Adam did. She wondered what possessed her to keep the large house, all the animals, and the eighty acres of land, she and Adam owned. She could never care for the farm on her own, and it wasn't fair to Luke or his family, expecting him to carry the burden for her. Leah prayed God would give her the direction in which He needed her to go. She didn't want to give up her home or Adam's dream, but she wasn't being realistic thinking Luke could continue working himself to a frazzle keeping her farm going.

Leah's mind came back to Benjamin Lapp and his family. Maybe she could hire Benjamin to run the farm for her. But, with as difficult as this man was, she really couldn't see herself working with him long-term.

Benjamin always took his meals out in the barn, which left Leah to eat alone with his three children. It was not an easy task taking care of three-year-old Beth and the twenty-month old twins, Caleb and Katie. The twins were much easier to take care of than Beth. She cried long and hard for her mother. Leah spent much of her time trying to comfort the child.

The girl's features were strikingly similar to her father's. Beth had the same dark curls and deep blue eyes like her dad, which was such an attractive feature in Benjamin. Leah felt the girl's pain, and as young as Beth was, she could tell Leah understood her grief. She wished their Daed would realize that Leah was no stranger to the heartbreak of losing a spouse. Benjamin was so angry. He had Leah in tears many times over his comments to her. She prayed for him daily and for the strength to continue to help his children. She reminded herself that everyone handled grief differently. Lyddie even told Leah how, not all that long ago, Leah herself had lashed out at Adam's sister-in-law while she was suffering through her grieving process.

Each day, Leah prayed for patience and the strength to deal with this stubborn, angry man. She tried encouraging to him, just as Lyddie had during Leah's time of grief. But, it only seemed to make Benjamin Lapp even angrier. There were times his blue eyes frightened Leah. Some days they seemed to hold only pain. While other days, he pulled his eyebrows down and drawn together, and his face held hostility, as though he was ready to attack her at any given moment. Leah had noticed a softening in his face and eyes a time or two, but that expression was always short-lived.

The promise of a hard winter was upon them, and the nights were cooler with each passing day. The frigid weather had arrived late this year, but now time was of the essence. Leah wondered what she would do about Benjamin Lapp. He couldn't possibly continue to sleep in the barn, with the temperatures dropping near the freezing point each night. The People offered many times to help him rebuild his house, but he refused. Leah truly did understand his disapproval, remembering how difficult it was for her to stay in her home after the death of her husband. However, he needed to start seriously thinking about what he would do for the winter.

Leah scolded herself for not wanting Benjamin to stay inside her house. She enjoyed caring for his children, and they were adjusting very well. She surprised herself by falling in love with each of them immediately. On the other hand, their father was a different story. He had changed ever so much from the man she once knew. During and before their Rumspringa, Benjamin was kind and always spoke in a respectful manner. He was now as unkind as a person could be. And, the truth was, Leah had no desire to keep company with him, much less deal with his attitude inside her home each day.

Now the Lord was for sure scolding her for her unkind thoughts. He reminded Leah of how she had behaved not all that long ago. Lyddie and Blake took her in without hesitation, and she should have a cheerful heart when it came to helping a neighbor in need. Leah sent up a prayer for both Benjamin and herself. She asked the Lord for a gentler spirit concerning Benjamin Lapp. Leah also asked God to heal Benjamin's heart and to give him the peace and comfort He had blessed her with during her time of sorrow. She looked to the ceiling as she spoke. "Lord, please help me find a way to get through to this man. Give me the words to help him understand that although he and his kinner have suffered a great tragedy, they are all very much alive, and his kinner need him."

While preparing the evening meal, Leah fretted, over asking Benjamin of his plans with the changing weather. She decided now was as good a time as any. When he came for his meal, she would ask him where he planned to sleep now that it was becoming too cold to sleep in the barn.

Leah was thinking too hard about Benjamin and wasn't paying enough attention to the meal, which Beth was helping her prepare. Beth knocked the flour bag over, and it spilled out on the counter and all over the floor. They were both covered in flour as well, and Beth now sat on the floor crying uncontrollably. Leah sat down beside her and pulled the girl into her arms.

As Leah held her, she assured Beth everything was all right. She explained how accidents happen all the time. She smiled and told Beth to look at the white powder, which covered a large area of the floor and pretend it had snowed here in the kitchen. Beth wiped her tears and looked up at Leah. Smiling, she said, "You are not upset with me?"

"Nee, I am not at all upset with you."

Beth hugged Leah tight. "I love you, Leah Beiler. I wish I could stay with you forever." Leah, in turn, told her how much she had come to wish the very same thing. Leah explained to Beth, "Eventually, you will have to leave with your Daed and the twins. But for now, my sweet maedel, we will enjoy every moment we spend together." After drawing a snowman in the flour, they rushed to clean up the mess and finish working on the meal.

They must have spent more time on the floor than Leah realized, because Benjamin came into the kitchen looking for his meal. As usual, he was angry and ranted on about how Leah should take care of her duties in the kitchen.

Leah promptly turned to Beth, "Please go upstairs and check on the twins. Go quietly. They may still be napping." Beth nodded and quickly left the room.

Leah turned back to Benjamin. He had hit a nerve and she reacted to him in a way which was unacceptable among the People, for sure and for certain. But, this was, after all, her house. He was a mere guest, not her husband, and she did not hesitate to make that fact known to him.

"As you are aware, Benjamin Lapp, this is my haus. And, I'm sure I do not need to remind you that you are not my ehemann, but rather a guest in my haus. You have no right to demand anything of me. You have been nothing but hostile to me since I opened my home to you and your kinner. I have enjoyed caring for them, and I will continue to care for them and feed you for as long as you need. However, Benjamin Lapp, I will no longer tolerate instruction from you as though you were my ehemann. If you wish to continue to stay here, I insist you start treating me with a little kindness and respect."

Leah swiftly turned to face the sink so he would not see the tears welling up. She heard his footsteps heading out toward the back door. When she turned back, he wasn't anywhere around.

She placed the meal on the table and went to check on the children. They were all playing on the floor. Leah changed the twin's diapers and headed back down to the kitchen. As she looked out the window, she saw Benjamin leaning on a fence post near the barn.

Leah asked Beth to run and tell her Daed the food was ready if he wished to come and get it. He still had never eaten a meal with them. He would come to the kitchen at mealtime and choose what he wanted. He would place it all on a tray and carry it out to the barn.

When Beth returned from the barn, she told Leah her Daed wanted her to bring his supper out to him. Leah fixed a plate for the children and asked Beth to try to keep them interested in their food while she carried the tray out to her Daed. As she handed him his food, he nodded and turned to go into the barn. When Leah started to walk away, she heard him whisper, "Danki."

She looked to Heaven and spoke to God. "Well, it's a start."

Leah had trouble sleeping that night. She found herself praying over and over for Benjamin Lapp. She never witnessed him being so harsh. He always had a smile for everyone. His wife, Annie, always spoke so highly of him. She often told how good he was with their children, always helping with whatever they needed. Unlike most Amish men, Benjamin helped her put their children to bed each night. He had never even been in their bedrooms at Leah's. As a matter of fact, he had never been any farther than her kitchen. Leah's home was large enough to support the many children she and Adam had planned to raise. The main floor had only one bedroom, and it was the one Adam and Leah had shared. She hadn't been able to bring herself to sleep in their bed since his death. Leah used the bedroom over the kitchen, Beth stayed in the one across the hall from her, and the twins shared one of the other two bedrooms.

Lately selling the farm consumed Leah's thoughts, especially during the night, while she tried to sleep. She knew why she wanted to hold on to it, but she also knew it would be a wise decision to sell it all. She did not plan to remarry, and the house was much too large for one person. The farm was something she could never care for on her own, no matter how much she wished she could. The thought even occurred to her to offer it to Benjamin Lapp for a fair price. She could always move back with her Mamm and Daed or stay in their small daadi haus until she decided what to do.

The sound of footsteps interrupted her thoughts. It was Beth, and she was sobbing. Leah held her arms out, and the child came running and climbed up on Leah's bed. Leah held her tight. Once again, Beth was unable to tell Leah what had frightened her. Beth asked to stay with her for the night. While tucking her in under the quilts, Leah asked. "Did your Daed ever tuck you in at night?"

"Jah, he did, till our haus got all burned up. He don't kiss and hug me no more, and he never plays with me no more either."

Leah's heart was breaking while listening to Beth try to explain, with her three-year-old vocabulary. Leah set her mind to have a talk with Benjamin Lapp about it first thing in the morning. He could not shun his children. It was as if he was punishing them, as well as everyone else, for losing his wife and his house. It was hard enough losing their mother, but it as though they had lost their father too.

Beth soon fell back to sleep and slept soundly for the rest of the night. Leah, on the other hand, was not so fortunate. Selling the farm weighed heavily on her mind. She knew it would be a wise decision, but it was all she had left of her Adam and the dreams they shared. Her mind wandered off to all the hopes they had for their farm and the land which surrounded it. She wanted Adam to send her a sign telling her what she should do. Out of respect, she discussed the matter with her brother-in-law, Joel, and asked him if he wished to buy the land and the house back from her. He wanted nothing to do with it. He was happy with their parent's farm and being close to care for his aging parents. Joel suggested she place an advertisement in their Amish newspaper, The Budget, offering the farm and the acreage for sale. And, if Leah wished to keep the house, he encouraged her to sell off or lease out the land.

In the morning, while dressing, it occurred to Leah why she was so restless about giving up their farm. She couldn't sell the place until she fulfilled the promise she had made to Adam. She never built the chicken coop as she promised him that dreadful night. "Ach, Adam, I do not wish to build anything without you here beside me. Why did you make me promise such a thing?" The lumber lay stacked in the barn where Luke had piled it all those months ago. Leah needed to build it before she thought of selling out again. Looking at Adam's pillow, which she hugged each night, she softly spoke. "I'm sorry my ehemann, I will build the coup as I promised you I would. But please do not be angry with me if I choose to sell the farm after I finish it. I can't even sleep in our bed, and you know I cannot take care of this farm on my own, for sure and for certain. Please understand my ehemann."

She talked with Adam often. It gave her peace and helped her feel a little less alone. Although Leah hadn't felt alone for some time now, Benjamin Lapp's children kept her busy. There wasn't much time in the day for her become lonely. However, when the children were all tucked in their beds for the night, the loneliness crept in. Hugging Adam's pillow somewhat helped her get through the night. She wished she could turn off her thoughts as she would the gas lanterns in her home. Her nights still brought many nightmares of that tragic day long ago. She desperately wanted to have delightful dreams with her and her husband walking through the fields as they once did. It would be a welcomed change from the evil which walked through her memories almost nightly. She sent up a prayer over the day and quietly headed down the stairs to the kitchen.

Leah was preparing breakfast when Benjamin walked into the kitchen. She poured him a cup of coffee and offered him a place at the table. Surprisingly, he accepted and sat down. The house was so quiet it sent chills through her bones. Finally, she broke the silence by telling him they needed to talk about the winter weather, which had finally come upon them. He must have misunderstood her intentions. He spoke in almost a whisper. "Do you wish for us to leave now?"

"Ach nee, it isn't what I meant at all. I do not feel you can continue to live in my barn with the cold nights we have been having." Leah took a deep breath and released it. "You are welcome to use a bedroom here in the haus."

She wasn't prepared for his harshness, even though she should have gotten used to it by now. "Let us be honest here, Leah Beiler, you do not wish for me to sleep in your haus anymore than I wish to sleep in a barn. I have found a warm and comfortable place to sleep. I do not need any more of your charity."

Remembering that Beth was still asleep in the room just above them, Leah tried to stay calm and keep her voice at a whisper. "Why must you be so harsh toward me? I was going to purpose to you, in exchange for the use of a room, you could work with me to raise a chicken coop. Before the Englisher killed him, my ehemann and I had planned to build it together."

The look on his face completely changed. Leah believed, at that moment, he remembered she too had suffered a heartbreaking loss. As fast as his expression softened, it turned hard again.

"I will have to think about it. Miriam Stoltzfus and I have talked of marrying. So, my kinner and I could be out of your hair real soon."

Leah couldn't believe how quickly her words came out. She shocked herself with the stiff tone of her voice. "Ach, nee, do you love her? It is too soon. Have you been spending time with her?" The moment the words came out of her mouth, Leah knew she crossed the line. There was no doubt Benjamin Lapp would scold her for her interference.

He quickly retorted. "You are out of line. And, this is none of your business, Leah Beiler, for sure and for certain."

Leah was in too deep and wasn't about to back down now. "Not where you're concerned, perhaps. But, you have permitted me to raise your kinner, for the past several months. Without any help from you, I might add. I believe you have made them my business, Benjamin Lapp." She willed herself to calm down. She spoke once again but in a softer tone. "You are hurt and angry over your Annie's death, and I better than anyone can understand what you are going through. You must remember it hasn't been all that long ago since my ehemann died in my arms. That Englisher stuck a gun to my Adam's chest and shot him right in front of me, and the vision still haunts me every night in my sleep. I'm begging you not to act in haste. I love those bopplin ever so much. The fact of the matter is I couldn't love them any more if they were my own."

Benjamin's voice was hurtful as he lashed out at Leah. "Still in all, they are not yours, they're mine. I will do what I wish, and you have no say in it whatsoever. It is not my fault you permitted yourself to get so attached to another woman's kinner."

As hurt as Leah was, all she could think about was, *"Did he love Miriam?"* For the life of her, she couldn't figure out why she would repeat her previous question. However, she was hoping he would answer her this time. "But do you love her?"

"What does that have to do with anything?"

"It has a lot to do with everything! You will be in partnership with Miriam Stoltzfus for the rest of your days. You will wake up to her every morning. You will eat every meal with her, and you will give her free will to raise your kinner. As she sees fit, mind you. You, as a man, can take care of yourself. However, those bopplin cannot. Has she ever been around Beth, Caleb, and Katie? Does she even know their names? Have you ever seen how she treats children? Do you truly know Miriam Stoltzfus?" Leah shocked herself by becoming so personal with this man. Still in all, he was completely crazy if he was to marry the likes of Miriam Stoltzfus.

He sat in silence. Leah had no idea how to get him to understand that Miriam had a mean and hateful spirit concerning children. Leah had known for some time Miriam was desperately seeking a husband. Given her dislike for children, Leah couldn't understand why she set her mind to a man with three small ones. The thought of it broke Leah's heart, and it gave her the strength to continue. "Benjamin Lapp, that woman hates children! If you have set your mind to marry her, and you can withstand it for the rest of your life, that is gut. But please, I'm begging you to leave your kinner with me." She didn't give any care to the tears which were now streaming down her face. The thought of Miriam Stoltzfus raising the children, she had come to love so dearly, literally put fear in her for their wellbeing.

By the look in his eyes, it seemed as though Benjamin's heart had softened. However, it quickly changed. Leah could now see the anger spread across his face as he spoke. "You have no right to speak such things. As I have said, this is none of your business. My kinner and I will be out of your haus by week's end."

He got up and turned to leave. Grabbing hold of his arm, Leah pleaded with him. "Wait. Please, don't leave Benjamin. I'm begging you to hear me out. I do not wish for you to go. I want you to take time to get to know Miriam Stoltzfus, spend some time with her. Watch her when she doesn't know you are watching. Please stay here, help me build my chicken coop, and take time to think this through. At least ask yourself why Miriam has yet to find a husband."

For the first time since coming to stay at her house, Leah saw half a smile come across Benjamin's face, and he replied, "Your bruder asked me something like that yesterday. His words were a bit harsher than yours, though. He questioned me about why I would wish to live in misery for the rest of my days by marrying a woman no other man in our district, or any of the other nearby districts, would have." Even though the others only saw the displeasing side of Miriam. Benjamin witnessed times when Miriam's heart softened. It wasn't often; however, he knew a kind soul was hiding within the shell of Miriam Stoltzfus.

Leah tried to stifle her giggle. Shaking her head, she responded. "Leave it to Luke. He isn't afraid to say what is on his mind, no matter how it sounds coming out. Seriously though, Luke is a wise man, and you would do gut to think on what he has said to you."

Benjamin sat back down. Leah poured him another cup of coffee, refilled her cup, and sat with him. It was then that Benjamin Lapp had a miraculous turnaround. His transformation astonished Leah. Surprisingly, after all these months, they sat together and had an enjoyable conversation. They talked about so many things, and then the conversation turned on a more personal level.

"Leah, you have been wunderbaar gut with Beth, Katie, and Caleb. Danki, I truly appreciate it. Please vergeef me for my actions. I will work on being friendlier from now on, I promise. And, I will do better at helping you with my kinner."

"This means you will stay, jah?"

"Jah, we will stay. I'll help you raise your coop, and I'll also work on getting to know Miriam Stoltzfus better."

For some reason, she didn't like what he had said. But, at least the children would be safe with her, for a while longer anyway. "Danki Benjamin, I feel it is for the best, especially for your kinner."

Benjamin went out to the barn to finish the chores. God knew he loved that woman, and it was a hard task being so close to her. It was easier for him to treat her with disrespect than to let his true feelings be made known. His attitude toward her helped keep his feelings in check. Now that he was alone with his thoughts, his emotions welled up inside him. He had loved Leah Zook Beiler for as long as he could remember. There was no doubt in Benjamin's mind; this was a test from God. He had no right to love this woman who continued to grieve the loss of her husband. God forgive him. He still should be in mourning over the loss of his wife as well. A part of him wished to get as far away from Leah Beiler as he could. Still, another part of him felt the need to stay close to her. Benjamin prayed daily for God to give him the strength to leave Leah.

CHAPTER 7
ം‌‌

"Be ye strong therefore, and let not your hands be
weak: for your work shall be rewarded."
II Chronicles 15:7

It was hard for Leah to offer Benjamin the bed she had once shared with Adam. Despite that fact, Leah had no wish to ever again sleep in the bed. She felt it was better anyway for her to stay as close to Beth as possible. The girl had nightmares nearly every night and ended up in Leah's bed often. Beth still hadn't been able to tell Leah about her dreams. All Leah knew was Beth slept better when she snuggled in tight with Leah. However, Leah felt it would make it harder for the child to leave when her Daed moved his family to a new house. She allowed herself to become too attached to Beth and the twins, and it would break her heart when they had to leave. Leah prayed for Benjamin to let them stay with her, especially if he set his mind to marry Miriam Stoltzfus.

When Leah got down on her knees for her evening prayer time, she prayed for just that. Leah begged God to put it in Benjamin Lapp's heart to let his children stay with her.

Most Amish men didn't do well without a wife, especially ones with small children. They usually remarried quickly out of necessity. Leah asked God to bring a wife for Benjamin Lapp but to let Beth, Caleb, and Katie stay with her. It wasn't likely to happen, but Leah told herself. *"The Bible tells us anything is possible with Gott. So Gott can make this happen."*

After finishing her prayers, Leah snuggled under the many quilts she placed on her bed. She may have liked having the bed to herself, but one thing she was sure of, she stayed much warmer when Beth came to snuggle in with her.

Leah tossed and turned, trying to get comfortable. For some reason, her prayer was nagging at her. She couldn't understand why asking God to bring Benjamin Lapp a wife bothered her so much. Leah passed it off as the fear of Miriam Stoltzfus not treating the babies in a kind manner.

Benjamin seemed to procrastinate when it came to starting the building project, and Leah couldn't understand why. Two weeks passed before they finally started the building. Things did not go well at first. Nearly a year earlier, Leah waited in anticipation to start the chicken house with her husband. Today, however, it was anything but exciting. Benjamin acted as though she was in the way and incapable of completing the task. It was starting to frustrate Leah. She prayed Gott would help her hold her tongue.

On the third day, Leah had enough. By mid-afternoon, she started to lose her patience. They were getting nowhere fast on the building. Had Adam and Leah been doing the work together they would have finished the chicken house in two days. She wanted to scream and almost did.

When she could take it no longer, Leah turned and snapped at Benjamin. "Benjamin Lapp, I am quite capable of working on this project. I have helped build many things in the past. The truth is, I could most likely build this coop on my own. And, I may have to if you don't stop treating me like I am helpless. So, tell me, do you wish for me to do it on my own, or are you willing to work with me?"

He stood staring dumbfounded at her, as she continued ranting. "My ehemann made me promise, just moments before he died, that I would build my chicken haus. And I aim to do it. So, with or without your help, I will get this thing built! Do you understand me?"

"Ach Leah, don't go all narrish on me. I do things my way, and I'm not used to having a woman working with me. It would be better and faster if you would permit me to do my work here, and you tend to your inside chores."

He said the wrong thing. Leah didn't hold back as she let him have it again. "Well, to start with, you are working with me and not the other way around. And if you are going to work with me, we are going to do things my way. As I have told you, my promise to my ehemann was I would build my chicken haus. I wished to raise my chickens and collect my eggs. It was what we called our special project because it would be the last project we would build together before we started having bopplin. I thought if you were to help me, you would feel as though you were working for your room. I was trying to help you feel your room was not charity. I am perfectly capable of doing this myself. So, tell me, are you willing to work with me?"

Something hit Benjamin hard. He liked the fire her spirit possessed. Those old feelings he had for Leah came rushing over him again. He had fought them for years. His feelings angered him because he felt like he was dishonoring his dead wife by wishing to get close to his first love again. Benjamin thought those feelings for Leah would disappear when he started courting Annie Glick. It had taken him some time to feel love for Annie. She was much different from Leah. They both had a shy way about them; however, Annie was much more submissive to everyone. He liked the fact that Leah could stand her ground when she felt passionate about something. She interrupted his thoughts when he heard her asking impatiently. "Well, Benjamin Lapp, are you willing to work with me or not?"

"Jah, Leah Beiler, I am willing. It will be a challenge working with a stubborn woman, for sure and for certain." He shot Leah a smile, which made her forget how frustrated she was. Still smiling, he continued to speak. "You tell me what you wish for me to do, and we'll get back to work, jah?"

"Jah, the sooner we get this finished, the less time you will have to put up with me."

As they worked, Leah couldn't help but notice how his eyes had recently changed. There was such a difference in them now. Before they were disquieting almost frightening; however, they had taken on the kinder tone she remembered from back when they were growing up. The warmth they held somehow got to her. His dark curls were in bad need of a trim, and his beard could also use some attention, but he was still quite handsome nonetheless. Leah realized what she was permitting her mind to settle on and tried to shake the thoughts from it. She had no business thinking about Benjamin Lapp in this manner. *"What would her Adam think?"* Leah scolded herself. She was determined once they finished the project, Benjamin Lapp would have to go. At the same time, the thought of not being with him day after day brought sadness to her heart.

They accomplished a lot that afternoon, and Leah felt they would finish the following day. Somehow, it didn't make her happy, though. It confused her. This man had been extremely loathsome to her when he first came to stay at her house. But now, here she was enjoying his company. Leah liked working beside him. As crazy as it seemed, she thought she actually might be falling in love with him, and that was not good.

Leah's heart dropped when Benjamin informed her he would not be having supper with her and his children. He would be sharing the evening meal with Miriam Stoltzfus. Leah could kick herself for arranging a union between Naomi Stoltzfus and Adam's older brother, Eli Beiler. Naomi and Eli were getting married in a couple of weeks. She would rather see Benjamin with Naomi than the likes of her cousin Miriam. The thought of him being with any other woman disturbed Leah. She was sure it meant only one thing; she had indeed fallen in love with this man.

The night dragged on without him. Benjamin never did come back to the house that night. It seemed like Leah had finally drifted off to sleep just before the sun peeked through her bedroom window. She went to start the coffee and put wood on the fire.

Thinking of Benjamin spending the night with Miriam tore at Leah's heart. She was sure it wouldn't be much longer, and they would be married. She begged God to give her the strength to overcome the pain of losing Benjamin and his children if it were God's will for Benjamin to take Miriam as his wife. Leah was angry for permitting her feelings to become too personal, and she scolded herself for wasting valuable time as she romanticized about Benjamin Lapp.

Benjamin entered the kitchen, looking half frozen. Leah's thoughts ran rampant. "He must have just returned from Miriam's. He had some nerve staying with her all night, and then coming into my house, sitting at my table, expecting me to wait on him as if I was his wife." She shook the thoughts from her head and turned to pour him a cup of coffee. Once she had poured it, she turned back to continue working on the morning meal. She knew the tears would flow if she went and sat at the table with him this morning. He didn't speak, and neither did she. It felt as though it was taking forever for him to finish drinking his coffee. Leah wished for him to quickly finish and go out to do his chores with her brother, Luke.

At last, he finished. He headed toward the door, turned back, and spoke. "I won't be able to help you with your coop today. Once I finish my morning chores, I will come and get my kinner. We will be gone most of the day."

When Leah didn't respond, Benjamin turned and walked out. Once the first tear fell, there was no holding back the ones that uncontrollably followed. She turned to the Lord and prayed. Thankfully, the crying stopped by the time Beth came down the stairs. Beth ran to hug her. Leah swept her up in her arms and held her tight. She feared the time for showing Beth affection was coming to an end. She was sure giving up Beth, Katie, and Caleb would be more than her heart could withstand. As she put on the best smile she could muster, Leah told Beth she and the twins would spend the day with their Daed. It was hard for Beth to control her excitement. It had been a long time since Benjamin had spent any time with his three children.

Leah got Beth ready for the day and then worked on getting the twins ready. They ate their morning meal without Benjamin. The table seemed empty without him. He recently started taking all his meals with them, and it had felt good to eat as a family would. The only problem was they weren't a family, and Leah needed to remind herself of this often.

When Benjamin came into the kitchen, Beth ran to him. He picked her up as she squealed in delight. "Leah says we are going to spend time with you."

"Jah, this is true, my maedel. We will spend the entire day together."

"Where will we go? What are we going to do?"

"You will know soon enough."

Leah put the twin's coats, hats, and mittens on them, all the while Benjamin struggled with Beth's scarf. Beth asked. "Why is Leah not getting ready to go with us, Daed?" She turned to Leah and continued. "Leah, you need to hurry. And, get your coat on, it's cold out there. She wrinkled her nose in the cute little way she had a habit of doing. "And, Leah, make sure you get your mittens, too."

Benjamin smiled at his daughter while answering her. "Leah has plans of her own. She has lots to do today. Don't you, Leah?"

Leah choked back the lump, which was forming in her throat. "Jah, I do have a lot of things I must do today."

Beth started to whimper, "But, you will be all alone. I do not wish to go without you, Leah."

Beth hugged Leah tight and told her she loved her. The twins each hugged Leah as well. They all headed out the door with their Daed. Leah watched as he tried to round them up to lift them into the buggy. The twins thought it was a game and ran in opposite directions. Leah stood at the window and watched as Benjamin frantically tried to catch them. When he got a hold on one child, the other one would take off. She decided to let him deal with them for a bit. *"After all, they were his kinner, and he would have to care for them once he left here. He would be a fool to think Miriam would take over the raising of his kinner"* She was certain Miriam would not take on the chore of raising three children. It saddened Leah knowing Miriam considered caring for children a distasteful chore. Knowing her the way Leah did, Miriam would unquestionably consider it more of a punishment. Under Miriam's guardianship, Leah was confident Beth, Katie, and Caleb would never receive the nurturing a child craves and deserves. Leah didn't think Miriam Stoltzfus was capable of love. She was a self-centered person, and it truly scared Leah to no end thinking Miriam would raise those babies the same way her mother, Adele Stoltzfus, raised her.

Hearing Benjamin Lapp scoffing at his twins brought Leah back to reality. Benjamin was not capable of controlling his children. He was getting frustrated, and the situation would most likely turn bad if she didn't intervene soon. She threw on her coat and hurried out to help him.

With ease, Leah gathered the twins up and placed them on the seat in the buggy. Benjamin smiled at her and said, "Danki, you are so gut with them, and you make it look so easy. Tell me, Leah, how do you do it?"

Leah spoke softly to him. "Patience Benjamin, you must have patience with them. You'll see, the more time you spend with them, they will learn they must obey you as well." When she turned to get out of his way, their hands brushed against one another. Her heart leaped in her chest and took her breath away. She hoped Benjamin didn't notice.

Katie slid down off the bench. Leah stood close to the buggy. She warned Katie to stay in the seat until her Daed helped her down. Katie nodded and threw her arms around Leah's neck. "Ich liebe dich, Mamm."

By the look on Benjamin's face, he was as shocked as Leah was. When he didn't speak, Leah did. "Katie, my maedel, I am Leah, not your Mamm."

Pointing at Leah, Caleb giggled. "Nee, you Mamm."

Leah looked at Benjamin. "You must explain it to the twins while you are with them today. It will be ever so confusing if we permit them to think of me as their Mamm. Do not allow it to become a habit, or it will be harder to break them of it once you take them away from me. You need to explain to them that Miriam will be their Mamm, and I am simply Leah."

In a whisper, Benjamin replied. "You are anything but simple."

"Ach, vergeef me, what did you say?"

Embarrassed, Benjamin lowered his head and lied. "I said I would do my best to explain it to them."

After cleaning the kitchen, Leah headed outdoors to work on the chicken house. Staying busy helped keep her mind off Benjamin and Miriam. Working on the chicken coop brought her joy and sadness at the same time. She was happy she was fulfilling the promise she had made to Adam. On the other hand, she missed Benjamin working alongside her. She also felt lost without the toddlers being underfoot. She tried to forget about everything else and concentrate on the task.

Hours had passed before Leah realized how late it had gotten. She let time get away from her. It would be dark soon. The sky was void of clouds, which meant another cold night was ahead of them. She quickly picked up the tools, stood back, and looked over her work. She told herself. *"My Adam would be well pleased."* The door would have to wait for another day. Before she could finish it, she would have to buy some hinges, a handle, and the latch. They had forgotten them when she and Adam picked up the lumber. She decided she would go early the next morning. She would hitch up the buggy and go into town for them, right after she finished her chores. She needed to deliver her baked goods and pick up her new bakery order as well. But as for now, she needed to get inside and finish baking the rest of the pastries. She was thankful she had already made the ten loaves of bread. They took the longest, and she would never have finished on time had she waited until now.

Leah fixed a sandwich and sat down to eat. It was the first meal she had to take by herself in some time. She looked around the empty table. Sadness filled her heart. She had to admit she didn't much care to eat alone. Although she reminded herself, it was something she would have to get used to again. And, most likely, it would happen sooner than she anticipated. With Benjamin now taking his children to spend time with Miriam, it could only mean one thing. Miriam becoming Benjamin's wife was inevitable, and it would probably take place within a month or so.

After Leah had taken the last of the sweet rolls from the oven, she went in to sit by the fire. She read the Bible and then prayed. She was somewhat annoyed with Benjamin for keeping the children out so late. It scared her having them out on the roads after dark. Somewhere in the middle of her prayers, Leah dozed off. She woke up to the sound of Beth's voice calling out for her. Beth explained the twins were sleeping, and her Daed was having trouble getting them out of the buggy. Leah quickly threw on her coat and ran outside to help Benjamin with the twins. The temperature had dropped considerably. Leah shivered when the cold air hit her chest. She wrapped her coat tighter around her body as she ran to the buggy.

Leah reached and picked Caleb up. He put his head on her shoulder and placed his arm around her neck. A look of disbelief crossed Benjamin's face. "How did you do that, he never even woke up?"

"You can do it too. Pick Katie up and hold her close to you. She will continue to sleep if she feels secure."

He reached in and picked Katie up just as Leah had Caleb. It surprised him when his daughter snuggled tightly against him. Benjamin looked at Leah and smiled. It melted her heart. She immediately told herself, *"Do not let your heart go there, Leah. He just spent the day with his future wife. At least he had enough sense not to spend another night with her. It would have been too confusing for the kinner."*

Leah carried Caleb into the house. When she started up the stairs with him, Benjamin was on her heels. She turned back to speak. Her heart leaped in her chest when, with his stature, they stood face to face. Leah tried to regain her composure quickly. "You can put Katie on the couch, and I will come back for her."

"I can carry her up to her room."

"Danki, but I would rather you put her on the couch, and when I have finished getting Caleb and Beth ready for bed, I'll come back for Katie. It will be easier this way. Besides, you must go take care of the horse and buggy."

Stumbling over his words, Benjamin said, "I am—I will be using the buggy again. But first, I wish to help you get the kinner ready for bed. Please let me help you."

It crushed Leah to think about him spending another night at Miriam's. She tried to keep her feelings in check but wasn't doing a good job. She was starting to lose her patience. "Honestly, Benjamin, it will go much quicker if I do it myself. I have had a long busy day, I'm ever so tired, and I wish to get ready for bed myself. It's late, and besides, you have someplace to go."

He went to the couch, put Katie down, and walked out into the kitchen. Leah continued up the stairs with Caleb, changed his clothes, and tucked him in his bed. When she came back down, Benjamin was rocking Beth in front of the fireplace. Leah picked Katie up and started for the stairs. "Beth, would you like to come now and get ready for bed too?"

Yawning, Beth answered. "Can Daed rock me more?"

Leah nodded and headed back up the stairs. It had been months since Benjamin had given Beth any real attention, and she needed this time with him. It touched her heart to see Benjamin rocking his daughter so lovingly. It was a sight she wished to see more often. Leah longed to have her home filled with love and family. Something she feared she would never experience after that night. Once Benjamin married and removed his children from her care, she would be all alone once again. Leah didn't want to think about the loneliness.

After getting Katie into her nightgown and all tucked in, Leah headed back down to the living room for Beth. She whispered, "I wish for Daed to put me to bed like he did before our haus burned all up."

Benjamin got up and headed up the steps. He turned to go into Leah's room. Leah ran up the stairs behind him. "Wait, that's my room. Do not go in there."

"But I want to sleep with you tonight, Leah. Can Daed tuck me in your bed?"

Leah's heart broke as she told her no. She also wished to have Beth sleep with her. Leah feared she would not have the sweet child there for many more days. "Nee Beth, you need to sleep in your bed. Your Daed can put you down and stay with you until you fall asleep if he wishes."

Before the tear trickled down her cheek, Leah turned and closed her bedroom door and headed back down to the kitchen for some hot cocoa. She had just finished making it when Benjamin came down. "Would you like a cup of hot cocoa?"

"First, I should take care of the horse. It has gotten so cold out there, and I have decided it would be best to stay in tonight."

Leah put more milk on the stove to heat. Once the cocoa was hot and ready, she poured it into a mug, placed it on the table, and went up to her room.

She was both physically and emotionally exhausted. The hot cocoa warmed her body, and she was able to relax. Leah fell to her knees and prayed. She finished and climbed under the warmth of the quilts and cried herself to sleep. With all the emotions she was feeling, it was surprising she slept through the night. As good as it felt to have the bed all to herself Leah missed Beth coming to her for comfort. Beth had slept through the night, which meant she most likely didn't have any nightmares. And, for that, Leah was thankful.

As she prepared breakfast, Leah wondered why Benjamin lied to her. Last night he had told her he wasn't going back out, but his bed had not been slept in again. Since his outings with Miriam started, he had not used his bedroom. Leah was still upset over Benjamin keeping his children out late the previous evening. There was no excuse for it. Nevertheless, they were his children and not hers. She was also upset over the fact of him still keeping company with Miriam Stoltzfus. She didn't know why she let it bother her so much. Benjamin came into the kitchen. Leah poured him his coffee and placed it on the table.

"Leah, will you not sit with me this morning?"

"Nee, Benjamin, I cannot. I am in a rush. I need you to care for your kinner this morning. I must go into Culver and run some errands."

"I have a few things I need to do in Culver too. We could take the kinner and go into town together."

"I am sorry, but as I said, I am in a hurry. I don't have the extra time to wait for everyone to get ready. It takes the twins a while to eat and then to get them washed and dressed. The threat of a storm is coming, and I have things I need to get done. I have breakfast almost ready, but you will have to feed your kinner, wash them up, and dress them for the day. You can take them with you if you wish, or you can wait for me to return and then go run your errands."

Benjamin's tone was somehow different, Leah couldn't quite put her finger on it, but something was undoubtedly different. "I was hoping we could talk this morning."

The sound of footsteps on the stairs meant Beth was up. Leah turned to Benjamin and said, "I'm sorry, but it will have to wait until later."

Benjamin went out to let Luke know that Leah needed him in the house and would have to finish the chores later. He was gone longer than Leah expected, and of course, Beth had gotten up earlier than usual, so nothing was going as she had planned.

Leah set the girl's breakfast in front of her, kissed her forehead, and assured Beth she would be back in a few hours.

When Benjamin finally came back inside, he tried to talk Leah into waiting until after they ate to leave. Beth kept trying to get his attention with the many questions of a three-year-old. Leah was thankful the girl distracted her Daed this morning. It made it easier to get out of the house.

"I will do the dishes and clean when I return. I am running too far behind now to worry about this kitchen."

"I'm sorry it took me so long, Luke needed my help fixing the barn door. He had to rush off this morning too. I got your horse and buggy ready for you, though. I hope that helps."

"Danki, it does. I will return as soon as I can." She reached down, hugged Beth, and headed for the door.

CHAPTER 8

❦

"For thou, Lord, art good, and ready to forgive; and plenteous in mercy unto all them that call upon thee."
Psalm 86:5

The air was cold and damp. It didn't take long before Leah could feel it down deep to her bones. She tucked the quilt tighter under her legs before encouraging the horse to move on. The sky looked threatening, with its gray hue. A gust of wintery wind caught her by surprise. She watched the steam coming from her horse's breath as it hit the cold air. Leah talked sympathetically to the animal. "I'm ever so sorry, girl. I should never have made you come out on a day such as this. I couldn't handle hearing about the kinner's day with Miriam, though. I needed to get away." Leah hoped she hadn't made the wrong decision, and the storm would hold off at least until she returned home. She spoke again to the horse. "I'll try to get us back home quickly. I promise. I'll give you some extra oats when we get back." Leah could hear the women's tongues wagging over her talking to her horse in such a personal way. She couldn't help it. The Lord had given her a heart for animals.

Leah scolded herself for getting so attached to Beth, the twins, and Benjamin. Now she had to deal with the pain of losing them, and she had no one to blame but herself.

As Leah passed the spot in the road where Adam died, the horrible memories of the day replayed in her mind. The young man who killed Adam had been caught and was facing the death penalty. When Leah found out, she pleaded for the young man's life. He ended up with life in prison without any possibility of parole. He had been in trouble several times in the past and was a known drug addict. Lyddie and Blake sat with Leah throughout the man's trial. The bishop frowned heavily on it; however, Leah begged him to permit her to attend the proceedings. She explained her need to hear what this man had to say for himself. She also wished for him to know she had forgiven him for taking Adam from her.

Leah gave a victim impact statement during the sentencing phase of the trial. With a trembling body, she stood before Liam Holden in the courtroom and addressed him by his given name. She explained why she fought to save him from the death penalty. Leah believed it would have been Adam's wish for the court to spare the man's life. Leah looked Liam in the eyes and asked him why he killed her husband. When he refused to answer, Leah went on to tell him she had forgiven him. The angered look on Liam's face gave Leah the courage to tell him her forgiving him was for her healing and not so much for his. Liam Holden showed absolutely no remorse for taking her Adam's life, but Leah still had to follow God's command and forgive him. She went on to share with Liam that once she had truly forgiven him for killing her husband, a sense of peace and healing flowed through her. This kind of peace could only come from God Himself. Leah finished by telling Liam Holden she would pray for him. And, it was her hope that he would allow God to cleanse his soul. She left the courtroom satisfied, knowing God and Adam were both well pleased with her.

It still bothered Leah to pass the area where it had all happened. But, she found comfort with the certainty of where Adam was. Her Adam was having a joyous time walking those streets of gold she had read about in her Bible.

After Leah found the hinges, latch, and handle she needed, she paid for the items and headed out to the fabric shop to buy the supplies on her list. She then stopped by the bakery to deliver her goods and pick up her next order, hoping it wouldn't be a large one. Since having Benjamin's children, she had tried to cut back on the baking she did for the bakery. Delia Daniels, the owner of the bakery, was in a talkative mood, and the morning was slipping away. Leah finally got the nerve up to explain her urgency in getting home. She hoped she still had time to visit Adam's gravesite before delivering an order for Delia. Praying again for the storm to hold off, she headed toward the graveyard for a quick visit.

When Leah returned to the house, her sister-in-law was there with her infant. She and Luke had stopped on their way back from the baby's appointment. The baby catcher suggested the baby needed antibiotics for his fever and congestion. Benjamin and Luke had gone into Culver for supplies and Sarah was left sitting with the children.

Sarah looked confused. "You didn't pass my Luke on the road? He and Benjamin Lapp only left about ten minutes ago."

"Nee, but they most likely took the short cut. I had to deliver bread to a customer for Delia Daniels, so I came around the long way." There was no need for Leah to tell of her visit with her dead husband. Sarah would have scolded her for it. So it was best to keep it a secret.

The women sat and talked for a while before putting the children down for their nap. Leah quickly did the dishes and cleaned the kitchen. She suggested Sarah go and take a nap in one of the beds. Sarah had also been under the weather lately, and the thought of a quick nap thrilled her. Before heading out the door, Leah told Sarah she would be outside taking care of her horse and working on the chicken house door.

Leah had gotten the handle and hinges on the door when she saw Benjamin and Luke pulling up to the barn. She couldn't believe what she saw. They were carrying chickens into the barn along with a load of supplies. Leah heard Luke telling Benjamin he needed to get Sarah and the baby back home before the weather got any worse.

Leah went into the house to help Sarah get the baby ready for the trip home. Leah handed Luke the extra quilts she had warmed by the fire to help them stay warm on their trip. Once Luke and Sarah started down the driveway, Benjamin headed into the house, and Leah headed back to her work.

With some degree of difficulty, Leah tried to attach the coop door. Benjamin came up behind her. Startling her, the door slipped from Leah's grip and fell to the ground. He bent over and picked it up. "Leah, please permit me to help you. I'll do whatever you need me to do."

She nodded in agreement. "Danki, I will hold it if you would like to attach it."

While they finished hanging the door, Benjamin started to talk. He talked to Leah more than he had talked since he came to stay at her house. He acted more like the Benjamin she once knew. He told Leah all about their time spent with Miriam. "Caleb and Katie repeatedly asked for their Mamm. Beth explained to Miriam that the twins meant you. Leah, she told Miriam, you were their mudder."

Leah knew this wasn't good at all. She was sure all of this infuriated Miriam.

Benjamin went on to say, "Leah, Miriam asked that we marry as soon as possible. She and her mudder have already discussed the matter with Bishop Miller. He has agreed to the vow exchange at any time."

Leah's heart was hurting, but she knew what needed saying. "It is for the best, Benjamin. The sooner your kinner realize, I am not their Mamm, and Miriam will be, the better it will be for them. They have been with me for too long. Even though Beth remembers your Annie, the twins do not. Benjamin, they truly believe I am their mudder."

"Permit me to finish, please. Miriam wants a man, not kinner. She wants me to leave Beth, Katie, and Caleb with you."

Leah wasn't the least bit shocked Miriam had suggested he give up his children. But, for Benjamin to agree to it was absurd. She feared her legs would no longer hold her up, so she sat on one of the boxes she had used while working on the door.

Aroused by anger, Leah interrupted him. "Benjamin Lapp, what are you thinking? You cannot give up your kinner. We need you."

"What do you mean, we?"

"I mean, I cannot raise your bopplin by myself. You are the only parent they have left, and they need you in their life."

"I told Miriam I would think about it. She has agreed to give it some time and try to get to know my kinner and see if she will become more inclined to raise them with me. If you would like us to leave, we will. But, if you can see fit to permit me to pay rent for me and my kinner and accept payment for caring for them, then we would be ever so grateful to stay with you until that time. I don't expect you to give me an answer right away, but maybe you could think about it some and let me know."

Leah was left dumbfounded by his request. It was as if Benjamin Lapp had hit her up the side of her head with a frying pan. She knew what she would like to say, but asked the Lord to keep His hand over her mouth. She hesitated a moment longer to get her wits about her before answering. "Jah, Benjamin Lapp, I will think about it and let you know what I decide."

The freezing rain was falling again with such intensity. The chicken house door would have to wait until another day. Benjamin suggested they get into the house and warm up with some hot cocoa.

Leah agreed. "Jah, there is no sense trying to do any more work on this today. Hot cocoa sounds ever so inviting."

The storm raged for much of the afternoon. Leah and the excited children watched from the window as the weather tried to decide what it wanted to do. One minute it was freezing rain, and the next, the biggest snowflakes Leah had ever seen fell from the sky. When it looked as though it would finally quit, it started all over again.

Leah went to the kitchen to prepare the evening meal, while Benjamin kept the little ones occupied. She enjoyed hearing the laughter coming from the other room while she worked away in the kitchen. It was a pleasant meal, and Leah found herself wishing it could be like that every evening.

It was apparent the children were getting tired. From the frequent yawns, coming from each of them, Leah knew she needed to get them ready for bed. She decided to quickly clean up the kitchen and call it an early evening. It would give her time to think about Benjamin's proposal.

Once the children were all tucked into their beds, Leah headed to her room. As exhausted as she was, she needed to come up with a plan, and she needed to come up with one quickly. By the time the morning light peeked through her bedroom window, she had come up with the perfect solution. It would benefit her and Benjamin Lapp. She would not have to keep company with him as much, but could still care for the children.

She hastily dressed and headed down to the kitchen to start the morning meal. She had the coffee ready and was putting the sweet rolls in the oven when Benjamin came into the kitchen. He appeared half-frozen. She questioned in her mind, *"Who does he think he's fooling? It's obvious he stayed out all night?"* He sat at the table and waited for Leah to bring him a cup of hot coffee. She placed two cups of the piping hot liquid on the table and sat with him.

Leah took a deep breath and let it out slowly before she began to speak. "I believe I have come up with the perfect plan, which would be best for all of us. I would like for you to hear me out completely before you respond. I have given this much thought, and I feel it will benefit you and your kinner while giving me a solution to my situation as well."

Benjamin smiled and spoke. "All right, I am listening and will do my best not to interrupt you."

"I will permit you and your kinner to rent my haus. It is not gut for you and me to continue sharing a home. Therefore, I will move into my parent's daadi haus until you marry Miriam and move into your own home. Keep in mind my offer is only gut until you marry. At that time, I will take over living here in my home again. I will come each day and care for your kinner as though I was working for you. I will prepare the meals and clean my haus. Once I finish with the evening meal and the cleanup is complete, I will go back to my parents. I will do this except on Sunday's. You will be on your own for the day. However, I will prepare enough food on Saturday for you and the kinner on our off Sunday. I do have one stipulation though; no other woman may come into my haus and cook or clean. After all, this is still my haus, and I do not wish to share my kitchen with another woman. We will figure out a fair price for your lodging and child care. We'll take into consideration the work you do around here with my bruder. If you and Luke agree, you may take over all the farm chores, and that will cover your rent. This is acceptable to you, jah?"

Benjamin stared straight ahead for what seemed like hours. Leah began to think he wasn't going to give her an answer. Shaking his head, he finally spoke, "I never thought you would leave us or your own home. I do, however, understand your point of us not sharing the same haus. Miriam did not like the idea, either. She wants me to live in her parent's daadi haus, but I'm not ready for that. Besides, my kinner are not welcome at this point. I can't say as though I'm fond of your plan, but I guess it is worth trying."

Leah had hoped he would have objected more than he had. She got up from the table and turned toward the counter before saying, "It's settled then. I will move over to my parent's haus today." When Benjamin didn't respond, Leah turned and opened the oven door to check on the sweet rolls. She heard the back door close, telling her he was gone. She looked back to the table, noticing he hadn't taken the time to finish his coffee.

Out in the barn, Benjamin tried not to think about Leah's leaving. It bothered him more than he cared to admit. If she would only give him a sign of being interested in him, he would fight for her. It was evident she was still deeply in love with her dead husband. He had followed her on a few occasions and found her at the cemetery, talking to and crying over her Adam's grave. She also made it clear one evening, she would never consider remarrying, and he had to respect her for her devotion. He desired to have someone so devoted.

Benjamin and Annie's marriage was a decent one, and he was thankful she was a good mother. He knew Annie was only a wife to him out of duty, and he appreciated her for it. He was left broken when Leah turned him away all those years ago. He was not Annie's first choice as a life mate, either. Annie thought she was pregnant when her English lover turned his back on her. For that reason, and because of Benjamin losing Leah, they decided to marry. Marriage would be beneficial to both Annie and Benjamin. Annie wouldn't have to face the shame of being an unwed mother, and Benjamin could get over losing his beloved Leah. After they married, Annie realized she was not pregnant after all. They grew to love each other in some respect, but it wasn't a passionate love. It was more of a survival love.

Benjamin and Annie understood each other, and it made for a favorable marriage.

Benjamin's thoughts ran rampant. *"Was he narrish to hope for a life with Leah? Was he willing to settle for less than what he and Annie had together? What was he thinking carrying on with Miriam Stoltzfus? Gott forgive him, but Miriam could be a beast of a woman at times. It was narrish for him to consider marrying her."* He wished Leah had a daadi haus where he could stay, and life could continue as it was. He reminded himself it would only get harder for him to watch this woman day after day. He loved her with everything in him and knowing he could not have her as his wife, left him broken. *"No, this plan of Leah's was for the best. He loved his kinner dearly, but they would be better off with Leah than the likes of Miriam Stoltzfus. Leah already loved and cared for them as if they were her flesh and blood. He now had to think of what was best for Beth, Katie, and Caleb."* Benjamin thought this was a sign from God to give his children over to Leah and try to make a life with Miriam. It would not be an easy life, but Benjamin had noticed changes in Miriam over the last month or so. *"Maybe a body could change. Maybe having a husband would soften Miriam and make her into a more charitable woman."* He was thinking about this too hard, and his head started to ache because of it. Leah made her wishes known, and it was best not to push her. He despised the thought of her leaving him and her own home, though.

Luke came into the barn shaking the snow from his coat. "It is going to be another miserable day with this weather. I had some trouble getting over here. Those old buggy wheels can't hold the road with all of this ice."

"Well, after today, you won't have come every morning. Leah has decided to rent me her haus, and I'll take over all the farm chores myself. She is moving back over to your parent's daadi haus today. It isn't a permanent solution, but she has decided it is what is best for now anyway."

"Gut for her. It's about time. I know she loves this place and doesn't wish to give it up. But, she is a smart maedel. And, I agree this is for the best. Besides, she will be closer to the graveyard. She doesn't think we know she visits Adam's grave much more than she should. Mamm is afraid if she says anything, Leah will go ahead with her plans to sell her farm and move to Ethridge, Tennessee, with our aenti there. It would break Mamm's heart to have her only daughter living so far away."

"I don't think she has any plans to leave. She will continue to care for my kinner, just as she has done. She told me she plans to move back into her haus once I remarry. I also know she will not sell this place until the chicken coop gets finished. She told me it was a promise she had made while her ehemann was dying in her arms. So, if we can keep her from finishing it, she will not sell out."

"Gut plan, but my schweschder is a strong-willed maedel, and she is more than capable of finishing that building on her own. It will be hard to keep her from finishing it if she sets her mind to do it. Maybe she will take heed to this weather and set it aside for a while."

Benjamin laughed. "I'll bring the door into the barn here and hide it. If she questions it, I'll tell her with the weather the way it is we should hold off finishing it. It may satisfy her for a time anyway."

Luke reached and shook Benjamin's hand. "Danki, I appreciate you looking out for my schweschder. Plus, it will be a tremendous load off me with you taking over the farm chores here. It has fallen to the wayside some. I haven't had the time or the energy to keep it up the way Adam and Leah did. It's simply too much trying to care for two farms."

"It will feel gut taking care of a farm on my own again. My old farm suffered in comparison to this one, but I will care for it as though it were mine, for sure and for certain. Come spring, there will be much work, and keeping busy will be a welcomed change."

"My fraa will be ever so pleased to hear this. I'm afraid I have neglected certain areas of our marriage while taking care of both the farms. I hardly have enough energy at the end of the day to make it to the bedroom. Sarah gave up on me months ago. She covers me up in my chair and goes off to bed alone. This will be a wunderbaar gut surprise for her, for sure and for certain."

The men finished feeding the animals and fixed temporary laying boxes for the chickens Benjamin had brought home. Luke climbed in his buggy and was on his way. Benjamin headed into the house for a hot breakfast. He was anxious to see Leah. He hoped she had changed her mind and would stay. He could fix up an area in the barn to use for his bedroom. And, he could put in a wood stove to keep him warm during the winter months. That way, Leah could stay in her home, and they would all still be together. If Leah was aware he was sleeping in the barn again, she never let on. He made sure to hide the quilts each morning, so she would not find out he was sleeping with her dogs to stay warm. A wood stove would, for sure, be a welcomed addition. If she hadn't changed her mind, he wouldn't have to worry about sleeping in the barn again.

As he came into the house, he noticed several bags sitting by the door. It saddened him to know she still planned to go. He would tell her of his plan to build a room in the barn. He needed to try something to get her to stay.

The children were already dressed and sitting at the table eating. Leah was at the sink washing her dishes. She didn't seem to notice he was even there. Beth, Caleb, and Katie were all excited to have him sit with them. Usually, he finished his breakfast and was gone before they were even out of their beds.

"Leah, you will sit and eat with us, jah?"

"Nee, I have eaten. I'm going to head out here soon and get the daadi haus cleaned up and ready for my move. I have already packed what I need. The kinner are anxious to see where I will be living. I have explained to them they will stay with you here, and I will come every day and care for them. They seem to understand things will not change much. I will just be sleeping elsewhere."

"I'm sorry, Leah. I feel as though I am chasing you out of your home. It doesn't seem fair."

"Do not concern yourself with it. I have chosen to leave, and I am gut with it. Maybe by the time you marry, I will be ready to sell. If you and Miriam like, you could purchase my farm, if I sell out. You would not have to uproot your kinner and move them into another haus. It will be hard enough on them, adjusting to someone other than me caring for them. You don't have to decide now. I'm not sure I will be ready to sell. We will see how the winter goes before I make such an important decision."

He was at a loss for words. It was not going the way he had it planned, that was for sure. He didn't want her to go. No, what he truly wanted to do was to sweep her into his arms. He wished to tell her how much he loved her and wanted them to live there as a family. He wanted her to know it was always her he loved. He would promise to continue loving her until his dying day. But alas, he couldn't bear the thought of her rejecting him a second time. The fear of that rejection kept him from declaring his love for her.

Beth brought her Daed back to reality. "Leah says we get to go see her new home today. She said her Mamm will be ever so excited to see us. You will come too, jah?"

"Nee, I cannot come with you. There's work here that needs doing. You keep an eye on your bruder and schweschder and don't get underfoot. Leah will need your help."

"Jah, Daed, I will help her. Leah says maybe we can stay with her in her new home sometime. She says the Englishers call it a *"sleepover,"* and it will be right gut fun."

"It does sound like fun." Benjamin then stood and went over to the sink. *"It feels ever so gut being so close to this woman."* He cleared his throat. "Leah, maybe I should come with you and help you get the daadi haus ready, or keep the kinner entertained while you clean. Luke said the roads were terrible out there, and I would never forgive myself if something happened to you and the kinner. I'll do whatever you need for me to do."

"Danki, Benjamin, but I think I have it all covered. Daed and Mamm will be there to help in any way. As you said, you have plenty to do here. If it gets too bad, I'll keep the kinner and stay at Mamm and Daed's until it is safe to come back. I noticed a few loose boards on the front porch that will need attention. I would appreciate it if you would take care of them for me. I didn't want to add the burden to Luke. Since this place is now yours, maybe you can give it the attention it needs."

Benjamin asked himself, *"Why must she be such a strong woman? Why can't she turn and tell me she feels about me the way I feel for her?"* He answered himself. *"Maybe it's because she doesn't feel the same way you do, you dumm kopp."* He cleared his throat and answered. "Jah, I will take care of it. Leah, I cannot make you stay here for the day, and I cannot force you to permit me to come along. However, Luke told me he had trouble getting here today. There is much ice under the snow. I feel it is too dangerous for you to go out, and I must insist on the kinner staying here."

Leah thought for a moment before asking. "It is that bad out there, jah?"

"Jah, Leah, it is. If you wish to go, please let me take you." It pleased Benjamin when Leah finally gave in and agreed to let him join her.

He went out and harnessed Leah's horse. He pulled the buggy around to the back of the house and loaded her bags. He looked toward the sky and asked God to change Leah's mind. His answer was, "No." Leah came out with the children, and together they helped get Katie, Beth, and Caleb into their seat. Leah talked of how things would change from that day forward. She would no longer be taking her meals with them. She was now the hired help, and it wouldn't be right for her to join them at mealtime. Benjamin was furious with this news. He would never consider her the hired help. But what was he to do? She was not his wife, and she had made that fact known on more than one occasion.

CHAPTER 9
ళంఆ

*"For evildoers shall be cut off: but those that wait upon
the L*ORD*, they shall inherit the earth."*
Psalm 37:9

She opened the door to the daadi haus and
stepped inside. It had been years since Leah
had been in the quaint house. The furniture still
sat as she remembered. A thin layer of dust
covered the furniture, which was not surprising
since the house had been empty for several years.
Leah soon learned her mother, Erma Zook, had
tried to keep it in decent shape, hoping Leah
would move into it after Adam's death. Erma
feared if she pushed Leah to come and live there,
it would drive her out of Pennsylvania and into
Tennessee. Erma was happy when Leah stayed in
their Somerton district. She was even more
excited when Leah decided to move back to the

family farm. However, she knew Leah would not be satisfied with the cramped quarters for long. Their daadi haus was smaller than the average grandparent's home. After Erma's mother had passed away, they built the house for her father, Ike. He wished to live alone but was not in good health, so Erma's husband, father-in-law, and son built the small house for him.

Once everything was in place and cleaned to Leah's satisfaction, they headed to the main house for lunch. Erma doted on the twins and Beth. They, in turn, absorbed all the love and attention Leah's mother gave them. As Erma was busy with the children and Jonah and Benjamin were talking, Leah's mind wandered off.

"This is how it must feel to have a husband and children of my own. We would come here often for an evening meal, and my Mamm and Daed would spoil our kinner something awful. My ehemann and I would scold them for their spoiling," but Leah would secretly love it. *"Was her heart healing? Was she ready for a husband and children?"*

"Leah, Leah?"

Jerking back to reality, Leah asked. "What is it, my sweet Beth?"

"Your Mamm says I can help set the table if it is gut with you."

"Jah, for sure, you can help."

Erma Zook looked at her daughter's tired eyes, "Leah, it will do no gut for you to get sick. Why don't you go lie down for a bit, and we'll call you when we have lunch ready."

"Danki, Mamm. I think I will do just that."

The nap had done Leah a world of good. Her body got the rest it needed, after a night with very little sleep. She felt better about the events of the previous evening and her leaving her home that morning. She was ready to face whatever it was the Lord had in mind for her. She would trust Him for guidance.

That evening, Leah prepared supper for Benjamin and his children. Once it was ready, she went out to the barn to let him know it was on the table, and the children were waiting for him to join them. She would now head to the daadi haus and return early the following morning. Benjamin cautioned her about going out on the road again. Even though the sun had come out earlier in the day, and the ice melted somewhat, as the temperatures dropped, the roads would be slippery again. Leah wouldn't hear of it. If she stayed the night, it would give Benjamin an excuse to disappear again. It bothered her something terrible, not knowing where Benjamin had spent his nights.

The next couple of weeks passed by, and the only time Leah saw Benjamin was while she served him breakfast. She missed him terribly. She didn't think she would ever hurt like this again. It seemed as though he was avoiding her. He was working hard around the farm and doing an excellent job. It impressed Leah. She never thought anyone would care for the farm the way Adam had. Benjamin did the repairs on the front porch, just as he promised he would. Leah couldn't ask any more of him.

Earlier in the day, Adele Stoltzfus stopped Leah in the fabric shop. She made sure Leah knew it was her daughter, Miriam, who held Benjamin Lapp's heart. Leah let her get everything off her chest before assuring Adele she was happy that Miriam, after all these years, was finally able to have the hope of marrying. Adele made a snide remark as Leah walked away. While Cora was ringing up Leah's purchases, she leaned over close to her and whispered, "She's so worried Benjamin Lapp will come to his senses and break things off with her dochder. Ach, Leah, do not pay her any mind. Everyone knows how impossible Adele and her daughter are, and I don't think either of them will ever change." Leah giggled and agreed with Cora. She then placed her hand on Cora's and thanked her for her kindness.

The run-in with Adele Stoltzfus had bothered Leah ever since it happened nearly three weeks earlier. Leah couldn't understand why Adele would attack her the way she had. It disturbed her terribly that the woman went out of her way to belittle Leah to anyone who would listen. Discussing the matter with Benjamin was tempting, but she thought better of it. What would burdening him with Adele's childish antics prove? He was not blind to her or her daughter, Miriam, which puzzled Leah about why he would continue to keep company with Miriam. He must have fallen in love with her somewhere along the way. The thought of it stabbed at Leah's heart. She wondered if her feelings were not for Benjamin, but rather the love she felt for his children.

The following morning, Leah's feet hit the floor with a feeling of joy deep in her spirit. She vowed nothing would ruin her day. She sang songs of praise and talked with God on her drive to her farm. When she pulled into the driveway, she noticed a buggy tied near the house. *"Who would be visiting so early in the morning?"* She was so shocked to walk in on Miriam Stoltzfus in her kitchen, preparing the morning meal. She did her best to contain the anger she felt. "What are you doing here in my kitchen?"

"This is my Benjamin's kitchen now, so I have every right to surprise him." With a smirk, she added. "Remember you have rented this place to him, which I might add includes this kitchen."

"Ach, so Benjamin doesn't know you are here?"

"He will when he tastes my delicious breakfast. He complains about what a miserable cook you are and wishes to have more of my tasty dishes. We are getting married soon, so I thought I would come each morning and cook for him. I don't know why it upsets you. It really would be a benefit for you. You wouldn't have to come over here so early every morning. Once Benjamin and I get married, this will be my kitchen anyway." Waving her arms around, she continued ranting. "I believe we will be ever so happy here. I have decided I will keep the kinner after all. Who knows, it might be rather fun having them around." Miriam's expression turned to one of pure evil. "It's too bad you and your Adam didn't have any bopplin together. If you did, it wouldn't get so lonely when you aren't needed around here anymore."

The Lord was testing Leah. Miriam was known for not always being truthful. She took several deep breaths to stay calm. Miriam's words cut deep into Leah's heart. It angered Leah that Miriam would bring Adam into her hateful games. It was hard to stay civil with this woman. "You are not Benjamin's fraa yet, and this is still my haus, so I have some say in the matter. Neither you nor any other woman will use my kitchen to make a meal for Benjamin or anyone else. You may marry Benjamin, but this will never be your kitchen. The deal with Benjamin was once he marries, he and his kinner must move from my haus. So, you would do best to keep that in mind. Now, you can wash your hands and be on your way. If Benjamin wishes to have you make his meals for him, he is more than welcome to it, but it will be in your haus, not mine."

"Well, we will see what my Benjamin has to say about all of this." She stomped out of the kitchen and through the door as a child who didn't get her way. Leah shook her head in disbelief. She giggled at the thought of Miriam running out to Benjamin to tattle on her.

It wasn't but a few minutes when Benjamin came through the door. Miriam was fast on his heels, barking orders as she followed him into the kitchen. "Tell her, Benjamin. Tell her I have every right to prepare a meal for you here in your kitchen. Tell her you no longer wish her to prepare your morning meals for you. Tell her I will be your fraa, not her."

Leah lost all patience with the woman. After hearing her last demand, Leah interrupted her. "Whoa, hold on there, Miriam Stoltzfus. You might be Benjamin's future wife; however, this is my haus. And, I will say who or who will not use my kitchen. Benjamin agreed to my terms, and I expect him to honor them. As I told you before you stomped out of here like a spoiled child, you can prepare a meal for Benjamin anytime you wish. You will not, however, do it in my kitchen. He is more than welcome to eat with you in your home, but no one else will use my kitchen for meal preparations. There is no debating this, so you are welcome to throw your tantrum elsewhere. I can promise you this; you will not get your way in this matter."

Leah looked at Benjamin and caught him doing his best to stifle a laugh. He looked as though he would blow up at any moment from holding it in. He winked at Leah, and she quickly turned to face the sink. She didn't wish to laugh in Miriam's face herself. Once she composed herself, she turned back to face both Benjamin and Miriam.

"Well, Benjamin, are you going to permit her to disrespect me in your home like this?"

"Miriam, the fact of the matter is, this is still Leah's home. And, as she has told you, there is an agreement. Part of that deal is no one will use the kitchen. I agreed to it, and we must abide by the terms. If you wish, the kinner and I will start coming to your Mamm's for breakfast, and you can prepare the meal each morning."

"I—I—Ach, I only wish to feed you. Let her prepare the meals for the bopplin. They will make a mess of my Mamm's kitchen causing her added chores. They will be underfoot and my Mamm will not put up with that."

Leah wasn't the least bit surprised at Miriam's change of heart concerning Benjamin's three toddlers. She was only trying to push Leah's buttons with her falsehoods of wanting to raise Benjamin's bopplin. Leah was about to let Miriam have it, but Benjamin promptly intervened. "Then we will leave everything as it is for now. You can start making meals for me and my kinner once we get married. We will continue to permit Leah to care for the kinner and their meals until you are ready to do so."

"As you wish, Liebchen." Miriam looked at Leah then turned and planted a kiss on Benjamin's cheek before ordering him to walk her out to her buggy.

When Benjamin returned, Leah was getting the twins dressed for the day. They were exceptionally active this morning. Leah welcomed it, though. It would not give any privacy for Benjamin to talk with her about the show Miriam put on in the kitchen. Her heart leaped as Benjamin's arm brushed against hers when he reached to pick Katie up into his arms. She scolded herself for letting her emotions get the better of her.

Once the children were all seated at the table, and Leah had placed their meals before them, Benjamin spoke up. "Leah, I'm sorry for Miriam's boldness. It will not happen again. She understands your kitchen is off-limits to her and everyone else."

"Enough said. It is over and done. I must get upstairs and tend to the bedrooms now."

"You could sit and eat with us just this once, jah?"

"Nee, danki. I have already had my meal, and I must get a start on this day. Thanks to Miriam's Stoltzfus' hysterics, I am running behind schedule. I have to make a delivery to the bakery, but I need to get the bedding washed first." Before Benjamin could say any more, Leah headed up the stairs.

Christmas was fast approaching, and Leah assumed Benjamin would be taking the Second Christmas meal with Miriam and her family. She wasn't sure how to approach him about the children. She and Benjamin hadn't had a personal conversation in over a month. Since the time she refused to eat breakfast with them, he had kept his distance and avoided her as much as possible. She decided she would leave him a note.

While the children napped, Leah sat to write the note. Before she was able to finish it, Benjamin came into the kitchen. He grabbed a cookie from the counter. "Leah, I need your help."

"What is it, Benjamin? Is something wrong?"

"I need help figuring out what to get the twins for Christmas. I built my Beth a sled, but for the life of me, I don't know what to do for Katie and Caleb. You will help me, jah?"

Smiling, Leah replied. "Jah, I will help you. I wish to ask you a question, but I'm not sure how to ask it without you feeling like I am overstepping my bounds."

Benjamin felt so much love for this woman. But at the same time, he felt the distance that had come between them in the last month or so. They had come so far before she moved out. Now it felt awkward being this close to her. He shook his head as if to shake the thoughts away. "Go ahead and ask me what you wish to ask."

"You will permit Beth, Katie, and Caleb to share the Christmas meal with me and my family, jah?"

Benjamin had hurt written all over his face. "Nee, I wish to spend the day with my kinner. You may come and see them if you wish, but they will spend the day with me."

"So you will take them with you when you share the Christmas meal with Miriam Stoltzfus? She and her Mamm are all right with that?"

Benjamin now looked confused. "Nee, they will not. But you do not need to concern yourself with that. I will make sure they eat gut."

Now it was Leah's turn at confusion. "Who will stay with them while you have your meal?"

"I have decided we will eat our Christmas meal here."

Leah started to protest but thought better of it. She could feel the anger growing inside thinking about Miriam Stoltzfus using her kitchen to prepare the Christmas meal for Benjamin.

Benjamin, being aware of the sudden change in Leah's expression, asked her. "What is it, Leah? Go ahead and say what is on your mind."

Taking a deep breath and letting it out slowly, Leah felt defeated. "Ach, Benjamin, it is nothing. Everything is gut. I hope you and the kinner all have a wunderbaar gut Christmas together. I will not interfere with your day of celebration. I will give their gifts to them when I come back to work. I promised Beth I would make her some of the peanut butter cookies with the kiss on top." Leah smiled. "She sure loves those cookies. Anyway, you will make sure she gets them, jah?"

"Jah, I will. Turning to head back out the door, Leah heard him whisper. "It might be the only thing the kinner get that's worth eating."

Leah was more confused than ever. She wondered what Benjamin meant by that comment. It tugged at her all afternoon. Then it hit her she would write a note asking him to come and have the Christmas meal with her and her family, if he decided not to share the meal with Miriam Stoltzfus and her family. She left the note on the table along with Benjamin's supper.

The following morning, Leah found a note on the table accepting the invitation. And asking if she had thought any on what he should get the twins for Christmas.

Later that morning, Luke and Sarah stopped in for a visit. Sarah offered to stay with the children, so Benjamin and Leah could go shopping for the twin's gifts. They rode over to Isaac Fisher's shop to see what toys he had in stock. They picked out a rocking horse for Katie. Isaac only had one set of oversized building blocks, and Caleb loved to build things. He would be excited when he saw this set. Benjamin spotted a child-sized broom and mop in the corner of the shop. Excitedly, he exclaimed. "Ach, Leah, we need to purchase these for our Beth. She enjoys helping you with the chores, and these are the perfect size for her."

Leah looked to make sure neither Isaac Fisher nor Levi Hershberger overheard Benjamin referring to Beth as "theirs." Thankful they were not within earshot, Leah relaxed.

Once they climbed into the buggy, Leah spoke. "We do not need to go into Lancaster now. We have the gifts you need for your kinner, so we should get back to the haus. I have much work to do yet."

Her tone and then her silence the rest of the way home confused Benjamin. He couldn't figure out what went wrong. He and Leah were enjoying their time together. At least, for a short time anyway. Now Leah was back to behaving appropriately. Without speaking a word, she reminded him she worked for him and must keep the relationship between them on a detached level.

January slipped by quickly. February brought icy weather, which carried over into March. The weather was unpredictable. The days brought thunderstorms, and the evenings were cold and held heavy frost. Leah's aunt's last letter told her of the strange weather Tennessee was experiencing. Plagued by an early tornado season, areas south of them had extensive damage due to the storms. It seemed the weather was unstable from the Midwest to the East Coast.

While dropping off a package, and a reply to her aunt's letter, at the post office, Miriam approached Leah. She was on a hunt for information. She quizzed Leah in a way to gain information about Leah and Benjamin's relationship. Leah was so angry and ready to confront Benjamin Lapp. By the time she returned home, Leah had calmed down.

Another couple of weeks had passed, and Leah was at her wit's end after a few more run-ins with Adele and Miriam. She couldn't be sure which tales the women told held truth in them, but she decided it was time to take control of her life and her house once again. Leah put blocks out for the twins to play with, while Beth sat at the table, still playing with her doll. A talk with Benjamin Lapp was long overdue. Putting her shawl around her shoulders, Leah opened the door to find Benjamin working on the loose porch railing.

"Ach, gut, you're here. I was coming out to find you. I'm sorry to interrupt your work, but we must talk."

He laid the hammer on the chair and headed into the kitchen. Leah poured them each a cup of coffee. She sat at the table with him and began. "Benjamin, I am going to go ahead and finish the chicken coop. Spring is just around the corner, and I need to get it finished. However, the door has disappeared. Have you done something with it?"

"Jah, I did. I put it in the barn until you were ready to finish it." He lied. "I didn't hang the door because I knew it would upset you ever so much. So I put it away until you felt ready to finish it."

"Danki, I would like to finish it myself before I sell this place." Looking around the farm, she continued. "Josiah and Rachael Miller are interested in purchasing the farm and all the farm equipment. You have not given me any reason to believe you and Miriam would like to buy my farm, so I told Josiah I would think about it."

Benjamin sat staring at her with a look of total shock on his face. Before he could respond, Bishop Miller came through the door and into the kitchen. "I apologize for the interruption, but I must speak with Benjamin. It is of the utmost importance."

Benjamin stood, placed his hat back on his head, and headed out the door with the Bishop following close behind. They had been gone for a few hours before they returned.

Leah and the children were upstairs when she heard Benjamin and the bishop come back into the house. She went down to the kitchen and told Benjamin their evening meal was warming and ready for them when he wished to eat. She was putting on her coat when Bishop Miller asked her if she would stay with the children while he and Benjamin went to have visitation with another member of the district. Of course, Leah had to agree. One didn't say no to a request from the bishop.

Leah liked the thought of having the extra time with Beth, Caleb, and Katie. She hadn't gotten them ready for bed and tucked them in for many months now, and she missed it terribly. They all fell asleep quickly, and she was left alone with only her thoughts. She wondered what was going on with the bishop and Benjamin. She sent up a prayer for their safety. The ice was building up, making a mess of the driveway. She dozed off in front of the fireplace and woke up a short time later. Benjamin still hadn't come back. Leah began to worry. *"What if he lost control of his buggy and was lying hurt out there somewhere?"* She began to pray again. Exhausted, she fell asleep.

Beth tugged on Leah's sleeve, startling her. Leah jumped. "Ach, Beth, what is it, my maedel?"

"Leah, can I cuddle with you? I woke up cold, and I got scared."

Smiling, Leah whispered. "Jah, for sure and for certain." Leah picked her up and carried her up the stairs to Leah's old room. She tucked Beth in and promised she would be right back.

She hurried down to the kitchen and stacked more wood in the stove. Passing through the living room, she threw a few more logs on the fire. Leah reached in the chest of drawers and found an old nightgown. She spread an extra quilt over the bed and crawled under with Beth. They snuggled together. Beth reached and touched Leah's face. "I missed sleeping with you, Leah. Ich liebe dich, ever so much."

"I love you too, my maedel."

It wasn't long before Beth was fast asleep. Leah, however, couldn't calm her nerves enough to fall asleep. She wished for Benjamin to come home. She couldn't imagine what could be so important that it would keep him away so long. She sent up another prayer for Benjamin's safety and asked the Lord to bring a night of restful sleep to her.

When sleep finally came, so did the dreams. It wasn't Leah's usual nightmare. She was walking through a beautiful field of flowers. The sun was brightly shining on her face. She could see a figure standing at the edge of the field but couldn't make out who it was. She put her hand to her forehead, trying to shield the sun. She was then able to see Benjamin Lapp standing with his arms stretched out to her, inviting her into them. She ran toward him. Just as she reached him, Miriam Stoltzfus appeared out of nowhere and pushed her to the ground. Miriam ran to Benjamin, all the while laughing at Leah. Benjamin kept reaching for Leah and calling her name, but he couldn't get away from Miriam. When it seemed like he had broken free, Adele Stoltzfus grabbed hold of him and pushed him into Miriam's arms. Leah ran toward Benjamin, and as she drew closer to him, he reached out his hand to her. Leah reached for his at the same time Adele Stoltzfus took hold of Leah's arm and pulled her away. Benjamin and Leah both struggled to get to one another. Finally, they were both free, and Miriam and Adele were nowhere in sight. They came toward each other with arms outstretched. All of a sudden, someone slapped Leah in the face. She jolted awake. It was Beth's arm, now resting across Leah's face, which startled her.

She tucked Beth's arm back under the quilt. Leah tried to figure out what her dream meant and why she would dream of such wild notions. *"Did Benjamin want her? Did she want him? Nonsense, if he wanted her, he would not be marrying Miriam Stoltzfus."* She tried to wipe the dream from her memory. Her mind needed rest. Something it hadn't been getting enough of for some time now. Then it hit her. *"What if the bishop came and took Benjamin off to marry him and Miriam? They were probably already ehemann and fraa, while Leah was dreaming of being in his arms."* She tried to shake the picture from her mind.

She looked over at the window. It was still dark outside. She pointed her flashlight at the windup clock on the nightstand. Of course it had stopped ticking; no one had used the room since Leah moved out. She slipped out from under the quilt and carefully went down the stairs. As quietly as she could, she tiptoed down the hall to her old bedroom. The door was open, so she peeked inside. It was obvious no one had slept in the bed. She whispered, "He didn't come home again last night." Leah went to the living room and threw some wood on the hot coals, hoping it would ignite, and she wouldn't have to fight to get it going again. She looked at the clock. It was nearly time to get up anyway, so she went back upstairs and dressed for the day.

She heard someone moving around downstairs. She rushed down the stairs and into the kitchen. Benjamin stood near the stove, trying to make coffee. Leah went and took the pot from him and finished getting the coffee ready. Benjamin never spoke a word. Leah poured him a cup of and left the room. She was suddenly uncomfortable around him, and for the life of her, she couldn't understand why. Leah found it hard to believe Benjamin was spending his nights with Miriam, but where else would he be staying? It was plain to see he slept in his bed when Leah wasn't around. After all, she was the one who made it up each morning.

When she heard him go out the door, she went out to the kitchen to prepare breakfast. Looking out the window, she was happy to see the clear sky. *"Perhaps the sun will come out today,"* she thought. Hopefully, it would get warm enough to melt the ice. As much as she liked being back in her own home, it was somewhat awkward. *"Was it because Benjamin went roaming when she was there? Would he tell her what the bishop wanted him for and why he hadn't come home? He couldn't even take time to say "guder mariye," to her, so why would he tell her about his business with the bishop?"*

Benjamin came in late for breakfast. Leah was busy upstairs. Caleb had taken ill and vomited all over himself and his bedding. Benjamin had left the house again, by the time she finished cleaning Caleb up and changing out his bedding. Benjamin didn't come in for lunch and spoke only long enough to ask Leah if she would stay until his son was feeling better. Caleb's fever spiked again before supper, and Leah worked frantically to bring it down. She wondered if he should see an English doctor for an antibiotic. Caleb clung to her tightly. She couldn't be out of his sight for long before he would start sobbing for her. She felt it was best to stay the night to keep an eye on him.

Once Benjamin found out Leah would be staying the night, he informed her he had supper plans and not to expect him until late. She assumed he was having supper with Miriam and her family.

Caleb's temperature finally broke again shortly before bedtime. Leah went to her room and dressed for bed. Benjamin still had not come home. Before climbing under the warm quilts, Leah went in and checked on Caleb. He was sleeping soundly. She went back to her room and curled up to sleep. She woke sometime later to Caleb's whimpers. Leah went in to find his fever had spiked again. She carried him down to the living room so he wouldn't wake the others. Leah prayed over him. She would let Benjamin decide if they should take him to the Englishers hospital, or make him drink the natural remedy the People often used. It was not a pleasant tasting tonic, consisting of honey, lemon, horseradish, and pepper, but it always seemed to work for bringing down a fever. Poor Caleb hadn't been able to keep the tonic down earlier in the evening. She gently tapped on Benjamin's bedroom door. When there was no answer, she knocked harder. Still, no answer came. She opened the door, only to find the bed empty.

She took Caleb to the kitchen and forced the tonic into him. She sat by the fireplace and rocked him. He soon fell asleep again. Leah dozed off and on throughout the rest of the night. Morning brought the reality that Benjamin never returned home. Caleb was still sleeping when she laid him on the couch and covered him with a quilt.

She breathed in the aroma of fresh coffee. It smelled particularly good this morning. Leah pulled out the potatoes to peel them for a breakfast casserole. She was finishing up when she heard Benjamin coming through the door. He appeared half-frozen to death. Leah thought to herself. *"That's what you get for spending the night with Miriam."*

"Leah, I was thinking, we could finish your chicken coop today."

"That would be right gut, as long as Caleb's fever stays down. It spiked again in the night. He has rested gut for a while now, but this is the way it was yesterday. His fever broke, and he seemed better, then suddenly, his temperature soared again. He may need an antibiotic. I strongly suggest you take him to an English doctor if his fever goes back up. For now, we'll keep a close eye on him and see how it goes."

"Whatever you feel is gut, Leah. You know more about raising my kinner than I do." He stood and walked to the coffee pot. Leah could feel his body close to hers, and she started to shake inside. She had to get out of that kitchen, and the sooner, the better.

She was thankful when she heard Beth's footsteps on the stairs. Leah took a deep breath, let it out slowly, and turned to speak to the child. "Guder mariye, Beth. Is my maedel hungry this morning?"

Throwing her arms around Leah's legs, she answered, "Jah, I am ever so hungry." Beth crawled up into her seat and asked, "Can I have some hot cocoa this morning, Leah?"

Smiling, Leah shook her head. "Jah, for sure, you can. Would you like me to put a little peppermint in it this morning?"

"Ach, please."

Leah tried working around Benjamin as he leaned on the counter near the sink. He had never done that before, and Leah wished he wouldn't have started it now. She was ever so nervous being this close to him. When she turned to reach for the pan of hot milk, she tripped over his foot. He reached out to catch her. Their faces were so close she could feel his breath on her face.

She would have liked nothing more than for him to kiss her. She quickly steadied herself, cleared her throat, and said thank you. *"Why was she feeling this way about him? Was she merely lonely? She had been without Adam for what seemed like an eternity."* She slapped her hand on her forehead. "Ach, nee, I forgot I had to go somewhere early this afternoon. I will have to work on the chicken coop another day. If Caleb is feeling better, I will need you to care for your kinner for an hour or so after breakfast. If you cannot do it, maybe Miriam could come and sit with them. It would give her gut practice."

"I can stay with them. I set the time aside today to work on the chicken coop, so I am free to care for them."

"Danki, Benjamin. We will keep a close watch on Caleb today. If he is feeling better, I will be staying in the daadi haus tonight."

Benjamin's tone grew sober. "Whatever you feel is best, Leah Beiler."

Leah had such mixed emotions. *"So, we are back to using our proper names again."* It was a custom among the People to call someone by their full given name. It was less personal but showed respect. Leah felt it was Benjamin's way of distancing himself from her. Was it possible he could sense her nervousness when they were close? No matter what his reasons were for using her given name, she would be more careful to keep her distance from him and treat him as if he were her employer, not the man she thought she might love. She scolded herself. *"That's absurd. I love my Adam, and I always will. There's no room in my heart for another man."*

Caleb was doing better, so she dressed to leave. She promised she would not be gone long. She went out to the barn to harness her horse. It was a chore Benjamin had done for her for so long, but he was nowhere in sight. *"No matter,"* she thought. *"I am capable of harnessing the horse myself. After all, I've done it enough times before Benjamin Lapp ever came along."*

CHAPTER 10

ॐॐ

"Trust in the LORD with all thine heart; and lean not
unto thine own understanding."
Proverbs 3:5

She tied her horse to the hitching post at the cemetery. She quickly made her way over to Adam's grave. She fell to her knees and began to cry. "I am ever so sorry, my ehemann. Please, vergeef me, for acting like such a fool. I still love you ever so much. I'm just so confused. Perhaps I'm lonely and think I am feeling something I'm not. Adam, I am so sorry for betraying you."

A voice seemed to come out of nowhere. "Why do you feel you are betraying him?"

Naturally startled, Leah jumped to her feet and turned to see who was speaking. Behind her stood a woman she did not recognize. Hesitantly Leah spoke, "Excuse me."

"Why do you feel you are betraying your ehemann, my maedel?"

Leah stood there, dumbfounded. She was at a loss for words. "Who was this stranger? It was obvious the woman was Amish. Her dress was similar, but clearly, she was not from their district. Only a prayer kapp covered her head. She wore no black stockings and no black bonnet. She wasn't wearing the customary black mourning dress, so she must not have lost her husband recently." Leah eventually found her voice. "You scared me half to death. Do I know you?"

"Nee, you do not know me, and please vergeef me for startling you. I was once a member of your district here in Somerton. That was before I lost my ehemann. I hurt so deeply, I ran away and married the first Amish man who would have me. I live over in Bird in Hand now, but I come now and then to visit with my ehemann." Pointing to the grave next to Adam's, the woman continued. "He's buried right here."

"Ach, I never paid any attention to the graves around my Adam's. Your ehemann died at a young age as well. How did he die, if I may ask?"

"His buggy was hit by an Englisher. They said he didn't suffer that he died instantly. We had only been married a month when he died. So many times, I wished I died along with my Zacchaeus. My world ended the day my ehemann passed away, or so I thought. I was hurt, angry, confused, and scared all at the same time. I didn't want to stay here and have everyone telling me what to do and how to do it. Nor did I wish for them to whisper about me and feel sorry for me, so I ran away. When I came to my senses, I couldn't believe I married a stranger. He was a widower with two young bopplin. He wasn't much older than I was when his wife died. He was as scared and hurt as I was. I promised to care for his kinner if he promised never to touch me. He agreed, and we got married."

Leah couldn't believe this stranger felt the same feelings she had felt during the months since her husband's death. "How did that work out for you?"

"Gott has blessed us with many years of love and happiness, my maedel. Once our grief had become more bearable, we permitted ourselves to open our hearts again. Before we knew it, we fell in love. We now have nine children and many, many grandchildren. As I said, Gott has blessed us, for sure and for certain. When I came to visit my Zacchaeus, I wondered if this Adam Beiler had a family of his own, and it is only natural for a body to wonder how someone died. I see it hasn't been all that long ago that you lost your ehemann."

With a tear in her eye, Leah responded. "My Adam has been gone just a little over a year now. I felt just like you did. I went as far as to contemplate taking my life. I also thought my world ended."

The woman's eyes held such compassion. She understood everything Leah had dealt with since her husband's death. "My name is Lora Raber. My Isaiah came to Bird in Hand, from Ohio after his fraa died of pneumonia. He wished to run away also. I believe it is our nature to run from things that hurt us. Nevertheless, running away doesn't solve anything. Our pain will follow us no matter where we run to, for sure and for certain. We have to deal with our hurt and our anger head-on. Something the lot of us cannot seem to do. So, let me ask you again, why do you feel you are betraying your Adam?"

"I might be in love with another man. I promised to love Adam until I die. I am so confused. And, here I am telling my most personal thoughts to a stranger."

"Sometimes it is better to talk to a stranger. Tell me something, are we truly strangers? We both know and understand the deepest hurt we each have had to deal with."

"Why do you still come to visit your Zacchaeus' grave?"

"Because I promised to love him as long as I have life within me, and I do still love him ever so much. I never thought there would be room in my heart to hold love for another, but I was ever so wrong. You see, my maedel, I love my Zacchaeus, but I also love my Isaiah. I love Isaiah more than I ever thought I was capable of loving. You are not betraying your Adam. In Gott's eyes, you have fulfilled your promise to both Adam and Him. You will never stop loving Adam, but time heals the heart to a point where we can move on in life. Do you truly believe Gott, and your Adam, wants you to go through the rest of your days here on this earth alone?"

"I'm simply not ready to say goodbye to my Adam."

Laughing, Lora retorted. "Do you think I have said goodbye to Zacchaeus? Goodness no. I have come to visit him here for the past thirty-eight years. My Isaiah understands. And, he knows how much I love and adore him. You can still hold love for your Adam and find new love as well. You can't live in the past, and that is what you will be doing if you do not permit your heart to love again. I must go now, but please, think about what we have discussed." Lora Raber slid into the back seat of the waiting car and was gone.

"Ach Adam, I must go now too. I have stayed longer than I should have. I love you. I will come again soon, I promise."

She entered the kitchen and immediately heard laughter coming from the living room. She quietly tiptoed to the door and watched as the children sat on the floor playing with their father. She was happy to see Caleb was feeling better. She went in and touched his forehead and was confident he was fever-free. Still, she insisted he take it easy for the rest of the day.

After hugging the children, she headed out to prepare lunch for them and their father. Benjamin stopped her and told her he had already fed them and was going to put them down for a nap. They would still have time to finish the chicken house door if Leah was up for it.

Leah offered to help get the twins settled, before going out to hang the door on the coop. She took yawning Katie into her arms and sat to rock her. The toddler was out before Leah ever got comfortable in the chair. She carried Katie up to her room and tucked her in. When she came back down, Caleb was already sleeping in his father's arms. Leah gave Beth the choice of who would rock her before her nap. Holding her arms up for Leah, she said. "I want you to hold me and rock me. I want you to come back and stay with us here. Or else, take me to live with you at your Mamm's."

Ach, my maedel, I'm sorry you are having a hard time with the changes in your life. But I must live at my Mamm's haus, and you must stay here with your Daed and the twins. They would miss you ever so much if you were to leave them."

Beth held tight to Leah's neck. Placing her head on Leah's chest, she cried herself to sleep. Leah's heart was breaking. She had to put a stop to all of this craziness. The children had become too attached to her, and it would only get worse. Leah needed to do something, but what?

By the time Leah got out to the coop, Benjamin had already brought the door out from the barn. He waited on Leah to give instructions about how she wanted the door hung. As they worked, they both made sure they kept a safe distance from the other. Leah was the first to speak on a personal level. "Miriam stopped me this morning while I was at the bakery. She informed me you both spoke with the bishop night before last, and you have set your wedding date. Will you be moving from here soon? The only reason I ask is I need to know if I should consider Josiah and Rachael Miller's offer. I do not wish for you to wait until the last minute to tell me you are leaving. You need to give me some warning."

Benjamin hesitated before speaking. "Jah, it is true the bishop had words with Miriam, her parents, and me the night before last. A wedding date has not been set, for sure and for certain. When it comes to other women, Miriam is very insecure. I wish she didn't feel like she had to run to you and wag her tongue all the time."

"Benjamin Lapp, it wasn't all that long ago you told Miriam you would think about giving your children over to me, once you and she married. I didn't think it was a gut idea at the time, but this arrangement isn't going to work here for much longer. It has gotten complicated around here. You haven't decided to purchase my farm, you haven't said any more about me raising your children, and you haven't made a move to marry Miriam. I asked you a question some time ago, and I'm going to ask you again. Do you love Miriam Stoltzfus, and if so, why are you putting her off when it comes to marriage?"

"Leah, I do not wish to speak ill of anyone, but Miriam Stoltzfus is an impossible, hard-hearted, selfish woman. She makes it hard for anyone to like her, let alone fall in love with her."

Giggling Leah asked, "So, does this mean you are not in love with her?"

He gave a hearty laugh, and it sounded good to Leah's ears. "Jah, it is what I mean, for sure and for certain."

"Have you told her how you feel?"

"Jah, I have. She does not care if I have no love for her. She wishes to have a husband so the People will quit wagging their tongues about her."

"Ach, that is sad. So, Benjamin Lapp, what are you going to do now? You cannot continue to live as you have. Your kinner have become too dependent on me. It is not gut for them. You need to figure something out and do it soon. I told you, I have thought about selling my farm and moving into my parent's daadi haus permanently. When I spoke with Josiah and Rachael Miller the other day, I told them I would give them a definite answer in one week. They are hoping to purchase everything I own here."

"Leah, please hear me out. I will offer my place to them. They can build their haus right where the old one once stood. I didn't think I could feel anything ever again. After losing my boppli, and then Annie and my farm, I became numb. It was as if I had only one emotion, anger. Leah, I looked at my kinner, and as hard as I tried, I could not feel anything for them. I admit I had thought about leaving them with you when I married Miriam."

The strangest thought came to Leah, and she shuddered at the notion. *"Does Benjamin Lapp think he can purchase my farm, marry Miriam, and keep me on to care for his kinner?"* She tried to shake the dreadful notion from her mind before speaking. "You are confusing me, Benjamin Lapp. What are you saying? Do you wish to purchase my farm?"

"Nee. Well, it's not exactly what I mean. Leah, you told me to watch Miriam in secret, and I have. But, I have also observed you over all these months. You have such a kind and loving heart. You have taken such wunderbaar gut care of my kinner. You have treated them and loved them, as though they were your own. I was angry. It was like Annie never existed. You immediately stepped in, and it felt like you were taking Annie's place in my kinner's lives. Katie and Caleb thought you were their mudder pretty much from the start, and it didn't take long for Beth to come to think of you as her mudder too. And then,

Miriam approached me and suggested we go ahead and marry and permit you to keep and raise my kinner—"

Leah interrupted him. "You are going to marry Miriam Stoltzfus and give up your kinner, for sure and for certain! How could you, Benjamin Lapp? How could you give them up for the likes of Miriam Stoltzfus? You will, for sure, come to regret this decision. It will haunt you every day of your life." As hard as Leah tried not to cry, it was a losing battle. The tears came like a flood.

Benjamin immediately knelt beside her. He started wiping her tears and spoke with a smile. "Ach, Leah, please don't cry. Hear me out. There is no way I am going to marry the likes of Miriam Stoltzfus."

"But you spent so many nights with her."

He jumped to his feet and started defending himself. "I have done no such thing. I have slept in your barn, and I about froze to death doing so. I was fighting the feelings I was having. I couldn't stay in your haus, knowing you were upstairs. You need to know that I stopped keeping company with Miriam on the day she took over your kitchen. I told her I needed time and space. She and her mother became so overbearing, and I could no longer deal with either of them. She holds to the hope and tells everyone we will eventually marry. But, I can tell you this, it will never happen. I have permitted her to carry on and even go as far as to bring the bishop in on her plan. Perhaps I am wrong in doing so, but it is impossible to get anything through the heads of the Stoltzfus women. They do not take no for an answer, for sure and for certain."

"I do not understand you, Benjamin Lapp. You talk in circles at times, so you had better explain yourself."

"Back when I was sleeping in your barn, I longed for you to invite me into your haus. Then you offered me a bedroom in exchange for the work I did. Well, that was the one and only night I slept in the haus while you slept in the room upstairs. I wished to have you beside me. I had no right to feel that way, and it shamed me. I tossed and turned all night, thinking about what it would be like if you were my fraa. The feelings were so strong I knew I couldn't sleep in your haus another night and go through it all over again. I decided I would go ahead and marry Miriam Stoltzfus, and it would fix everything. However, spending time with her was torture for the kinner. They wished to come home and spend the time with you. Last night, I came to a decision; to stop being prideful and ask you to marry me and continue carrying for my kinner. I never figured out a way to tell you how I felt. I do not wish for you to raise my kinner without me. You have never given me any inclination that you would consider marrying me, but if we were to marry, it would solve everything."

Leah was out of her comfort zone. Their talk became too personal, and it made her anxious. She wished she could become Benjamin Lapp's wife, but not this way. She did not want to marry, simply because he needed a mother for his children. Leah wanted more; she wanted Benjamin Lapp to love her as Adam had loved her. Abigail Stauffer was sure Benjamin Lapp loved Leah when they were young teenagers. But, not once did Benjamin speak of love. She couldn't imagine sharing a bed with a man when there was no love.

They finished hanging the door, and Leah stepped back to look over the project. It was finally completed. Sadness swept over her. Now that she fulfilled the promise she had made, nothing was keeping her there. She was free to sell her and Adam's home and land. It wasn't cold outside, but chills ran through her body, nonetheless. It wasn't the air causing the chills, and she knew it. Leah had so many mixed emotions, and she felt uneasy being alone with Benjamin. She suggested they go inside for a hot drink.

"Jah, for sure, something hot sounds wunderbaar gut."

Once inside, Leah asked him, "Kaffi, or hot cocoa?"

"Hot cocoa would sure hit the spot and maybe some of your cookies to go along with it."

Smiling, she said, "Benjamin Lapp, I like the way you think."

Leah prepared the cocoa, grabbed a plate full of cookies, and they headed in by the fire. After adding a few logs, Benjamin turned back to Leah and asked, "Well, Leah, are you going to marry me?"

Leah hesitated a few moments and then answered, "Please vergeef me Benjamin Lapp, but I cannot answer you at this time. I am ever so sorry. You are a gut man, but I will need time to think about this."

"I hope you are not putting me off merely because you are afraid to hurt my pride by saying no. Leah, I ask that you seriously think about it."

"Jah, Benjamin Lapp, I will think on it, for sure and for certain."

Benjamin couldn't blame her for being so formal with him. He was the one to start pushing her away and calling her by her full given name again. *"Maybe she was afraid he would force himself on her. He would never do that, but did she know it?"* "I promise I'll be a gut ehemann, Leah. I will not force you to share a bed with me, and I will treat you with much respect."

Leah's heart dropped. She now knew he was not in love with her. *"How can I marry him? If I don't agree to it, I will eventually lose Beth, Katie, and Caleb, though."* It was a no-win situation for Leah. She already told him she would think about it, so she decided to give it some time before telling him no.

"Danki, Benjamin Lapp, for clarifying your intentions. As I have already told you, I will consider it and let you know."

The next few weeks were miserable. The days were busy with the children, and Leah loved every moment they had together. It was the evenings which she dreaded. In the quiet of the night, all alone in the daadi haus, Leah's thoughts ran rampant. She wished there was an easy answer. Lora Raber told her there was no reason she couldn't love again. However, Leah still felt she was betraying Adam with her feelings for Benjamin Lapp. Leah kicked at the quilt, exposing her leg to try to cool her body down. The nights were much warmer now with spring upon them. She couldn't get comfortable. Maybe if she threw the quilt from the bed. It didn't help. She got up and went to the window. The full moon shone brightly in the night sky. She opened the window. The coolness of the breeze, hitting her face, felt good. Leaving the window open, she climbed back into the bed. Maybe now she could fall asleep. She tossed and turned for a short time before her mind finally gave in to sleep.

Leah woke with a start. She jumped from her bed and quickly dressed. *"Why am I feeling so stressed?"* She hadn't overslept, and she didn't have to rush. Then why was she feeling so anxious? Her heart told her something was wrong. She dashed off to the main house to check on her mother and father. Everything was fine. She quickly ran out to the barn to harness her horse. Her dad came out and took the contraption from her shaking hands. "Here, let me take care of your horse for you." He tried calming her down before sending her off to take care of the Lapp children.

Once she arrived, she hurried into the house and up the stairs. She peeked in on Beth, who was sleeping soundly. She opened the door to the twin's room, she gasped. Caleb was not in his bed. She looked over to Katie's bed and felt relieved to see the twins cuddled up together. She quietly closed the door and headed back down the stairs.

At the bottom of the steps, she met Benjamin. He whispered, "Leah, what are you doing here so early?"

"Ach, I don't know. I woke up with a jolt and had such fear as though something was wrong. When Mamm and Daed were gut, I came here as quickly as I could, for fear there was something wrong over here."

"Everything is gut. Come to the kitchen, and I'll start some kaffi. We'll see if we can calm you down some."

"Danki. I will be gut, though. I will start the kaffi and make some sweet rolls since I am here so early."

"Gut, it will give us some time to talk before the kinner come down."

Leah became nervous. "I haven't made my decision yet, and I would prefer not to discuss it."

"Ach, don't worry Leah, I was not planning to discuss my proposal at all. I do, however, need to discuss something ever so important with you."

They headed into the kitchen, and Benjamin lit the gas lanterns. The daylight had barely made its appearance. "You really shouldn't have come out this early, something could have happened."

"Something could happen any time I come out. I trust Gott to keep me safe." She quickly changed the subject. "Why don't you tell me what is weighing so heavily on your mind, Benjamin Lapp?"

"Come sit with me. Last evening, I had a visit from Bishop Miller. He, Deacon King, and the preachers had a meeting and came around the district asking for volunteers to travel out to Shipshewana, Indiana. A tornado ripped through the Shipshewana district, causing much damage. They are seeking unmarried men to go there to help rebuild the community. Bishop Miller asked if I would be willing to go. The only way I will consider going is if you agree to come back to your house here and care for our kinner."

Leah didn't miss the fact that he referred to his toddlers as their children. She doubted he ever realized the mistake he made. She let it slide. "Of course, I will help in whatever way I can. For them to ask for the men from here in our Pennsylvania district to travel that far to help, the damage is for sure bad."

"From what I understand, the devastation to the homes is unimaginable. Most of them were badly damaged or destroyed. I feel the need to go, Leah. What do you think?"

"If you feel Gott is nudging you to go, then you must follow His leading. Your kinner will miss you something awful, but I will take gut care of them, I promise."

"I know you will. Leah, will you not miss me?"

"Benjamin, please do not do this."

"But Leah, we are already living as though we are a family. I told you I would not force you to share a bed with me. I would never force you to do more than you are already doing."

"Ach, Benjamin, you deserve so much more. Do you not wish to have a marriage filled with love? Do you not wish to have that feeling of excitement knowing after a long day you will come home to the one you love? Someone you cannot bear the thought of being away from for even a moment? Someone you feel comfortable with, enough to share your most personal thoughts? You did not settle for Miriam Stoltzfus. Please, Benjamin, do not settle for me either."

"But Leah, I feel the way you say. I cannot stand being away from you. I think about you all the time. I even dream about you. I like the way I

185

feel when we touch accidentally. I like the way I feel when we are working together. I have tried to hide my love for you all these years. I hated myself for being here so close to you when I had only just lost my fraa. I almost married Miriam Stoltzfus to escape my feelings for you. How narrish is that? Please, Leah, do you not think you could ever love me? Maybe even after some time? If you feel you could learn to love me someday, then please say you will marry me. Ich liebe dich ever so much, and I can live with you not loving me, but I do not wish to try living without you."

Benjamin's confession shocked Leah. She heard him correctly; he said he loved her. Did he truly love her? Or did he merely want a mother for his little ones? Lyddie's words came rushing back to Leah. "You complicate your life by overthinking things too much, Leah." Lyddie was right. She had to stop overthinking this. Leah was sure she loved this man as well. She felt the need to visit with Adam again before giving Benjamin Lapp her answer. She never got the chance to say anything else to Benjamin. Beth came into the kitchen, sobbing.

Leah hurried to Beth's side. "What is wrong, Beth? Are you feeling ill?"

"Jah, Leah, my tummy hurts bad."

"Leah felt her head. Thankfully, there was no fever. Leah picked Beth up into her arms and held her close. Would you like some warm tea with peppermint?"

"Jah, I would like that. Will it make me feel better?"

"I for sure hope so, my maedel."

CHAPTER 11
ഗ്രൂ

Therefore, my beloved brethren, be ye stedfast,
unmoveable, always abounding in the work of the Lord,
forasmuch as ye know that your labour is not in vain in
the Lord.
I Corinthians 15:58

Leah put the water on the stove to warm for
Beth's tea. Benjamin had disappeared, and
she didn't know why. As she tucked Beth in on
the couch, she wondered if Benjamin would come
back in before the day got too crazy.

"Leah, you will ask Daed to come and sit
with me, jah?"

"Jah, I will go ask him."

Leah found Benjamin on the back porch
with his kaffi. "Beth would like you to come in
and sit with her while she waits for her
peppermint tea."

He stood up and started for the door. Leah reached out and touched his arm. "I promise to give you an answer soon, Benjamin Lapp." He smiled and disappeared through the door.

The twins were sleeping in later than usual this morning. Leah was thankful for the extra time. She and Benjamin needed to discuss his leaving for Indiana.

He went in and picked his daughter up and carried her to the rocking chair. Leah leaned over Benjamin while she held the cup for Beth to sip on her warm peppermint tea. Benjamin loved the smell of her. He loved everything about her and had for so long now. He wished she would have loved him back when they were courting. She never led him on, though. He knew from the start her heart belonged to Adam Beiler. She was just as unselfish now as she was back then. She worried about him being unhappy going into a marriage where she felt no love for him. He thought to himself, *"If only she could learn to love me."* Little did he know, this woman who was leaning so close to him had lost her heart to him months ago. He wanted to reach out and touch her face, to kiss her lips. He cleared his throat and spoke softly to his daughter. "Is the tea helping you, my maedel?"

She reached up and touched his cheek. "Jah, I think so. I'm ever so sleepy, though."

"Close your eyes, and I'll rock you until you fall asleep."

"Ich liebe dich, Daed."

"I love you, my maedel."

Curled up in her father's arms, Beth slept peacefully. After several minutes Benjamin stood up, placed Beth back on the couch, and covered her with the quilt. Looking up to Leah, he asked, "Can we talk over a cup of kaffi?"

"Jah, for sure, we can. I wish to know more about this trip to Indiana."

With hot coffee and some sweet biscuits in hand, they sat at the table together, while Benjamin explained what he knew about the forthcoming trip.

"How long will you be gone?"

"Bishop Miller says to prepare for a month, but it might take longer depending on how bad things are. I wouldn't think it would take more than a month, with all the men pulling together. Once we get the supplies and get organized, I feel the houses will go up in no time." The thought of spending a month away from Leah and his little ones brought sadness to him. But, it would give Leah time to think about his proposal without him underfoot.

"Will we have time to celebrate Beth's birthday before you must leave us?"

He liked the way she included herself in the question. "Jah, if we can do it tonight or early tomorrow. I wish we had the time to do it when she feels better, though. I can't believe our Beth is going to turn four next week. I'm ever so glad I finished the doll cradle yesterday. I wish to give it to her before I must leave."

It suddenly hit Leah, and it hit hard. She would be without him for a month, perhaps longer. Leah did not like the idea of him being away from them for so long. It would make for a long hard month. "I made her a set of faceless dolls for her birthday. She will be ever so excited to have a cradle to put them in."

Benjamin had a questioning look on his face. With his eyes squinted and his head tilted to one side, he asked. "Why two dolls?"

Leah smiled and answered, "Ach, Beth wanted a buwe and a maedel just like her Caleb and Katie. She loves her bruder and schweschder, for sure and for certain."

"Leah, I wish things were different with us. I can't find the words to explain what I mean. I just wish things were different is all." What he hoped for was to marry her before he had to leave. He longed to know she was his wife and would be anxiously waiting for his return from Shipshewana. If he pushed her, it would only make her distance herself from him. And, that was the last thing he wanted.

"Benjamin, I'm sorry I cannot give you what you want. I need some time, and I can't explain it either. I promise, when you return, I'll have an answer for you. That is gut, jah?"

"I have no choice but to wait."

Benjamin tried to convince himself he would be too busy rebuilding the homes in Shipshewana and wouldn't have time to think about Leah. He knew, when the time for sleep came, she would be heavy on his mind. She already consumed his thoughts without end, and he missed her already. He was close to his children once again, and he didn't relish the idea of leaving them either. He wished for a way to take them all with him. He had to stop this self-centered way of thinking. *"The district in Indiana needs help, and they are much worse off than I am. I'm feeling sorry for myself, and I am sure it is ever so displeasing to Gott."* He felt shame for his petty thinking.

Interrupting Benjamin's thoughts, Leah asked him if he would like a refill of coffee.

"Jah, that would be gut."

The sound of footsteps worried Leah. It was too early for visitors. The anxiety welled up in her chest again. *"What is wrong with me? Please, Gott, give me peace over this day."*

Her Grossdaadi, Preacher Zook, entered the kitchen. "Guder mariye, my maedel. You are gut this morning, jah?"

"It depends, Grossdaadi; do you have gut news or bad? It would be wunderbaar gut if you were only here to visit with no news at all."

"I am here to see Benjamin Lapp about the Indiana trip."

Leah filled a cup with coffee for her Grossdaadi. After refilling Benjamin's cup, she placed more sweet biscuits on his plate and turned to go.

Benjamin quickly spoke. "Leah, please stay with us. I wish for you to hear the plans." He immediately added, "This way, you will know the details for how long you will have my kinner."

Leah was grateful he clarified his wishes. It would do no good for her grandfather to know something was happening between the two of them. She sat at the table with the two men, and respectfully answered, "As you wish, Benjamin Lapp."

Preacher Zook gave Leah a strange look before he explained the English driver would arrive at five o'clock the following morning to pick up Benjamin. Altogether, about twenty men would be heading out to Indiana. He still had no details to give on how long they would be gone but hoped it wouldn't be more than a month. Preacher Zook talked about the trip and the bishop from Shipshewana's account of what he experienced. He stated he had never witnessed such devastation in his lifetime. Thankfully, there was no report of any deaths. After the second cup of coffee, the preacher was on his way.

"Benjamin, I do need you to walk out with me."

It puzzled Benjamin about what the preacher wished to say out of earshot of his granddaughter. He nodded his head and got up to follow the preacher out the door.

They went down the steps and stood near the preacher's buggy. "Benjamin Lapp, only a fool would not know what is going on with you and my granddaughter."

Defensively, Benjamin answered. "Ach, Preacher Zook, I promise you nothing ungodly is going on between Leah Zook and me. I have the highest respect for your granddaughter and would never do anything to bring shame to her."

"I believe you, Benjamin Lapp. But, I also believe you are in love with my maedel. So, why would you not wish to marry her?"

"I would marry her today if she would only agree to it. She does not love me. She has already told me I should not settle for her."

"Are you so sure?"

"I don't know what you mean. Am I sure about what?"

"Are you so sure she doesn't love you?"

"She has made the fact pretty clear to me, I believe."

"Maybe she doesn't know it herself. I believe this time away will do you both a world of gut. However, I must insist on a different arrangement when you return if you are not to marry her."

"She has been living in the daadi haus at her parents. She only stayed here while the bopplin were sick, and the roads were too bad for travel. And, I slept in the barn. I have only slept in the haus one night while she was still living here. But, it didn't feel right, so I never did it again. Your Leah Zook has never done anything to break the Ordnung or to dishonor herself."

"I am ever so happy to hear this; however, it is not what I meant. I was getting at the fact of you two moving on with your life if you are not going to marry. The arrangement you have going here will not work as a permanent solution." The preacher reached out and shook Benjamin's hand. He then climbed into his buggy and turned the horse toward the road.

Benjamin slowly climbed the steps. He stood on the porch for a time, thinking about what the preacher had said. It would pain him to leave there with his little ones if Leah turned his proposal down. Not only would Benjamin be devastated, but his children would be heartbroken as well. He took a long deep breath, released it, and headed back inside. He nervously thought to himself, *"What will I tell Leah if she asks why her Grossdaadi wished to speak with me in private?"*

Leah was the first to speak. "Well, I guess that means we will have to celebrate Beth's birthday today. I had best get to work on a cake for her. I, for sure, hope she is feeling better once she wakes up."

"Jah, that would be a wunderbaar gut blessing. Last night, I asked my bruder if he would help Luke with the farm chores here while I am gone. He said he would do whatever needed doing." Placing his coffee cup on the counter next to the sink, he said, "I need to get out to the barn and get to work. Give me a yell when breakfast is ready, and I'll come back in. Maybe the smell of those sweet rolls will be a pleasing smell to our Beth, and she will be able to eat when she wakes."

Benjamin was ever so relieved when Leah didn't ask about the private conversation. It is not the Amish way for a woman to question such matters. Leah indeed was the proper Amish maedel.

Beth was feeling better after she had something to eat. The thought of having her birthday celebration a week early excited Beth. She wished to help Leah make the cake. Leah loved having the child help her in the kitchen. It was their time together, and she hoped Beth would never get tired of it.

"What kind of cake would you like to bake?"

"Pineapple, no wait, I think I would like a coconut cake. But I like pineapple too. Ach, Leah, it is too hard for me to choose."

"Why don't we make a pineapple cake with coconut icing? That sounds gut, jah?"

Wrapping her arms around Leah's legs, she stated excitedly, "Ach, Leah, it sure sounds wunderbaar gut to me."

"Okay, my maedel, that's just what we will make then. What do you say we get started on it? Then when it cools off, we will decorate it together, jah?"

The biggest smile spread across Beth's face, as she nodded her head.

As Leah slid the cake into the oven, Miriam Stoltzfus came rushing into the kitchen. Half out of breath, she exclaimed. "I need to see Benjamin right away." Looking around, she spoke with a high-pitched voice. "Is he here?"

Wiping her hands on her apron, Leah answered. "Nee, he is out in the barn working."

Placing her hand on her hip, Miriam demanded Leah to bring him to the house so she could have a private talk with him.

Leah wasn't about to let this woman come into her house and order her around. "If you would like a private conversation with Benjamin Lapp, here is not the place to have one. Most private talks take place in the barn. Perhaps you could go find him yourself."

"I'm not going into that barn. There are animals in there, and besides, it stinks something awful out there. Nee, you go get him. After all, hanging around in a barn comes naturally to you."

Maintaining her patience with this woman wasn't an easy task. "Look, Miriam, if you wish to speak with Benjamin, you go look for him. This is my house, and you will not order me around in it. You are wasting your time if you think I am going to go out looking for him for you."

Miriam stomped her foot and turned to go. As she turned, she stumbled into Benjamin.

Stuttering, Miriam tried to compose herself. "Ach, Benjamin, there you are. I was sending Leah out to find you. I need to have a private talk with you immediately. Please ask Leah to go upstairs or outside while we discuss an important matter."

"Miriam Stoltzfus, this is Leah's home, and I will not ask her to leave. Whatever it is you wish to say, you can discuss it in front of her."

Miriam pouted. "Nee, Benjamin, I can't. It is too personal."

"As I said, I will not ask Leah to leave her own home so you can talk to me. We can go to the barn if you wish to have a private talk."

Ach, it is ever so dirty and smelly out there. I couldn't possibly talk in such deplorable conditions."

"Well then, it isn't that important."

Leah interrupted. "Perhaps you could take this out to the porch. Miriam has something heavy on her mind, and I have no desire to hear what her problem is."

"Ach, that would be gut. Leah could bring us a nice glass of lemonade or tea while we talk."

Leah spoke under her breath, "Jah, I just bet I'll make a fresh pitcher of lemonade and serve it to you. You must think I have nothing better to do with my time."

Once Benjamin and Miriam disappeared out the door, Leah shook her head in disbelief. This woman had a lot of nerve. Miriam Stoltzfus pushed many of the People to their breaking point. And Leah was no exception. She tried to push Leah's buttons every chance she got. They set aside the day to celebrate Beth's birthday, and Leah wasn't going to allow Miriam to spoil it. Leah looked to the ceiling. "Lord, please forgive my wicked thinking. But this woman is exasperating, for sure and for certain."

Miriam pulled two rocking chairs close together. She sat in one and patted the other for Benjamin to sit with her. When he declined to sit next to her, Miriam started pouting. This behavior always annoyed Benjamin. He refused to give in to her childish antics.

He adjusted his hat to shade the sun as he leaned against the porch. He could have easily moved to the front railing where his back would block the sun. However, talking face to face with Miriam was too personal for his liking. He made sure the distance between them was proper. If someone were to see them together, they would have nothing ill to say about the situation.

"Tell me why it is you felt the urgent need to come over here this early in the day. Although I must warn you, I have very little time. There is much to do today."

With pleading eyes, she stated. "All I ask is that you hear me out before giving me your answer, jah?"

Benjamin feared she was going to push for a union between the two of them again. The thought of having her for a wife sent a scare through him as he had never felt before.

"Jah, Miriam Stoltzfus, I will listen as long as it has nothing to do with the two of us being together."

Her facial expression turned to one of sadness. "Benjamin Lapp, don't you think I know what the People say about me. I know it isn't gut to feel this way, but I blame my mudder for it all.

She pushes me ever so hard to do the things I do not wish to do. Over the years, it has become easier to do what she wants. She makes my days extremely miserable if I go against her wishes and act in a way that displeases her. Now, I believe my behavior has become a habit. I do not mean to say and do the things I do." Miriam pointed toward the house. "Like how I just addressed Leah in there. I permitted my mudder to make me treat Leah as if she were an enemy. I like Leah, I always have. She is such a kind, thoughtful, and strong person. I admire her, especially for the way she didn't hesitate to take you and your kinner in after the fire. I admire the strength she had after her ehemann died. I would have crumbled. Jah, Leah Beiler is a strong woman, for sure and for certain. I'm not like the other women in our district. Benjamin, I'm not strong at all; I am weak indeed."

When Miriam hesitated, Benjamin asked, "Why are you telling me all of this, Miriam? Shouldn't you be talking to your mudder or Bishop Miller?"

"I have tried talking to my mudder over the years, many, many times. Ach, Benjamin Lapp, you have personally seen my mudder in action. Would you go against her if she was your mudder?"

Benjamin gave a hearty laugh. Nee, I don't suppose I would go against her. What is it you want from me, Miriam? I hope you do not wish for me to talk to your mudder for you. Frankly, the woman scares me half to death." It was now Miriam's turn to laugh.

From inside the house, Leah heard them laughing and carrying on together. She didn't like the thought of Benjamin enjoying Miriam's company. She wondered what they could be talking about that would make them laugh and carry on so. Leah scolded herself. It was, after all, none of her business. She went into the living room, where she wouldn't be able to hear their laughs. She didn't want to know he was having a gut time. She sat with her pen and paper and finally started to answer her Aenti Abby's letter. It was long overdue.

Back on the porch, Benjamin waited for Miriam to explain the real reason for her visit.

"I overheard Preacher Zook talking with Elias Yoder about going to Indiana to help rebuild the community there. I'm ashamed to admit it, but I continued listening in on their conversation. When I heard the preacher tell Elias the names of the men who had agreed to go, a wunderbaar gut idea came to me. Please, take me with you, Benjamin Lapp."

Benjamin choked in shock. "What would I do that for?"

Miriam begged him to take her to Indiana with him. "Please, Benjamin, surely there would be something for me to do there to help in some way."

The last thing Benjamin wanted was to ride in a vehicle for nine hours with Miriam Stoltzfus. On the other hand, if Leah had asked him to take her along, he would agree without any hesitation whatsoever. The harder Benjamin tried to get Miriam to change her mind, the more determined she seemed to become.

Benjamin understood why Miriam felt the need to get out from under her mother's control. Adele Stoltzfus demanded her way no matter the cost. Although this time, Adele's overbearing ways could cost her dearly. Miriam was willing to run away from home and expected Benjamin to help her. It was a shame the way Adele Stoltzfus raised her child. Miriam was a beautiful girl. Her copper-colored hair, peeking out from under her prayer kapp, glistened in the sunlight. Her eyes were almost turquoise blue. Her skin had a smooth texture and appeared porcelain. Yes, she was quite lovely. If her mother hadn't interfered all the time, Miriam could have easily gotten a husband on her looks alone. Determined for her daughter to marry, Adele didn't seem to care if it destroyed her relationship with Miriam. Her selfish, prideful ways pushed Miriam so far that she was willing to run away. It brought a certain amount of sadness to Benjamin's heart. He was starting to feel sorry for this woman he despised not all that long ago. He tried to decide if he should help her or turn her away. *"Maybe I should take her along. It would give Miriam a fresh start, a chance for happiness, and possibly even love."* Benjamin laughed as he realized he had talked himself into taking her along on the trip.

"Why are you laughing?" Tears welled up in her eyes. "This is no joke to me, Benjamin Lapp. It could change my life forever. Maybe even be the opportunity for me to break the hold my mudder has on me. I fear I have become my mudder. And it is not something I am proud of, for sure and for certain. If you don't help me, I fear I will stay in my mudder's shadow for the rest of my days. Please, Benjamin, say you will help me."

"Jah, Miriam Stoltzfus, I will help you."

"Danki, Benjamin, this means ever so much to me; more than you will ever know." She eagerly jumped up from the rocking chair, almost toppling over. She moved close to Benjamin, kissed him on the cheek, and hugged him. Leah came through the door, witnessing the entire scene.

Benjamin immediately pushed Miriam away. Miriam turned and excitedly exclaimed to Leah. "Benjamin is taking me with him to Indiana. I must go home and pack." She sidestepped Leah, ran down the steps, and climbed into her buggy. "See you in the morning, if not later this evening." She pulled away, smiling and waving as she left.

Leah rushed down the steps and headed out toward the mailbox with her letter in hand. "I must hurry and get this in the box before the mailman comes. I have waited too long to mail it as it is."

Benjamin hurried after her. "Leah, please, let me explain."

"Benjamin Lapp, you do not owe me an explanation. I'm sorry I interrupted your time with Miriam. I needed to mail this letter. I haven't had the time to respond to my aunt's letter. With the kinner sleeping, I finally had the extra time. She worries about me when I do not respond to her letters promptly."

"You didn't interrupt us, and I want to tell you all about Miriam's visit."

"Benjamin, what you and Miriam discussed is not my business. Why do you feel you must tell me about it?"

"Because, Leah, I do not wish to keep any secrets from you."

"You have every right to your own business. You owe me nothing. But, if you feel you must tell me, then go ahead."

Benjamin went on to tell her all of what had transpired on the porch with Miriam.

"Are you telling me Miriam Stoltzfus wishes to run away from her mudder, and you are willing to help her break her Mamm's heart by taking her only child so far from home? Are you sure this isn't one of Adele's schemes? You know, to push you and her Miriam together."

"I suppose it could be a plot. I mean, Miriam was like a different maedel. It might have been an act. Ach, Leah, now what am I to do? I am a dumm kopp, jah?"

"Nee, you are not a dumm kopp, for sure and for certain. You have an extremely kind heart. I hope I'm wrong about Miriam's motives. It would be wunderbaar gut if you indeed had a glimpse today of the true Miriam. And if she is genuine, then I truly hope she can have a happy life in the Shipshewana district. I'm sorry I planted a seed of doubt in your mind. You know Miriam Stoltzfus better than I do."

"I don't know Miriam as gut as you think I do. If you are right and this is just another game Adele Stoltzfus is playing, what am I to do? Will you help me out here, Leah?"

"Help you? I don't know what I can do."

"You could go visit Miriam and find out if she is telling me the truth. Miriam did tell me she felt terrible for always treating you the way she does. She said it was her mudder who made her act spoiled and entitled. Those were the words Miriam used. She may talk to you. Or maybe you can tell if she's trying to deceive me." He shot Leah a crafty look. "I have heard women can tell these things."

"Ach, Benjamin Lapp, you are asking a lot of me, for sure and for certain."

"I know I am, and I'm sorry. Leah, seriously, I don't have any idea what to do. I do not wish to spend a day with Miriam, let alone a month away with her in Indiana."

Leah let out a huge sigh. "All right, I'll go visit her. But, mind you, only after the cake comes out of the oven."

"Danki, Leah. I'll harness your horse for you, and I'll stay here with the kinner."

CHAPTER 12
৩৯৫

"Have not I commanded thee? Be strong and of a good courage; be not afraid, neither be thou dismayed: for the Lord thy God is with thee whithersoever thou goest."
Joshua 1:9

Leah had no clue what she would say to Miriam. She knew, without a doubt, her visit would not be a welcomed one. At least it wouldn't be welcomed by Adele. Aware of how sweaty her palms had become, Leah steered the horse up to the back of the Stoltzfus' house. She sent up a prayer for God's guidance before slowly climbing down from the buggy and heading to the door. Before she reached the steps, Adele came out to the porch carrying a rug.

"Guder mariye, Adele Stoltzfus."

The disgruntled tone of Adele's voice was no shock to Leah. "Leah Beiler, what reason do you have coming here?"

"I came to see Miriam."

"Nee, you will not. You may just as well climb back into your buggy and be off with yourself. My Miriam will have no dealings with you."

Before Leah could think, she blurted out, "Benjamin Lapp sent me with a message for Miriam."

Adele's facial expression changed from that of contempt to one of surprise. "I'll get my dochder. You wait here."

When Miriam came outside, she had a genuine look of fear on her face. It was as if her eyes were pleading with Leah not to give away her secret. Leah sympathized with the girl and tried not to give too much information.

"Guder mariye, Miriam. Benjamin Lapp sent me to talk to you."

Miriam stumbled with her words. "Ach, jah, we had a wunderbaar visit this morning. I was expecting him to come by, though. Why did he send you?"

"His dochder woke up this morning with a stomach ache. But then, you probably already knew that. Anyway, Benjamin stayed with her and sent me."

Miriam wondered how she and Leah could talk in private, without interference from her mother. Her answer came when her father appeared and stood next to Leah.

"Guder mariye, Leah Beiler, what brings you here this day? Did you bring me any of your wunderbaar gut sweet rolls?"

"I'm sorry, Henry Stoltzfus, but I did not. I hadn't planned on coming by today."

Miriam interrupted. "Ach, Daed, she came to deliver a message to me from Benjamin."

"Then, I will leave you to your business." He placed his hand on his wife's back and continued, "Come, my fraa, I am ready for some kaffi and something sweet to go along with it."

Miriam breathed a sigh of relief. "Come, let's talk quickly. I don't know how long my mudder will permit us to talk in private. Please, tell me Benjamin hasn't changed his mind about taking me to Indiana." She grabbed Leah's arm and pulled her toward the barn. "Ach Leah, danki, for not ratting me out to my mudder. She would throw a fit that would make a snow blizzard seem calm, for sure and for certain." The two women giggled.

"Nee, Miriam, he has not changed his mind. He does feel you should tell your Mamm and Daed of your plans, though."

Pulling a piece of paper from her apron pocket, she showed it to Leah. "I wrote everything in this letter. I intend to leave it on the table. My mudder will never let me go if she finds out what I have planned."

"I know it will upset her, for sure and for certain. However, you are old enough to make your own choices, Miriam." Leah held the letter in her hand. "The decision is yours to make, but your Mamm deserves to hear it from you, not from this letter."

"You are right, if only it were that easy, Leah. You know how she is; even my Daed won't stand up to her." Shaking her head, Miriam continued. "I can't talk to her. I promise you it will not end gut. It is better for me if she learns from my letter why I felt the need to leave."

"It's apparent your mudder doesn't feel you can take care of yourself, Miriam. Make her see that you are a strong, capable maedel who can handle life without her mudder interfering."

"If I agree to tell her, will you go with me?"

"Ach, Miriam, I am not your mudder's favorite person, for sure and for certain. You should do this on your own."

"Nee, I'll leave the letter. As I said, it will be better this way. I do not wish to deal with her punishment if I were to tell her."

"I'll go with you, but we must hurry. I have much to do today and need to get back home."

Once they were inside sitting at the Stoltzfus' table, Adele immediately put up her guard, insisting her daughter tell her what was going on. Miriam stuttered as she tried to find her words. Leah's heart went out to Miriam while Adele scolded her daughter for stuttering and for bringing the likes of Leah Beiler into their house.

All at once, it was as if Miriam snapped. Her voice held strong and courageous. She stood up and paced back and forth in front of the table. "I'll tell you what is going on, Mamm, but you must sit and listen. You have no say in this matter. The decision is mine to make, and I have made up my mind to go to Indiana. I will be accompanying Benjamin Lapp in the morning."

Just as Miriam had predicted, her mudder began to throw a fit. "You will not go anywhere without the bishop marrying you first. We will arrange it for later today." She started to get up from the table. Miriam put her hand on her mudder's shoulder.

"Sit down, Mamm, I am not finished. You know it takes more time than a few hours to arrange the ceremony. Besides, I am not marrying Benjamin Lapp before we leave. I am going to help out in the community. They need all the help they can get."

"Nee, I will not permit you to go. I need you here."

"I am going. I am old enough to make my own choices, Mamm, and you need to understand that."

When Adele became enraged, Henry put his hand on his wife's arm. "Adele, hush." She stood up and protested. Henry spoke firmly. "Adele, sit down and hush. Our dochder has spoken. She has made her decision, and we will respect it."

Adele's face brightened. It then took on the sinister smile Leah had become accustomed to long ago. "Ach, you need permission from Bishop Miller to go. He will never permit you to travel with all those men."

Miriam rebelliously spoke out. "I'll go talk with Bishop Miller now."

Adele quickly snapped back, "And, I'll go with you."

"Nee, Mamm, you will not. Leah will go with me."

Miriam stood her ground as her mother continued to protest. Henry motioned for his daughter and Leah to go. As Adele tried to follow them, Henry took hold of his wife's arm. "You will stay here with me."

It shocked Miriam to see her father stand up to his wife the way he did. She had never witnessed anything like in all the years she could remember. What shocked Miriam, even more, was the fact that her mother listened when Henry Stoltzfus took control. It was surprising to Miriam that her father supported her decision to leave their district. She would have to remember to thank him for it later. Miriam hoped her mother would calm down by the time she returned home. She didn't wish to leave with her mother so angry at her. But she would leave for Indiana come morning, with or without her mother's approval.

As the girls walked down the steps, Miriam apologized. "I'm sorry to put you through all that with my Mamm and Daed. Thank you, though, for staying with me. You don't have to go with me to see Bishop Miller if you don't wish to. I only said it to stand my ground with my Mamm."

"You did a gut job standing up for yourself back there. Your mudder is right Bishop Miller will frown heavily on you going off to Indiana with the men."

"I will do my best to make him understand why I must go. If he says no, I don't know what I'll do. I do know, for sure and for certain, I will find a way to leave Culver County."

"It is on my way home, so if you want me to, I'll stop at the bishop's house with you." Leah chuckled. "But, I cannot stay long, so plead your case quickly."

"Danki, Leah. Danki, for everything. I'm ever so sorry I have treated you poorly. I have always liked you, really I have."

"Miriam, I truly hope you find happiness in Indiana. I believe you are doing the right thing. It will be a chance to turn over a new leaf. In Indiana, you will have a fresh start. You must make the most of it."

"Ach, Leah, I am ever so excited about it. No one will know me there, and I'll be able to show the real me. My mudder cannot force me to act the way she wishes if she is not there. I'll get a chance to have friends. I hope I will even find love. Like the kind of love you and your Adam had." Miriam's expression changed from hopefulness to one of fear.

"What is it, Miriam. Why in all the world the sudden sadness?"

"My Mamm is right, Leah. Bishop Miller will never permit me to travel all that way with only the men accompanying me. Ach, Leah, what am I to do?"

"Don't go borrowing trouble, Miriam. You have given up before you have even talked to Bishop Miller. Our bishop is a kind and compassionate man, and I believe he will understand this situation with your mudder and give you his blessing. I'm sure he will scold himself for not taking the matter into his own hands long ago. He is not blind or deaf. He knows the way your mudder has controlled you your entire life. I believe he will feel this is best for you since the damage she has done will be ever so hard to undo."

"Ach, Leah, I for sure hope you are right."

Bishop Miller was in his buggy when the girls pulled up beside him. They all greeted one another before Miriam got to the point of her visit.

"Bishop Miller, I am hoping you will give me your blessing on going to Indiana tomorrow. I must tell you this; if it all goes gut for me there, I do not wish to return here to Somerton. Please understand, if I have any hope of getting married and having a family of my own, I feel I must leave here."

Bishop Miller ran his hand down the length of his beard. "Have you discussed it with your Daed and Mamm?"

"Jah, I have. My Mamm threw a fit, just as I anticipated. However, my Daed gave me his blessing. Please give me your blessing too. I can't stay here any longer. This is for sure a wunderbaar gut opportunity for me, Bishop Miller."

"You are hoping for an answer this instant, jah?"

"Jah, Bishop, I would appreciate it."

"Maybe you could go at a later time when there's a woman along for the trip."

Leah piped in. "Benjamin Lapp has promised to accompany her on the drive, and he would look after her."

Miriam added, "And, not only would the People in Shipshewana be helping me, but I could be a gut help to them now too."

Bishop Miller smiled at Miriam, letting her know he fully understood her plight. He didn't hesitate any longer before giving her his permission. "I will be over later today to talk with your Daed. I'll give my permission for you to become a member of the church there in Shipshewana when the time comes."

"Danki, Bishop Miller. You cannot begin to understand what this means to me. Danki, ever so much."

Overtaken by the excitement, Miriam turned and hugged Leah. Leah, on the other hand, was in total shock over Miriam's jester. Leah could come to like this side of Miriam. She felt they could, in reality, become good friends.

They all said their goodbyes. Leah offered to drive Miriam back to her house. She even offered for Miriam to spend the night with her if she wished to. Miriam refused the offers and decided she would enjoy the walk back to her house. They parted ways, and Leah headed for home.

Benjamin was waiting on the steps when Leah pulled up. The twins were playing together on the porch, and Beth was playing with her tattered faceless doll. The doll had seen better days. It had barely survived the fire at the Lapp's home. Benjamin found it the morning after the blaze. One leg was partially missing, and it showed signs of scorching in other places. Benjamin wanted to throw it away, but Leah refused to let him. She sewed the leg up and cleaned the doll the best she could. Leah thought it would help Beth through the ordeal. It had only been a couple of weeks ago that Beth asked for new dolls. And Leah was more than happy to make them. She couldn't wait for Beth to see them.

Leah sat in a rocking chair. As Katie climbed on her lap, Leah told Benjamin the outcome of her visit with Miriam. It was all set;

Miriam Stoltzfus would be leaving with Benjamin Lapp come morning.

Today though, they would celebrate with Beth and enjoy their last day together. The children, of course, had no concept of the amount of time their father would be away, but Leah knew. And she didn't like it, for sure and for certain.

It had been a magnificent day. Leah felt so close to Benjamin that evening as they tucked the children in for the night. Her heart was so torn. She longed to love Benjamin and be loved by him. Nonetheless, she still carried such heavy guilt within her heart, and she didn't wish to betray Adam. Maybe Benjamin's leaving was a good thing. It would give them time to sort out their feelings and see if they really would be able to build a life together.

Leah tried to turn off her thoughts. *"Who was she kidding? They had already built a life together. The only part missing was the marriage. Somewhere along the way, they had become a family."*

Neither of them had a restful night's sleep. They consumed each other's thoughts throughout the night. Leah had packed Benjamin's clothes and personal items earlier that evening, so the only business left to do was to say their goodbyes.

Leah went down to the kitchen and prepared a hearty meal for Benjamin. She wasn't sure how long it would be before the men would stop to eat. She fixed up a basketful of sandwiches and snacks. She made a batch of Benjamin's favorite cookies. The man, for sure, loved his pecans. With the amount of damage they suffered, who knew what the food supply would be like in Shipshewana. She wondered if Benjamin would get enough to eat. She grabbed a few extra jars of her canned fruit and packed them into his food bag. She had no idea where the closest market was. Surely the neighboring districts would help. After all, the People always took care of anyone in need.

She heard Benjamin coming into the house. She hated he felt the need to sleep in her barn. She was afraid of what his sleeping conditions would be like in Indiana. The poor man needed a bed to sleep in, not a pile of straw. Benjamin would now have to hurry since he overslept. *"At least one of us slept gut."* Leah told herself.

When Benjamin came into the kitchen, he looked ragged. It was apparent he hadn't slept well after all. He apologized for coming in so late. "I didn't get any sleep and had trouble functioning this morning. He quickly added. "Must be anxious over this trip, I reckon." He sniffed the air. "Ach, Leah, something for sure smells wunderbaar gut in here. It smells like my favorite pecan cookies."

"I made plenty of them for you to take on the trip. I also made enough sandwiches and other goodies for you to take along. It will be a long day, for sure and for certain."

"Leah, did you pack paper, a pen, envelopes, and stamps by any chance? I promised Beth I would write her letters for you to read to her."

"Nee, I didn't, but I'll quickly gather it all together while you eat your breakfast. Your driver will be here soon. I forgot to tell you the bishop was making arrangements for the driver to pick

Miriam up at her haus. So she won't be coming here to meet him after all."

Leah gathered up the supplies Benjamin had asked for and tucked them away in his bag. She caught the headlights in the window as she set the bags by the door. The driver was early. She wasn't ready to say goodbye. She wished for a little more time with Benjamin. "Driver's coming up the drive," she called out.

He quickly took one last bite of his food before pushing his chair away from the table. He wished he had the nerve to kiss Leah before he headed out the door. He would be away from her for so long. He couldn't stand the thought of it. He didn't know what the greater torture was for him. The night he slept in the room below her, forbidden to hold her in his arms. Or, not seeing her for the next month or more.

As he swept by her, he said, "Tell the kinner each night before they go to sleep that their Daed loves them and will come home as soon as he can." He repeated himself on a more personal level. There was sadness in his voice as he asked pleadingly. Leah's heart broke for him. "You will tell them each night that I miss them, jah? And kiss them for me before they close their eyes?"

Smiling sympathetically, she replied. "Jah Benjamin, I will, for sure and for certain."

They each picked up a bag and headed out to meet the van. The driver had already picked up most of the men. Benjamin was happy to see Miriam sitting proudly in the front seat. He was sure she would keep the driver entertained on the trip. The van was large and could easily hold fifteen people. Benjamin let out a sigh. The only empty seat was the one directly behind Miriam. He glanced farther into the vehicle until his eyes fell on another available seat. The last row of seating already held three men, but he decided on it anyway. He would have the luxury of stretching his long legs in the aisle. Another advantage was it allowed him to distance himself from Miriam Stoltzfus. Even with this change in her, he imagined she could still talk up a storm.

Miriam got out while the driver loaded Benjamin's bags in with the rest of the men's baggage. She reached out and hugged Leah. "Danki, again for helping me out yesterday. It was ever so kind of you, Leah, especially since I have never treated you with respect. I will write to you and tell you how it is going. My Mamm is still ever so angry with me and has told me she will not write. You will let her know how it is going for me when I write to you, jah?"

Two days earlier, Leah was sure of two things. Miriam Stoltzfus would never change and would never make a move to hug her. She was wrong. In a single day, Miriam was able to become a kind heart, and Leah would enjoy their new friendship. "Jah, Miriam, I will tell her. Do not worry so. Your Mamm will come around. She will be writing to you in no time, for sure and for certain."

"I'm not so sure about that; she's more stubborn than a mule." She giggled and added. "Leastwise, that's what my Daed always says."

This time it was Leah who reached to hug Miriam. "I look forward to hearing all about your new life in Indiana. Remember, you can always come back home if you wish. Don't let pride stand in your way."

The two hugged one last time before Miriam climbed back into her seat. Leah waved goodbye and headed back inside. Benjamin's leaving was affecting her more than she ever thought it would. She missed him already.

Benjamin told the driver he forgot something inside and would be right back. The driver assured him it was no problem as they were ahead of schedule anyway.

He ran up the steps and into the house where he found Leah standing at the kitchen sink. "Were you not going to say goodbye to me, Leah?"

Leah turned to face him. Before she could speak, she found herself in Benjamin's arms. He kissed her tenderly at first. When she didn't try to pull away, he kissed her with more intensity. When he stopped and backed away, he said, "I love you, Leah Beiler. I will be back for you."

Leah stood there, dumbfounded. She couldn't speak. Benjamin turned and left. She ran up the stairs and threw herself across her bed. She cried hard. The guilt was overwhelming. "Forgive me, Adam. I am ever so sorry for betraying you and our love." She cried herself to sleep.

The days were slowly passing, and Leah was miserable. The guilt she felt over betraying Adam, and the love she had for Benjamin was taking its toll on her both physically and emotionally, and it showed. She was losing weight she couldn't afford to lose, and her eyes held dark circles under them. It was her mother who suggested Leah leave the children with her for the day, so Leah could rest and take care of herself. Erma feared her daughter was coming down with a virus of some sort. Leah was sure it was no virus. She was aware it was her guilt-ridden heart causing all the issues.

Leah avoided visiting Adam's grave because of the remorse she held inside. She decided she had to confess what was in her heart, and she needed Adam to hear it.

As weak as Leah's body felt, she chose to walk to the cemetery anyway. She admitted two miles had never seemed so far before. The air wasn't moving that unusually warm spring day. She was fortunate though that the trees hung over the road giving her much-needed shade for her walk. Still, she wished for a breeze to come through the blossoming trees. There was a stream that flowed along the edge of the cemetery. Perhaps she would immerse her feet in the water after she finished her talk with Adam.

At the cemetery, she spotted Adam's resting place and forgot all about the heat. The limbs of the cherry tree, which hung over Adam's grave, were in bloom, and the sweet aroma filled her nostrils. She closed her eyes and breathed it in. She knelt beside the grave as she often did. She pulled the wild weeds from around the grave marker. Visiting the dead was not something the Amish practiced, yet it made Leah feel closer to him. It was hard to believe her Adam had been gone over a year now. In some ways, it seemed much longer. As much as she missed him, her heart held joy for all she had learned over the past year. Not to mention, the Lord had opened her heart to love again, something she thought impossible.

This man from long ago found his way deep into her heart. As a young teen, Leah liked Benjamin Lapp, but she wasn't in love with him. Even though she felt she could learn to love him, she refused to settle for a man for the sake of marrying and having a family. Now, this same Benjamin Lapp completely consumed her thoughts and controlled her heart. She longed to feel his touch, and she hungered for him to kiss her again like he had the morning he left for Indiana. Now, her heart was so heavy with the feeling of betrayal.

She threw herself across her husband's grave. Her heart held so much pain and confusion. She softly spoke, "Ach, Adam, what am I to do? Am I wrong to move on with my life, to love another man? I have loved you for so long, and I miss you ever so much. I do not wish to betray you. If only you could let me know I'm doing what's right. Adam, I need to know you approve of me marrying Benjamin Lapp."

At that moment, a beautiful yellow and black butterfly fluttered above her. Leah watched as it came and landed on her hand. There had only been one other time in her life when a butterfly landed on her. Through her tears, she whispered. "Danki, my ehemann, danki, ever so much." She wiped the tears from her cheeks, stood up, blew him a kiss, and turned to go.

At the edge of the creek, she sat down, removed her shoes, and placed her feet in the cold stream. Leah shivered as the cold water immediately brought her body temperature down.

She leaned back, looking at the cloudless afternoon sky she dozed off.

Leah slept nearly an hour before opening
her eyes to the bright sun. The nap had done
wonders for her. She stood and brushed the grass
from her dress. Dangling the shoes in her hand,
she turned to head for home. It would be the first
time this year she went barefoot through the
grass. As she walked among the trees toward the
road, she recalled the day she and Adam walked
through the field beside his parent's house. It was
shortly after they had gotten married. Adam had
such high hopes, and unfortunately, his father's
farm was much too small for Adam's plans. He
and his brother, Joel, decided to trade farms.
While Leah and Adam discussed it, Leah had
mentioned it would be nice to have a sign
confirming they were doing the right thing.

Adam spoke. "Ach, you say you wish for a
sign? Well then, if a butterfly comes and lands on
your hand before we finish our walk, we will know
we are doing what is right, jah?"

"Ach, Adam that will never happen. And, if
it did, it would be a miracle."

"Exactly. I'm asking Gott to permit this to
happen. If He does, then it is our sign."

When a butterfly landed on Leah's hand,
Adam insisted it was the sign. He was confident it
was the Lord blessing their decision. Leah could
now see Adam's face so clearly. It was as if he was
there with her, speaking his words once again.
"Leah, the butterfly will be the sign we will always
look for when we face a serious decision. It will be
a sign of blessings, for sure and for certain."

Leah spoke out loud. "Adam, was the butterfly your blessing as well as our Lord's? If you approve of me marrying Benjamin, please send me another sign."

The day was unusually warm for early spring. The air was quiet, with no movement whatsoever. All of a sudden, a breeze blew across Leah's face, and such calmness swept over her. She was confident Adam was releasing her to love again. He wanted her to have a happy marriage and children with Benjamin.

"Danki, my ehemann. I will always hold your love deep in my heart. I am not saying goodbye, because we will meet again, for sure and for certain."

Leah returned home, feeling more relaxed and rested than she had in months. She was now ready to give Benjamin Lapp an answer to his marriage proposal.

CHAPTER 13
ဖွာ

*"So do not fear, for I am with you; do not be dismayed,
for I am your God. I will strengthen you and help you; I
will uphold you in my righteous right hand."*
Isaiah 41:10

The following day, a letter from Benjamin waited for her inside the mailbox. Her heart leaped within her chest. It had been nearly two weeks since he left, and she missed him terribly.

Her joy lasted briefly. After reading about how much Benjamin missed his children and how he couldn't wait to see them again, he went on and on about Miriam. She tucked the letter into her apron pocket after partially reading the letter to Beth, Katie, and Caleb. They surely didn't need to hear their father go on about Miriam Stoltzfus. Leah would read the rest of the note after she put them all down for a nap.

It was as though the letter kept calling Leah's name from the apron pocket where she had tucked it away. There was a part of her that didn't want to read the rest of the letter. However, curiosity was killing her. She was glad when the three rambunctious toddlers finally fell asleep.

She pulled the letter from her pocket and began to read where she left off earlier.

"Ach, Leah, Miriam has been a completely different maedel since we've been here. Being away from her mudder's influence has been ever so gut for her. I'm sure you will find this hard to believe, but I have enjoyed spending time with her. Something else you will find unbelievable is her behavior around the kinner here. She has taken such gut care of them and has expressed to me her desire to have bopplin of her own. The change in her is amazing, for sure and for certain. She has confided in me about so many things in her life. She now feels strong enough to come back home with me and live her life without her mudder's interference. I must stop writing now, Miriam says supper is ready. Jah, it is true, Miriam is, in fact, a wunderbaar gut cook. A talent she has kept hidden from the People there in our district. I haven't learned the reason behind her keeping it such a secret. But, as much as she has opened up to me, I am sure I'll learn more of her secrets in time. Please give Beth, Katie, and Caleb another kiss for me. Tell them I love them and hope to come back to Somerton soon."

It crushed Leah's spirit. She fell to the porch steps. She couldn't believe Miriam Stoltzfus won over Benjamin's heart in the short two weeks they were gone. His letter was so impersonal concerning her; however, his praises for Miriam left Leah nothing to mull over. She looked out across the field while pondering the thoughts running crazy in her head. *"He didn't even say he couldn't wait to come home. It was he hoped to come back to Somerton soon. Am I reading too much into this letter? Am I borrowing trouble? Either I misread the signs from my Adam and Gott, or else I wasn't supposed to give my heart to Benjamin Lapp. Ach, Lord, how will I ever overcome the hurt of losing another love?"*

The rest of the afternoon, Leah walked around in a daze of non-belief. All the while, asking the many questions she had. *"How could kiss her the way he did, if it meant nothing? And, if it meant something, how could his heart change in just two weeks? How could he fall in and out of love in such a short amount of time?"*

While tucking the youngsters in for the night, Leah repeated what Benjamin had asked her to do. She told them how much their father loved each of them and how much he missed them and couldn't wait until he was with them once again. Of course, they all missed him. However, the twins were oblivious as to his absence. They seemed to adjust to Benjamin not being around. Beth, on the other hand, started having nightmares again and ended up sleeping in Leah's bed more often than she did her own. Being separated from her father was weighing heavily on the girl. Leah decided against letting him know the impact his absence was having on his daughter.

Leah sat at the kitchen table with a pen in hand. She wrote several words before crumpling the paper and throwing it away. On her next attempt, she kept the letter very impersonal and wrote only about Benjamin's children. She told him his children loved him and missed him ever so much. Leah finished writing the letter by telling him how delighted she was to learn about Miriam's transformation. She signed it and stuffed it in an envelope. She determined it would be best to mail it quickly before changing her mind and writing the words she wished she had the nerve to write.

Erma Zook stopped by to visit with her daughter. After some coffee and sweet rolls, she insisted Leah deliver her baked goods to the English bakery. It would give Erma time with the three Lapp children. She adored children and only had one grandchild, who she didn't get to see nearly as much as she liked.

Delia Daniels and Leah had just finished their conversation when Henry Stoltzfus entered the bakery. He talked so fast it was hard for Leah to keep up with him. "Ach, Leah Beiler, you are gut, jah? Have you heard the wunderbaar gut news?"

"Nee, I suppose I haven't."

"My Miriam is in love and will soon marry. She is ever so excited. Benjamin Lapp has been so gut to her—."

After reading all about Miriam Stoltzfus in Benjamin's letter, Leah couldn't stand to hear Henry go on about her. She interrupted him. "Ach, I'm ever so happy for Miriam, but I must run. I promised my Mamm I would be back long before now."

Leah kicked herself for not hearing Henry Stoltzfus out. She talked to herself on the trip home. "Surely there is some mistake. Why would Benjamin ask me to marry him if he was going to go after Miriam? There must have been more to Henry's telling, and I should have allowed him to tell it. I'm such a dumm kopp." She wondered how long it would take Benjamin to tell her about the marriage between them if he did indeed plan on marrying Miriam Stoltzfus. She hadn't gotten another letter from him, and it had been over two weeks since she mailed her last letter. "I am sure Adele Stoltzfus has wagged her tongue to everyone in the district already about her daughter's upcoming marriage." It comforted Leah to know this was an off Sunday, which meant no church services. Now, she wouldn't have to hear all the tellings about Benjamin and Miriam during the meal preparations.

Beth was having an especially hard day. She was whining and wanted her father. Another week had passed with no word from Benjamin. Each day Beth asked Leah if a letter had come. And, each day, Leah had to crush the little girl's heart by telling her there had been no more letters. The twins were already down for their nap, so Leah suggested they go for a short walk to the mailbox. Beth was eager to get the mail and ran out ahead. Leah prayed to God for the mailbox to hold the much-needed letter. Beth jumped up and down with excitement when she pulled a large envelope from the box. "Does it say Daed on it, Leah?"

Leah sent up quick praises for the answer to her prayer. "Jah, Beth, it does, for sure and for certain." She grabbed the girl's small hand and said, "Let's rush back to the haus, and we'll read the letter."

The envelope was much thicker this time. Leah assumed he was writing to tell her all about his and Miriam's plans. She ripped open the envelope and unfolded the pages. A separate folded up paper fell out from among the other pages. She picked it up. It had her name written on it, along with the word *private*. She slipped it into her apron pocket. Beth climbed up on Leah's lap. Smiling, Leah said, "Okay, let's see what Daed has to say today."

Beth spotted her name. "Read it, Leah. Does it say he is coming home to us? Does it, Leah?"

"Calm down, my maedel, and we will find out."

Beth had trouble containing her excitement as she wiggled around on Leah's lap. Leah read the letter. It said nothing about when he expected to come home. Beth's face grew sad. Leah tried to lighten her mood. In a cheerful voice, she said. "Ach, Beth, see here." She showed the child the extra pages. "Daed wrote to you, Katie, and Caleb. Look, it's a bedtime story for me to read to you tonight. That was ever so thoughtful of him, jah?"

The child nodded. "Leah, will you read it now, before my nap?"

"Jah, for sure, I will."

Leah hugged Beth tightly and began reading the story. Benjamin impressed her with his telling. She hadn't gotten very far into the story before she realized Beth was sound asleep. Leah carried her inside, laid her on the couch, and covered her with a light sheet. She kissed Beth's forehead. "I love you, my maedel."

Back in the kitchen, Leah poured a glass of lemonade, grabbed a piece of her famous lemon bread, and headed out to the porch to read her private letter. She feared it was the news of Benjamin and Miriam's marriage plans.

Leah's tears threatened to blind her, and she fought to finish the last few words written on the page. She folded the letter and held it tight against her chest.

She had misinterpreted the meaning of Benjamin's last letter. She had also misunderstood Henry Stoltzfus that morning in the bakery. She could have saved herself the heartache had she let Henry finish his telling that day. It relieved her to know Benjamin was not in love with Miriam, and Miriam was not in love with him.

She unfolded the letter once again and reread parts of it. "I have the most wunderbaar gut news. Miriam has found love here in Shipshewana. She told me to tell you she promises to write all about it soon.

Things have gone gut here with the rebuilding of the district. We are now working on the schools. The Englishers have been a blessing. Leah, they have brought furniture and kitchen supplies like you can't imagine. Many of them have offered help with the carpentry work. The gut news is we may come home within the week.

I know I told you before I wouldn't push you, but I hope you have thought about us and will have an answer for me when I return. You consume my thoughts day and night. I long to fall asleep with you in my arms, and I wish to wake up each morning with you there beside me. My heart is so full of love for you, Leah. It is easier for me to pour my heart out to you in this letter and not face to face. This way, you can't stop me from telling you all that is in my heart. If your answer is no, then it won't be because I didn't say how I truly feel. Ich liebe dich, Leah Beiler, and I have loved you since we were kids. I have carried that love all these years. I pray I will get the chance to show how much I love you as we grow old together.

I can't wait to see you. I think about our kiss often. And no, I am not sorry I kissed you the way I did. I wish to hear you say you enjoyed it as much as I did. I pray each night Gott will grant a miracle, and someday you will love me as deeply as I love you. As I said before, I am willing to live without your loving me. I promise I'll be a gut husband and treat you with much respect. I cannot wait to see you. But Leah, part of me is ever so afraid to come home. I do not wish to pressure you, but a man can hope, jah?"

This man had no clue how deep Leah's love was for him. Determined he would know soon, she rushed into the kitchen, gathered up her stationery, and sat at the table to answer his letter. She opened her heart up to him. Her words flowed smoothly across the paper. She held nothing back.

"My dearest Benjamin, when Adam died, it left me crushed. I wanted to die too. I'm ashamed to admit it, but I thought ever so hard on how I could take my life. I ran away from our district, my family, and my friends. Lyddie and Blake kindly took me into their home for nearly a month, while Lyddie helped me through my grief. She led me to the saving knowledge of Jesus Christ, and I accepted Him as my personal Savior. I know this is something the People do not talk about openly. Nevertheless, I need you to know these things to help you understand me better. It is because of Christ I was able to overcome my anger and grief over Adam's death. I believed I would spend the rest of my life alone, and I was all right with that. I knew I would never love again, remarry, or ever have a boppli of my own. I did not think I could overcome it all and feel that deep emotion ever again. Benjamin, I was wrong, and I didn't even know it. I'm not quite sure when it happened, but the night you mentioned Miriam's name for the first time, I knew I was in love with you. It broke my heart to think of you with her. I had to get out of my haus as quickly as I could. It was to save me the pain I would face night after night, knowing you would soon be her ehemann and not mine. I thought you would possibly permit me to share your kinner, but Miriam would be the one sharing your bed. So, to answer the questions you have asked, jah, I love you. And Benjamin Lapp, I will marry you, for sure and for certain."

Satisfied with her thoughts, she folded the letter and slid it into an envelope. She addressed it and placed a stamp in the corner. Maybe she would harness the horse, and after the children woke from their nap, she would take them with her to the post office. Her letter would arrive earlier if she got it out today. The twins would be excited to take their evening meal in a restaurant over in Bird in Hand, but not as excited as Beth would be. She loved to go in the buggy, as much as she loved to go through the shops.

The days continued to pass slowly. Leah wondered if her letter had arrived on time. Benjamin and the others were due to leave Indiana early the following morning. Soon he would be home where he belonged, and they could begin their life together. She couldn't wait for him to take her in his arms again and kiss her the way he had the day he left. This time would be different, though. She would be more prepared and respond to his kisses.

The marriage ceremonies took place in November. However, there were circumstances when marriages took place in the spring, before planting season. There were exceptions made to these times, though. Benjamin and Leah were already members of the church, so there would be no waiting period for them. The only delay would be the requirement the Englishers had when applying for a marriage license. And, that was only three days. She and Benjamin could be married very soon. The thought sent tingles racing through her body. She couldn't wait to become the wife of Benjamin Lapp.

The children were sleeping when Benjamin arrived home. Leah went weak in the knees when she saw him standing at the door. He set his bags down and quickly went to her. He kissed her long and sweet. They held each other for some time before Leah spoke. "Ach, Benjamin, you got my letter."

"Jah, I did. It was the best surprise I could have received. I thought once I came back to Somerton, you would tell me you didn't want to marry me. I thought I would be looking for a new home when I returned. I never imagined you would tell me you loved me and couldn't wait for me to come home."

"I'm ever so sorry it took me so long. I had so much unnecessary guilt built up inside of me, and I couldn't think straight. I prayed and prayed about it, but it wasn't until I was silent that I heard the answer. The Lord has given me His blessing on us, and Adam has given his blessing as well. I know this is all hard for you to understand. And I hope my belief in Jesus Christ doesn't cause problems for us in our marriage. But, I do believe with all of my heart, Benjamin, Jesus is the only way. And, Gott is the only one I have to answer to in this life. He has authority over me, not the church. If this will be an issue, you must tell me now."

"Nee, Leah, it is not an issue, for sure and for certain. I know what you are saying. It was my faith in Jesus that brought me through all these months. I did not act like a child of Gott at first. I was angry, and I quit praying. I was so in love with you and angry with you at the same time. You were the only one who welcomed us into your home so unselfishly. I didn't want to come into your home, which is why I chose to sleep in your barn. The last thing I wanted was to live under the same roof with you knowing I could never have you as my wife. I was also guilt-ridden. I had just lost my fraa and the mudder of my children, and yet I was still in love with you. Annie and I knew we were not in love with each other. But we had deep respect for each other, which would carry us through our life together. I never expected to stay here in your haus as long as we have. But once I was here close to you, I didn't wish to leave. And, I saw how you were with my kinner and how they fell in love with you immediately, I felt as though we were a family and I didn't wish to give such a wunderbaar feeling up. One night, something you had said reminded me I could talk to Gott, and He would listen. That night I prayed, poured my heart out to Him, and asked for His forgiveness. I also asked for Him to heal my broken spirit. It was then that He was able to work in me, and I was able to let go of all the guilt I had stored inside of me. So, Leah Beiler, I do understand so much more than you think."

"Danki, for sharing your thoughts with me, it means ever so much. I believed I would spend the rest of my life alone. I didn't think I would ever be this close to a man again and share such personal thoughts. I'm almost afraid to love you, for fear I'll lose you."

"Leah, Gott does not promise us tomorrow. Nevertheless, He has blessed us with today. Let us live each day thanking Him for the time He allows us to have together, jah?"

"Jah, Benjamin, it is a wise way to spend our days."

"I plan to talk to Bishop Miller later today about our plans to marry. You are gut with it, jah?"

Benjamin had never seen Leah smile as she did at that moment. She reached and hugged his neck and answered. "I am gut with it, for sure and for certain."

Benjamin kissed her lips. It was too much for him, being this close to her. He pulled back and moved to the table. After regaining his composure, he spoke in a matter of fact tone. "I can't stay here with you anymore, Leah. I will have to find a place until we get married."

"Ach, Benjamin, I do not wish for you to stay away from me again. But, if you wish, I'll go back to my parent's daadi haus until we are married."

"I do not wish to go away either, but it won't be gut for me to stay here. The talk your Grossdaadi had with me before I left for Shipshewana was about me finding another place when I came back. The bishop will know of a place I can stay."

"Would you be willing to stay in my Daed and Mamm's daadi haus? They will be ever so pleased over our plans, and they will, for sure and for certain, permit you to live there."

"Jah, I would be willing. We could visit them before we speak with Bishop Miller. How soon will the kinner wake from their nap?"

"It shouldn't be long now. Ach, Benjamin, the daadi haus is not big enough for the four of you. Please, stay here with the kinner, and I will go back to the daadi haus."

"Nee, Leah, I will not permit you to leave your home again. I have chased you away once, and I do not wish to do it again. It will only be for a short time. You can keep our kinner here with you, jah?"

A warm feeling swept through Leah. He referred to the kinner as theirs once again. "Jah, Benjamin, whatever you say will be gut."

He reached for her hand, "Leah, I have done much thinking, if you agreed to marry me; well, I had another scenario if you refused my proposal, but it's not important now. I must ask you, are you still thinking of selling your farm here?"

"I don't know, Benjamin. I figured I would sell the haus and land when you and the kinner moved out. But now, I will leave the decision to you. Josiah and Rachael Miller are still very much interested in purchasing it all. We have options. I would like for us to continue living here, but only if that is what you want also. I think it would be gut for the kinner. The twins do not remember their old home, and Beth has come to think of it as her home. If it is too much, though, and you wish for a farm with less acreage, then we will leave. What do you think?"

"We could sell my old land and barns to Josiah and Rachael Miller. They could build a house to their liking. Josiah had asked me at one time if you decided not to sell if I would consider selling my farmland to them. We could stay here and sell them my old farm, jah?"

"Jah, that sounds wunderbaar gut. I went to visit Isaac Fisher's shop the other day. He had just finished a bedroom suit. It was beautiful. We could purchase it and move the furniture from our bedroom to a room upstairs."

"I, for sure, like the sound of you calling it our room. Soon we'll share it as husband and wife. Leah, I'm gut with us keeping the furniture in the bedroom, we do not need to purchase another set."

"Jah, Benjamin, we do. I cannot bring myself to sleep on that bed again. We need to make a fresh start. It will be gut to move it upstairs for now. I'm not ready to give it up, but maybe Josiah and Rachael will want it for their new haus. Besides, Isaac Fisher put a hold on the set for me. He told me to take some time to think about it.

The talk with Leah's parents was a welcomed one. Erma had known Leah was in love with Benjamin Lapp for some time now, but her daughter needed to realize it for herself. It wouldn't have done any good to push her. She knew the Lord would open Leah's heart up when the time was right. The way Benjamin Lapp had looked at Leah since he was a boy, left no doubt in Erma's mind that he had loved her for many years. A woman could tell such things. That is why Adele Stoltzfus always belittled Leah. She knew Leah held Benjamin Lapp's heart captive, and she did not like it at all. She frequently commented about Leah conducting herself in a way to draw attention from Benjamin. Erma learned the tongue-wagging only came from Adele Stoltzfus and no one else. During many meal preparations, the women urged Erma to push her daughter toward Benjamin Lapp. Erma reminded them it was not their business to do such pushing. Adele Stoltzfus had high hopes it would give her the time needed to push Miriam and Benjamin together. She seemed to think it was her last hope of her daughter ever having a husband.

Leah tugging on Erma's sleeve brought her back to the present. "Ach, Mamm, you were so deep in thought. Do you care to share your thoughts with us?"

"Jah, I was thinking about the wunderbaar gut blessings the Lord has given us. I am ever so delighted you have opened your heart up to love and happiness once again. I am ever so happy to have three more grandchildren to call my own. They will liven up this haus, for sure and for certain."

The days were busy ones for Leah and Benjamin. They hired a driver and went into Lancaster and applied for a marriage license. They stopped to visit with Lyddie and Blake. Leah couldn't wait to share the wunderbaar gut news with her dear friend. Leah had confided in Lyddie months ago of her feelings for Benjamin. Lyddie tried to convince her to talk with Benjamin. But she understood when Leah said she wasn't ready to move forward. It was one of the qualities Leah loved most about Lyddie; she never pushed her to do anything Leah was uncomfortable with doing. When it was time to leave, Lyddie and Blake assured them they would attend the services, when Leah and Benjamin exchanged their vows. Blake prayed a prayer over them before they got into the vehicle to leave.

Leah pulled the envelope from the mailbox. She unfolded the letter and began to read it. Leah was somewhat disappointed when Miriam wrote very little about her and her husband. "I promise to tell you about my ehemann when there is more time. For now, I want you to know how happy I am about your upcoming marriage. I feel so honored you wish for me to stand with you when you say your vows. I have known all along that you and Benjamin belong together. I am excited about introducing my new ehemann to you. I must admit I'm ever so nervous about bringing him with me to Somerton. I've told him what a horrible person I was growing up. And I am sure there will be some who are eager to share the horror stories about me. My only hope is they will be kinder toward me than I deserve. Ach, Leah, it has been nearly two months, and my Mamm still refuses to write me a letter. My Daed has written and keeps me informed of the changes in Mamm's attitude. Sadly, they are not gut changes. He fears Mamm is in a state of deep depression. I don't know what I can do about it, for sure and for certain."

This was Miriam's second letter to Leah, and she still hadn't written much about the man she married. She did write he was a widower and the bishop of their district. Leah overheard some of the women wagging their tongues about the man. They assumed he was a lot older than Miriam and most likely had grown children. They scoffed at the idea of Miriam marrying a man of advanced age. Leah refused to become a part of the gossiping. However, she did tell them it was a shame they never got to know the real Miriam. Of course, not many of them wished to hear how she had changed for the better. Adele refused to discuss her daughter with any of them, which fueled their fire. Leah prayed Adele Stoltzfus' heart would soften, and she would welcome Miriam and her husband. It would take a miracle, but God was in the miracle business, after all.

When Miriam confided in Leah it was almost certain Adele would not permit her and Peter to stay in their house, Erma and Jonah Zook suggested they stay with them in their daadi haus. Benjamin would move into the main house with them.

CHAPTER 14

❧

"For I know the thoughts that I think toward you, saith the Lord, thoughts of peace, and not of evil, to give you an expected end."
Jeremiah 29:11

Leah couldn't believe it, in just five days she and Benjamin would be husband and wife, and they would start their new life together. Benjamin wanted to take Leah on a honeymoon, but Leah was afraid to leave the children. Of course, it excited Beth, Katie, and Caleb when they found out they could spend the time at Leah's parent's house. Beth had already started calling them Grossdaadi and Grossmudder Zook.

The twins had called Leah "Mamm" since they had first arrived at her haus. Beth had recently asked if she could now call her "Mamm." The idea of being their mother thrilled Leah.

Everything was in order. While the women were preparing some of the foods for the wedding meal, the men were busy rearranging the house. Benjamin, Blake, Josiah, and Luke moved the old bedroom furniture and carried it to the spare room in the far corner of the upstairs. They placed the new bedroom suite in the downstairs bedroom. It was now ready for the newlyweds to use on their wedding night. Benjamin decided they would wait a day before heading off to the beach for their honeymoon. It had taken Benjamin some coaxing, but Leah finally agreed to spend four days away from the children.

After the men had finished arranging the furniture to seat all the wedding guests, the men and women headed home. Leah and Benjamin sat on the porch while the children played. Soon they heard Beth shouting. "Car's coming. Car's coming."

The Englisher pulled up between the barn and the house. The back door opened, and an Amish man climbed out, holding a sleeping child in his arms. Benjamin stood to his feet and headed down the steps to greet the man. It was soon clear to Leah, who the man was. Miriam's face was glowing as he helped her from the car. It was Miriam. She ran and hugged Leah. Beth immediately ran and hid behind Leah. Miriam's happy face turned to one of sorrow. Beth was afraid of her and with good reason. Leah took Beth up into her arms and explained Miriam was no longer someone she needed to fear. Miriam talked soothingly to the girl, and soon Beth relaxed and allowed Miriam to hug her. Leah and Miriam chattered on while Benjamin helped the

Englisher remove the bags from the trunk of the car.

Still cradling the child, the man reached out with his free hand, took hold of Benjamin's hand, and shook it hard.

"Ach, Benjamin Lapp, it is wunderbaar gut to see you again. I am happy to come and attend your wedding celebration."

"Danki, Bishop Hochstetler. It is ever so gut to see you again as well. Welcome to Somerton, please come, meet my Leah and the kinner."

The men walked over to where the women were talking. Benjamin interrupted them, knowing if he didn't, Miriam would go on forever. She could still talk up a storm. Only now, it was more enjoyable. "Vergeef me, but I wish for your ehemann to meet my Leah. Leah, this is Bishop Peter Hochstetler, and this is my Leah."

The bishop nodded. "Ach, it is gut to meet you, Leah Beiler. Benjamin talked about you ever so much. It feels as though I already know you. Miriam tells me you are about the only friend she has here in your Somerton district. And you were a big part of her coming to Indiana. I thank you for helping her. If she hadn't come with your Benjamin, we would not be married today."

"It is gut to meet you too, Bishop Hochstetler. It is true; Miriam and I have become gut friends. I enjoy hearing her tellings of living in your Shipshewana district. Would you like something cold to drink? Perhaps some lemonade and some freshly baked lemon bread? The trip has been tiresome, jah?"

"Jah, it was for sure. My Ella didn't care much for having to sit still for so many hours. It was a blessing when she finally gave in to sleep. Some lemonade and your fresh bread sounds wunderbaar gut. I have heard about your famous baking skills, not only from your Benjamin but also from my Miriam. She tells me you sell your goods to a local English bakery."

"I do. I guess I have sold my baked goods to them for seven years or more now. I do have my little stand here, but I mostly take orders through the bakery. The business has been wunderbaar gut."

"My Miriam prepares some delicious meals, but she admits she has never liked to cook. I try to remind her now and then that I did not marry her for her baking skills. She stole my heart from the moment I met her." He winked at Miriam as she smiled from ear to ear. "As you have probably already figured it out, I am not an Old Order bishop. I believe it is gut to compliment your fraa from time to time."

At first, Leah was somewhat uncomfortable with the bishop. However, she soon relaxed. He was not as strict as she thought he would be. *"Oh, and how the women's tongues will wag when they finally meet this right handsome young bishop."* Leah smiled at the notion. They already pegged him as an old man. They couldn't have been more wrong. Bishop Hochstetler was a young man of twenty-six. His eyes were as blue as the sky, and his hair was the color of the golden hay. He was a nice-looking man, and the girls would be in envy of Miriam. Leah worried it would cause problems for Miriam with the young women. Jealousy can turn the sweetest of souls into hateful spirits. Leah hoped they would not embarrass Miriam in front of her new husband.

Leah spread a quilt on the porch for the sleeping child. Peter gently laid Ella down, while Miriam told Leah all about her new daughter. The child was the same age as the twins, and her eyes and hair were a similar color to Peter Hochstetler's. Miriam adored her. When the girl woke up, she ran into Miriam's waiting arms. Ella hugged her hard; she seemed to have adjusted well to having Miriam take over as her mother. Ella's mother died in childbirth not long after Peter Hochstetler became the bishop of their district. They were not an Old Order community, so Peter was given the time needed to find a new wife.

It was a blessing to see the way Miriam was with Ella. "Did you have a gut sleep, my maedel?"

Ella shook her head. She then said she was hungry. Miriam and Leah took all the little ones inside, leaving the men on the porch to talk. Once the children were at the table, Miriam poured milk into their cups, while Leah placed some cookies on a plate for them to share. The women continued to talk.

"Ach, Miriam, why have you not gone to see your Mamm and Daed yet?"

"I could not bring myself to go see my mudder. Ach, Leah, she told Daed to tell me in my last letter, not to bother coming to their house. I am not welcome there. I wish to see my Daed, for sure and for certain. But if Mamm refuses to see me, what can I do?"

"Have you told your ehemann? He could speak with Bishop Miller about a visit to your parent's haus to take care of this matter once and for all."

"Nee, I do not want to push my Mamm into a visit. But, as I said, I do wish to see my Daed. I know he will enjoy meeting my ehemann and Ella. I'm afraid they will not come to church knowing I will be there. They will most likely visit with Mamm's sister over in Lancaster. I want to have a relationship with my Mamm. But if she wants nothing to do with me, then I am gut with it. I do not wish to lose my Daed over it, though."

"I know you are probably tired of hearing me say this, but Miriam, do not borrow trouble. Wait and see if they are at services come Sunday and go from there. Once your Mamm sees you and how happy you are, maybe she will have a change of heart."

Smiling, Miriam replied, "I do not wish to borrow trouble, as you always put it. Truthfully, I am worried she will cause a terrible scene. Something we all know comes easy for her. You do remember we are talking about my mudder, jah?"

Leah snickered. "Jah, I know. But, seriously Miriam, she has become a different person too. She doesn't talk much anymore. She helps prepare and serve the meals, but she no longer gets involved in any of the women's tellings. The other women quit asking about you. And they stopped trying to strike up conversations with her because quite frankly, she let them know she didn't wish to talk to anyone. My parent's daadi haus is ready for you if you decide not to stay with your parents. But may I suggest something?"

"Ach, please do."

"Since you are afraid of her making a scene, why not try to visit with them today. If your Mamm turns you away, then stay in my parent's daadi haus. If she greets you with love, then you know you will be welcome to stay with them. Whatever you decide, do not let your mudder's attitude spoil your time here. I, for one, am ever so happy you have come. If you do not wish to use the daadi haus, then you are welcome to come back and stay with me."

Benjamin and Bishop Hochstetler came in, and Benjamin announced. "We have harnessed the buggy so you can visit with your parents."

The look of fear moved across Miriam's face. "I'm not sure I am ready to go out to my parent's haus quite yet. Maybe after we rest some, we will go, jah?"

Bishop Hochstetler took his wife's hand. "If you wish to go alone, I understand. I do feel it is ever so important you go now, though. The longer you wait, the harder it will be on you, my fraa."

Miriam lowered her head as she spoke. "Nee, I do not wish to go alone. I do not wish to go at all. Mamm has made it clear I am not welcome there. I do not wish to cause trouble. Maybe we should go stay in the daadi haus and see my parents at the next church services."

"Ach, my fraa, do not punish your Daed because of your Mamm's stubbornness. It is not fair to him."

"You are ever so right, my ehemann; it is not fair to my Daed. He has expressed how anxious he is to meet you and our Ella. Maybe we could invite him here or to the daadi haus. We could enjoy a comfortable visit with him and not have to face the wrath of my Mamm."

"I believe you are worrying for nothing. Surely your Mamm will not make a scene with a stranger in her presence, jah?"

Benjamin inadvertently choked. Miriam quickly uttered, "Ach, see, even Benjamin Lapp doesn't believe that."

Benjamin apologized before saying, "Adele Stoltzfus knows no fear, for sure and for certain."

"I do not wish to force you to do anything, my fraa. However, I feel it would be best to go and confront the issue. If she turns us away, we will go. Your Bishop Miller should have disciplined her a long time ago for her haughty spirit."

"Jah, he should have. But, on the other hand, I was as guilty as she was, and I too deserved punishment. I hoped my leaving would open her heart to become a more humble person. I never expected her to shun me or my family."

Bishop Hochstetler finally talked his wife into going to her parent's house. Miriam fretted the entire trip. When they reached the door, she froze. "I cannot go in there. I wish to see my Daed, but I can't go into the house knowing my mudder has forbidden it."

"I'll go in while you wait out here, jah?"

"As you wish, my ehemann."

Before he could enter the haus, Henry Stoltzfus came out of the barn. "Miriam, my maedel, is that you?"

"Jah, Daed, it is." She ran to him.

Henry took his daughter into his arms and hugged her hard. "Ach, my maedel, I have missed you ever so much. How was your trip?"

"Long, Daed, it was long and tiresome. Come, I wish for you to meet my ehemann." Miriam introduced the men.

"Where is your dochder, Ella? I was hoping to meet my granddaughter."

It was Bishop Hochstetler who explained. "Miriam and I thought it was best under the circumstances to leave her with Leah Beiler until we found out how your fraa would react to our visit."

"Jah, it was most likely a wise decision. My Adele has made her feelings very clear about our Miriam. Be ready for a hostile woman when you go in there. That is if she even comes out of her room."

After some time had passed, Miriam asked her Daed about her Mamm.

"Daed, can't you make her see me?"

Her Daed expressed his sadness about the way he was sure his fraa would react to Miriam and her husband being there. "You know how your Mamm is, Miriam. I have not been able to get through to her at all. I must admit I am at a loss with how to deal with my fraa. I'm afraid our bishop will have to come and try to deal with her."

"If you feel we should leave, Daed, we will go. I do not wish to bring trouble. Tell Mamm I love her, and I am ever so sad she will not meet my ehemann and my new dochder, Ella."

"Please, do not leave. Come in, sit, and visit with me a while. We will see how your mudder handles the news of your arrival. However, I will not permit her to prevent my dochder from visiting with her Daed. I am ever so excited to meet my granddaughter. I wish to come by the

Zook farm and spend some time with her and get to know her before you head back to Indiana. That will be acceptable, jah?"

"Ach, Daed, I want you to meet her. You will fall in love with her immediately. And she will love you too. I'm sorry we couldn't bring her with us. But as Peter has said, we felt it was best to leave her with Leah until we found out what kind of reception we would get from Mamm. I did not want Ella around if Mamm goes to throwing a fit."

"I understand. Come, let's go inside and sit, it is too warm here in the sun."

They hadn't been sitting long before Adele appeared in the kitchen. She looked to her husband and asked, "Why is she here?"

Nervously, Miriam blurted out. "Mamm, you have finally gotten what you have always wanted. I have a husband and a dochder whom I love ever so much, and they love me too. I am ever so happy, Mamm."

Adele never once looked at her dochder. Instead, she focused on Henry, as if they were the only two in the room. "Tell her, Henry. Tell her she is not welcome in this haus. You tell her, she is no longer our dochder."

Henry spoke in a tone that shocked both his wife and his daughter. "Adele Stoltzfus, you will keep silent. She is my dochder, and I love her, ever so much. Miriam will always be welcome in my home. If you would let go of your anger and hate for me, Gott, Miriam, and yourself, you could be a happy person again. You have carried around this heavy burden for way too long. For the last twenty years, you have been a miserable woman, for sure and for certain. What happened was not Miriam's fault, and yet you continue to punish her. You have tried to ruin her with your hate. Come on, Adele, the poor maedel doesn't even know why you treat her as you do. The gut Lord saw fit to give our Miriam a chance at a happy life and a family. I will not permit you to keep her, her ehemann, and our new granddaughter, out of my life. If you choose to continue to live with anger and hate, I can do nothing about it; nevertheless, I refuse to take part in it. I should have taken care of this all those years ago. I knew you needed help, and I didn't make you get it. That is on my shoulders. But you can turn it all around now, and start anew. No one else can change you, Adele, the choice is yours. Will you welcome your dochder, her ehemann, and their Ella into your heart, or will you choose to walk away and stay in the joyless life you have hidden in?"

Adele spoke not a word. She stood stiff, her body appeared frozen, and her face held no emotion. Then without a word, she turned and walked away.

Miriam tried hard to suppress the tears which threatened to fall. Peter took her hand and tried to comfort her. The three of them sat in the kitchen, talking for over an hour. When it didn't look as though Adele would join them again, they decided it was time to go.

Henry assured Miriam she had done all she could to make amends with her mother. It was now time for Miriam to move on and try to get past Adele's behavior. Henry begged his daughter not let her mother's attitude discourage her. He reminded Miriam she was finally living a contented life, and she deserved to enjoy a life of love and happiness with her new husband and daughter. "Your Mamm will have to give an account one day to our Gott for the way she has chosen to live her life. It worries me, for sure and for certain. I have asked Gott to forgive me for permitting her to behave this way for far too long. I am also asking you to forgive me. I am ever so sorry."

They all got up from the table and headed out the door. Miriam hugged her Daed. "Ich liebe dich, Daed, ever so much. And I love Mamm too. I wish she knew that. I wish you would tell me what it is she blames me for."

"Your Mamm owes you a telling, for sure and for certain. I have wished she would come to you on her own and explain it all to you. We will talk soon, I promise."

"Before Peter and I leave, jah?"

"Jah, my dochder, before you leave, I promise." He reached and hugged his daughter again, before helping her into the buggy.

Over the next couple of days, Adele refused to come out of her room much. Henry had no idea what to do. She had decided to shun him as well. She hadn't talked to him since the night of their daughter's visit when they had argued. They never had such harsh words between them in all their twenty-three years of marriage. She continued to feed her husband and complete the chores. She still slept in their bed but had no contact with Henry whatsoever.

Sunday morning, Henry Stoltzfus sat at the table. His heart was ever so heavy. Bishop Miller would heavily frown when Adele didn't show up for the Sunday preaching. He wouldn't lie for her. If the bishop or any of the preachers asked of her, he would tell them the truth. Something needed done about his wife's behavior. They would both receive a stern warning. Henry was finishing his breakfast and was drinking one last cup of kaffi when his fraa entered the kitchen dressed for church. When Henry started to speak, Adele stopped him, "Do not speak a word, Henry Stoltzfus. The only reason I'm going today is to avoid the wrath of Bishop Miller. He would place the ban on me if I didn't show up for services without having a gut reason."

Henry decided talking to his wife would prove pointless. He didn't know who she thought she was fooling. The bishop never shunned anyone for missing one Sunday preaching, even if there wasn't a good reason for missing the service. He wondered what it was she was up to, although he was sure he would know soon enough. His Adele never minced words, and she was a determined woman when it came to getting her way. He only hoped whatever it was, his wife planned, she wouldn't cause irreparable damage. Her actions had brought enough hurt to their family. After the argument they had the night of Miriam's visit, he warned her that she was driving him away, just as she had their daughter. He informed her he had tolerated her behavior long enough, and threatened to go on an extended visit to Indiana if Adele continued to treat him in a disgraceful way. He decided to ride back with Miriam and Peter if Adele hadn't made a move to mend their broken family. Miriam deserved to know the truth, and if Adele wouldn't take the initiative to explain it, then he would on the trip to Shipshewana.

The drive to the Zook farm seemed to take longer than usual. It was a quiet ride. Henry looked over at his wife several times, but her face remained hidden behind the wide brim of her bonnet. It was making him crazy; not knowing what it was she had planned. He knew, without a doubt, she was up to something. And he was out of his mind with worry over it. During the sermons, he looked over at Adele. She was staring straight ahead. He doubted she even heard what the preachers were saying. He silently prayed for God to do a work in her heart.

His mind wandered back to a time when they were happy. It seemed like a lifetime ago. Adele was a sweet, thoughtful, and beautiful girl when they were courting. Their Miriam was the spitting image of her mother at that age. It wasn't until after the tragedy that Adele's appearance seemed to transform into an aged and ragged looking woman. Her personality immediately changed that morning; she was no longer loving and caring. She became angry with her husband, her daughter, and herself. Her heart hardened, and she became someone no one wished to associate with, including her husband. If the Amish permitted divorce, the temptation might have overtaken Henry, but he felt she would eventually come around. After twenty years, Henry had learned to put up with his wife. He let her have her way and kept his distance as much as possible.

He knew it was wrong to permit her to continue in her destructive behavior. However, when he encouraged her to talk about her feelings, she went into a rage. It didn't take him long to realize his life was more peaceful if he didn't push the issue. As time went on, he hated himself for allowing his wife to poison their daughter.

When Miriam announced her wishes to leave with Benjamin Lapp for a new life in Indiana, Henry was all for it. He knew it was the only way his daughter would stand a chance at a happy life. Now here she was, married with a child of her own and radiating with contentment. Henry wished to take part in her life. He made up his mind. If his son-in-law and Miriam permitted him to go with them, he would make the trip back to Shipshewana.

When Deacon King made the announcement for everyone to bow their heads in prayer, it brought Henry's attention back to the service.

CHAPTER 15

❦

*"Remember ye not the former things, neither consider
the things of old. Behold, I will do a new thing; now it
shall spring forth; shall ye not know it? I will even make
a way in the wilderness, and rivers in the desert."*
Isaiah 43:18-19

The church service was the usual three-hour
service, which ended with the exchanging of
vows between Leah and Benjamin. Because they
were the only couple who would recite vows at
this service, the ceremony was short. The meal
would not be the ordinary wedding feast; however,
it was somewhat more elaborate than the typical
Sunday service meal.

It pleased Leah when she looked to the back
of the room and saw Lyddie, her Mamm, and all of
her sisters sitting there. On the opposite side of
the room with the other men and boys sat Blake,

Lyddie's Daed, her brothers, and her brother-in-law. Of course, they stood out from the others with their English clothing and hairstyles, but other than that, it seemed like old times.

Leah and Benjamin were both beaming with happiness. Family and friends surrounded them, congratulating and giving them their best wishes. Benjamin was impatient. He wanted some time alone with Leah, but it was clear it wouldn't happen any time soon. The celebration would last the entire day.

Once the guests had calmed down, the men gathered into their little groups to discuss the happenings since the last Sunday preaching, and the women prepared to serve the meal. Benjamin grabbed Leah's hand and pulled her to the side of her parent's house. Looking around, making sure they were out of view from all the others, he took her into his arms and kissed her. They stayed out of sight for some time, enjoying the closeness. "Benjamin, we are acting like we are still in Rumspringa and hiding our courtship from our parents."

"Ach, Leah, I feel like I am still in Rumspringa and kissing you for the first time. You don't understand how long I have waited for this. God has blessed me with the love I thought I would never have. When we were courting, I thought we would spend the rest of our lives together. And then when you turned me away, I was crushed. You are the love of my life, and I am ever so happy for this day. So I wish to have some time alone with you now that we are permitted to do so." He pulled her in tight against him and kissed her again.

"Benjamin, we must go and join the others. How will we explain our absence? Surely they have noticed we have gone missing. Do not fret so much; it won't be long before we can leave. Then we will be alone for the entire night."

"It will seem like forever, for sure and for certain."

Leah smiled and kissed his cheek. "My ehemann, be happy they will not treat as they do the other newly married couples. We wouldn't be permitted much time alone whatsoever. But tonight, my ehemann, we will spend the night alone in our own haus and not our parent's home. It will be ever so nice, jah?"

"Jah, my fraa, it will be wunderbaar gut to have you all to myself." He pulled her into his arms again.

"You two are hiding out, jah?"

Leah jumped at the voice she heard. Embarrassed, she turned to see who had caught them. She breathed a sigh of relief when she saw Rachael Miller smiling.

"Ach, I caught you two love birds hiding and making out."

"Rachael Miller, please vergeef us."

"There is nothing to forgive. I know how wunderbaar gut it feels to have some alone time. It is not something Josiah and I have the pleasure of very often with as active as Sadie is. And she shares a bedroom with us as well. So, get all the alone time you can." She lightly hit Benjamin in the upper arm. "Keep that spontaneity; it will keep the fire burning in your marriage."

With a mischievous grin, Benjamin commented. "Ach, believe me, I plan to. Leah will always feel loved, for sure and for certain."

Rachael giggled and winked at Leah. "Carry on then." Waving her hand, she walked away.

Leah and Benjamin burst out laughing. They were both relieved it was Rachael Miller who saw them and not someone who would try to cause trouble over their behavior. They needed to get back with the People before someone else caught them carrying on in such a manner.

Back among the group, Leah spotted Miriam standing alone. She looked as though she was carrying the weight of the world on her shoulders. Benjamin nudged his wife to go to Miriam and talk with her. Leah started toward Miriam. She stopped dead in her tracks when she saw Adele Stoltzfus approaching Miriam. Leah continued to watch them closely until they walked away together. When Leah was sure Miriam did not require her help, she went back to join Benjamin and the others.

"Ach, Leah that was ever so quick. What happened to you going to talk with Miriam?" He snickered. "I've never known Miriam to end a conversation so quickly."

Leah told her husband what she had witnessed and how she watched until Miriam and her mother walked into the field toward the creek.

Adele's voice was unstable when she asked her daughter if they could talk. As shocked as Miriam was, she readily agreed to a private conversation with her mother. They walked through the Zook's field in silence until they reached a secluded spot near the stream. Adele sat on a large rock at the edge of the water.

Miriam waited for her mother to say something. When it didn't seem like Adele was ever going to talk, Miriam asked, "What is it you wished to talk to me about, Mamm? Surely you didn't bring me out here so we could look at one another."

Adele licked her parched lips before speaking. "This is ever so hard for me, my maedel. Please, come and sit."

Miriam sat in the grass. "It is that bad, jah?"

"Jah, my dochder, it is that bad, for sure and for certain. It is an ever so sad telling, one I should have told you many years ago. And now, I wish I would have. We wouldn't be here today if I had more faith. I have wasted many years to hate and to anger. And I destroyed your life because of it."

"Nee, Mamm, you have not destroyed my life. I am ever so happy with my new life. I love my ehemann and Ella, and I truly like living in Indiana."

"Jah, you are happy in your new life. You could have had a gut life here had I not raised you the way I did. You could have gotten married years ago and had bopplin of your own by now."

"But, Mamm, I would not have found my Peter and Ella if I had stayed here. Like I told you, I love them ever so much, and they love me too. I never imagined I could be so happy. It is as if Gott has smiled down on me. I, for sure, do not deserve His blessings with the attitude I carried for so many years."

Adele smiled. It wasn't one of the sinister smiles Miriam had grown accustomed to over her lifetime. "I'm sorry, my maedel. I'm sorry for everything. I'm afraid your attitude is the one I forced on you. You had no choice but to behave the way I forced you to act. I asked Gott to punish me for it, not you. You were what I raised, and I am ever so ashamed of myself for never giving you a chance at a gut life here in Somerton."

"My life is gut now, so will you tell me what Daed meant about a tragedy? I wish to understand you and your anger. What happened all those years ago, Mamm?"

"You were not an only child as I have permitted you to believe. Before you were born, Daed and I had a son. Your Daed was overjoyed. He longed for a buwe. Ach, don't get me wrong he wanted a maedel too. As a matter of fact, he wished for many, many bopplin. He just hoped for a buwe first. And, our Daniel stuck to your Daed like molasses. He was always at your Daed's heels, no matter what. At night though, Daniel loved for me to lie on his bed, cuddle him, and tell him bedtime stories. But as for the daytime, he was your Daed's shadow. We loved our little buwe ever so much." Miriam watched in silence while the tears fell from her mother's eyes. She had never seen her mother cry. She also had never seen this side of her before. This woman had always been hard and unfeeling, but here she was pouring her heart out. Compassion filled Miriam's heart. She wondered how her mother kept this secret hidden for so many years. Miriam was stunned by the fact that she once had a brother. She wished she could have known him. Miriam was about to learn what happened to her brother and also the reasons behind her mother's hate and anger throughout Miriam's lifetime.

"We thought Daniel might be the only boppli the Lord would give us. It took over two years for me to conceive again. Your Daed and I were ever so happy when you came along. Your Daed had wished for a maedel from the moment he found out I was carrying another child. Your bruder loved you ever so much. He would play with you and try to get you to smile. He gave you an old faceless doll he had found in the chest at the foot of our bed. He would sit with you after supper and tell you the stories he had learned from our bedtime tellings. He would kiss you good night each night, whether you were awake or not. He refused to go to bed until he was able to kiss you and tell you he loved you."

Adele coughed and cleared her throat. She hesitated for too long. Miriam asked, "You will tell me what happened to our Daniel, jah?"

"Jah, I will. It is still ever so painful. You must understand I have never spoken of this to anyone except your Daed. And I had only spoken to him once, that just after it had happened. I have relived that dreadful morning every day since. I have blamed and hated myself all these years. But, I'm not the only one I held responsible for Daniel's death. I blamed your Daed, and my maedel, I blamed you. More so though, I faulted Gott, for losing my buwe. I blamed Him that morning, and I have charged Him every day after. For twenty years, I have continually blamed Gott for not saving my Daniel."

Adele clenched her teeth and tried not to start crying all over again. Miriam reached for her hand while speaking in a compassionate voice. "Mamm, I believe talking about it will make you feel ever so gut. And, I also believe Gott gave us our tears as a cleansing. So, go ahead and cry Mamm. It will do you a world of good. I can't imagine the weight this grief has caused you to carry."

"We will see how gut it makes me feel, my maedel. I have carried this burden for so long now; I can't imagine anything making me feel better about what happened that morning."

"Go ahead, Mamm, please, tell me about the morning my bruder died."

Adele nodded. "I had been ever so sick with a headache. It had lasted for days. Your Daed's sister suggested I see an English doctor, but the thought of going to see an Englisher made me ever so uncomfortable. I sent for the baby catcher to see what she had to say. Ella Mae showed up and listened to what my symptoms were. She called it a *migraine headache* and would normally suggest I take in more caffeine. But I was nursing you, and we didn't wish to put you in danger. I had the headache for days, and it wasn't getting any better. The pain wore my body down, and I was ever so tired. Daniel had just turned three, and you were only a month old. I had been trying to get the morning meal made, but wasn't making much progress with all the vomiting I was doing. Daniel was hungry, so I gave him some eggs and a biscuit. I told him he would have to wait until I was able to cut his ham into small pieces for him. You were crying and ever so hungry too. I told

Daniel to eat his eggs, and I would get him his ham as soon as I finished feeding you. I left him at the table to eat while I went into the living room to nurse you. You hadn't much more than started nursing when I heard a crash in the kitchen. I called out to Daniel. When he didn't answer, I carried you out to the kitchen. The chair Daniel had sat on was on the floor, and he was lying beside it. His face was turning a strange color of blue. I laid you on the floor and grabbed him. I beat on his back, and then I reached my finger in his mouth, but couldn't find anything. I beat on his back again, but nothing happened. I screamed and screamed for your Daed. He came running into the kitchen and took Daniel from me. He worked to clear Daniel's throat. He couldn't save Daniel any more than I could. Our Daniel was dead. He choked to death on a piece of ham."

Adele was sobbing uncontrollably. Miriam held her mother in her arms. Once Adele was able to gain control again, she continued, "I blamed myself for leaving Daniel alone. If I had taken the time to cut up some ham for him, he would not have climbed up to the stove and got it for himself. I blamed your Daed for being so late coming in to eat his breakfast that morning. If he had been at the table, he would have been able to watch Daniel and help him with cutting up his food. I'm ever so sorry my maedel, but I have also blamed you all these years. I blamed you for crying and demanding to nurse at that very moment. Your next feeding wasn't for another hour, but for some reason, you woke up early. My mindset was if you had only waited an hour longer, my Daniel would still have been with us. And, then there's Gott. I have blamed Him because, after all, He is all-powerful and all-knowing, and He could have prevented it all. Gott took our Daniel from us, and I vowed never to forgive Him, for sure and for certain."

"Ach, Mamm, it saddens me you have held on to this for so many years. Does this mean you have forgiven yourself, and let go of the anger and hate you have had for Daed, me, and Gott?"

"Jah, my dochder, I have. It took losing you to realize I have wasted so many years being angry, and quite frankly, I have been a miserable person, to put it mildly." Adele gave a slight chuckle.

Miriam rose to her feet again and hugged her mother. "Mamm, you haven't lost me. I'm here. I came home hoping we could talk, hoping you would be happy for me, and hoping you would accept and love me for me. Ach, Mamm, I like the new me. Please, tell me you will try to love me again?"

"Ach, my maedel, I have always loved you. Even as you grew inside me, I loved you. I was afraid to show it for fear Gott would take you from me too. I have been ever so wrong, and I am so ashamed of myself. I have asked Gott to vergeef me, and now I am asking you to forgive me as well. You will forgive me, jah?"

"Jah, Mamm, I forgive you."

"Has your Daed talked to you about going back to Shipshewana with you and your ehemann?"

Miriam's expression saddened, she looked to the ground. "Jah, Mamm, he has. Do you really think he would up and leave you behind, for sure, and for certain?"

"Jah, my dochder, I do. And, who could blame him? I have treated him with such disrespect. I fear I will never be able to make it up to him. I pray your Daed will be as forgiving as you have been."

"I believe he will forgive you the moment you ask if he hasn't already. Ach, Mamm, let's go back and join the others. You need to talk with Daed, and I wish for you to get to know my Peter and Ella. You will love them ever so much."

Adele stood to her feet, took her daughter's hand, and together they walked back through the field. As they walked, Adele continued confiding in her Miriam. "I would, for sure and for certain, like nothing more than to go back to Indiana with you and your Peter. I wish to spend time with you and my new granddaughter. I wish to help you when you start having bopplin of your own. I do not want to miss out on your new life."

Miriam leaned into her mother's shoulder, "Our new life, Mamm. Why don't you and Daed come home with us? You could live in our daadi haus, and Daed could work the farm with Peter."

"That sounds wunderbaar gut. However, I feel it would be best for me to stay put, at least for now. I have to make amends to the People here. And I must make a public confession in front of the church."

"Ach, not so, Mamm. Bishop Miller has never disciplined you or placed the ban on you, so there is no reason for you to make a public confession."

"The bishop should have disciplined me years ago. And, although he never enforced Meidung on me, I still know what I did was wrong. Nee, it is true, the bishop will not require a public confession; nevertheless, it is something which I feel I must do. You understand, jah?"

"Jah, I understand. Ach, Mamm, I love you ever so much. It is a gut decision you have made, for sure and for certain. Promise me you and Daed will come to visit, and if you both like it in Shipshewana, please say you will think about coming to live with us."

"We will come for a visit, for sure and for certain. And I can see us coming to live there too, but I will make no promises about how soon it will be. Bishop Miller will have to approve the move, and so would your bishop." She gave a quick laugh. "But, then again, I guess we already have your bishop's approval. How is it being married to the bishop of your district?"

"Ach, Mamm, it is ever so wunderbaar. My Peter is more loving than I could have ever imagined. And our Ella is crazy about me too. I can't envision my life without them."

Adele raised her eyebrows in surprise. "I see your vocabulary has broadened since leaving me. I suppose that is a gut thing." They continued walking arm in arm back to the house.

The meal was well underway when they returned. The men had finished eating. And the women now sat around the tables, talking and eating. As hungry as Adele and Miriam were, they went to find Henry and Peter instead of joining the others to eat. The four of them chatted for a while before Leah and Benjamin brought Ella over to meet her Grossmudder. Adele was in tears when Ella hugged her and wanted the woman to hold her. Before Adele put her down to join the other children, Ella hugged her neck again and spoke. "Ich liebe dich, Grossmudder Stoltzfus." They all laughed at her mispronunciation of the name, before Adele replied, "I love you too, my maedel."

CHAPTER 16

ഗ്രൂ

*"Do not let my heart turn to any evil thing or perform
wicked acts with men who commit sin. Do not let me
feast on their delicacies.*
Psalm 141:4

The festivities were finally winding down, which
pleased Benjamin. He finally convinced Leah
to say goodbye so they could be on their way.

The evening breeze felt good on Benjamin's
face. Leah, on the other hand, snuggled closer to
her ehemann as a chill went through her. She
liked the feel of being close to him. He kissed her
forehead, and Leah whispered, "Let's hurry home,
my ehemann."

He grinned mischievously. "That's what I've
been trying to do all day, my fraa." He made a
clicking noise to get the horse moving faster.

As they pulled up to the barn, it surprised them to see another buggy sitting close to the house. It shocked Benjamin to see Elmo and Greta Glick. They didn't attend Leah and Benjamin's ceremony that morning. It didn't surprise him in the least, but to see them sitting at his house left him confused. Annie's parents didn't have anything to do with Benjamin since the fire that killed their daughter. Benjamin asked, "Wie geht's, Elmo Glick?"

Taking his wife's hand, Elmo answered. "We need to talk to you, Benjamin Lapp."

Benjamin was understandably curious. Annie's parents blamed Benjamin for their daughter's death. The last time they spoke to him was the day he told them about Annie's death.

"Come into the haus, and we will talk, jah?"

"Nee, Benjamin Lapp, this does not concern Leah Beiler, We will talk to you in private."

"It is Leah Lapp now. But then, you already knew that, or you would have attended the preaching this morning. Nevertheless, she is my fraa, and if you have something you wish to talk about, you will discuss it with both of us."

Elmo Glick protested but to no avail. Benjamin stood firm on his decision. Leah would sit in on their visit, or there would be no conversation at all. Elmo eventually gave in, and he and his wife followed Benjamin and Leah into the house.

Leah was the perfect host, offering drinks and snacks which Elmo and Greta refused. Leah poured Benjamin a glass of lemonade. All the while, wondering why the Glick's would choose now of all times to come for a visit. She sat at the table beside Benjamin, waiting for Elmo Glick to tell them the reason for their visit. Her mind trailed off. *"They couldn't have picked a worse time to come for a visit. Have they come to ruin our wedding day?"* She wished for him to say what was on his mind and be on their way. It was not how she pictured her wedding night, for sure and for certain.

Benjamin scratched his forehead. "Something tells me you are not here for a pleasant visit, Elmo Glick. Please, just come out and say what is on your mind so we can take care of it, and you can go on your way. Neither of you have spoken a word to me since the day you accused me of letting your dochder die."

Leah gasped. "Ach, say it is not so? He ran back into that burning house to save your Annie. You did not see Benjamin the night of the fire. He almost died himself, trying to save Annie. He took in so much smoke and the burns on his hands were horrible and were proof he did not give up on his fraa."

Benjamin placed his hand on Leah's to calm her. His blue eyes held such love for her. She took a deep breath and slowly released it. "Vergeef me, Benjamin."

Greta Glick let out a loud grunt. "It was no secret to me that Benjamin Lapp was in love with you when he married my Annie. She had told me all about it long ago. She also told me his heart broke for you when you lost your ehemann. It seems awful strange that after you lost your husband and was free to marry again that my dochder dies in a fire. She was the only one who lost her life that night. How is it the kinner and

Benjamin Lapp got out, but not my Annie?" She was now sobbing uncontrollably. Her ehemann put his arm around her shoulder as to comfort her.

Since Greta Glick talked such nonsense, Leah felt it was only fair they listened while she spoke her piece. She held nothing back as she let the Glick's know what was on her mind. She finished with, "You both should feel such shame for thinking these despicable thoughts. I believe your grief has blinded you to the truth." Shaking her head, she added. "Gott help both of you."

When Leah finished, Benjamin spoke. "I am ever so sorry you feel that way, Greta. It is obvious you never heard the truth about how your dochder ended up back in the house. Do you wish to hear what happened that horrible night?"

Elmo spoke abruptly. Nee, Benjamin Lapp, we do not wish to hear anything you have to say about our Annie's death."

Trying to show no emotion, Benjamin turned to Elmo and spoke directly to him. "Then tell me, exactly what is it you want, Elmo Glick?"

"We wish to have our grandchildren."

A deafening silence fell over the room. Benjamin finally shrugged his shoulders and asked, "And?"

"And nothing, that is it. We wish to have our grandchildren."

"You have not had any dealings with them all these months. And now, out of the blue, you wish to take them from me?"

Leah shrieked. "Nee, you simply want to visit them, jah?"

Benjamin turned to Leah. "Nee, Leah, they wish to take them from me."

Leah's tears fell. "They cannot take the kinner, right Benjamin?"

He squeezed her hand. "Nee, Leah, do not worry, they cannot take them."

Elmo became defensive. "They are our Annie's bopplin, and we have a right to them."

It took all the power Benjamin could muster not to lose his temper with his former in-laws. He took a long deep breath and held it. When Benjamin finally released it, he spoke in a firm voice. "Elmo Glick, the bopplin are my flesh and blood, too. Ever since their Mamm's death, you have ignored them at the Sunday preaching and the community meals. You could have visited them anytime you wished. But not once did you try to see them. It was you, Elmo Glick, who refused to permit me or my kinner to live with you after the fire. Even after I said I would find another place to sleep, you still refused to keep my bopplin. So tell me, why is it, after all this time, you wish to take them away from me?"

"You have a new fraa, and together you can have bopplin of your own. These are our Annie's kinner, not Leah's."

Benjamin was slowly losing his patience. "Leah opened her home and her heart to my kinner when you would not. She has done everything for them. They have loved her and have come to think of her as their mudder. Leah loves Beth, Katie, and Caleb as though they were her flesh and blood."

Elmo's fist came down hard on the table. "She is not their mudder."

Benjamin pushed his chair back and stood up. "We are finished here. If you wish to continue with this nonsense, we will discuss it with the bishop present. You will leave now."

Benjamin took Leah's hand, and together they followed Elmo and Greta Glick out the door. Before they stepped off the porch, Greta spoke out. "Beth is not your dochder. She belonged to our Annie. She told me she was with child before you and she married. Therefore, we have every right to take Beth with us. She does not belong to either of you."

Elmo Glick almost fell down the porch steps. He looked to his wife in total shock. It was clear his wife had never told her husband about their daughter's affair with the Englisher. Elmo quickly tried to regain his composure.

Benjamin was on the verge of losing his temper with this couple. Leah reached and touched her husband's arm, hoping to calm him down. "I refuse to discuss this matter with you. We will finish this conversation in the presence of the bishop. You will leave now."

Once the Glick's were on their way, Leah cried out. "Ach, Benjamin, what are we to do?"

"Nothing. It is our wedding night, and I do not want any more of it spoiled for you."

"Nee, Benjamin, we cannot enjoy our night with this hanging over our heads. We need to see Bishop Miller, and then we must get Beth, Katie, and Caleb from my parents. You don't think Elmo and Greta Glick will try to take them from my parent's care, do you?"

Benjamin pulled Leah into his arms and held her tight. "Ach, my fraa, I am ever so sorry about all of this. I never imagined Elmo and Greta would try to pull such an act. I believe you are right though, this will eat away at us all night, and it will make for a miserable wedding night." They headed back over to the buggy. Benjamin helped Leah in, and they drove to the bishop's house.

After explaining the reason for their visit, the bishop suggested they all make a call on Elmo and Greta Glick.

Once inside the Glick home, Bishop Miller did the talking for Benjamin. He scolded Elmo and Greta Glick for taking such matters into their own hands. He reminded Elmo such behavior could result in discipline. When the bishop finished speaking, Elmo demanded to have his say. Bishop Miller honored his request.

"Benjamin Lapp was in love with Leah Zook when he married my Annie. She told us so herself. Do you not find it strange that not long after Leah's ehemann died, our Annie mysteriously dies in a fire in which Benjamin and the kinner survive? Then, he moves his kinner and himself next door to Leah Beiler's haus. And, now they are man and wife. He let our Annie die so he could be with Leah Beiler. Where was your discipline when all of this happened, Bishop Miller? Why were they not disciplined for carrying on together all these months?"

The bishop spoke in a comforting manner. "Elmo Glick, do you hear what you are saying? Do you truly believe this of Benjamin Lapp? You did not see him after the fire, but I did. Had you seen him, you would not be making such outlandish accusations. Confused, Annie ran back into the burning house to find her dead buwe. When Benjamin went in after her, he almost lost his own life. He could not save her. You have to let it go and move on. It was an unfortunate accident. You must let go of your hate and your anger. Gott is not pleased with such behavior. You have blamed Benjamin Lapp and his kinner for living while your Annie perished. It is time to let Gott heal your broken heart. Your Greta came to me after Annie and Benjamin became published. She knew Annie did not love Benjamin, and she was concerned the only reason for the union between the two of them was Annie was already with child. She had carried on with an Englisher. I talked with both Annie and Benjamin before they were to marry, and they both assured me they wished to marry and have a family together. After I married them, Annie realized she was not carrying the Englisher's child, after all. They had a gut marriage and had a certain amount of love and respect for each other. Greta, did your Annie ever confide in you anything different?"

Greta continued looking at the floor and shook her head to signal Annie had not confided anything being wrong in the marriage. She knew, once everyone left, her ehemann would be scolding her for keeping such secrets from him.

"As for your accusation about Benjamin not being Beth's Daed, you are ever so wrong and surely blind. Why the maedel is the spitting image of Benjamin. And now, I will address the charges you have unfairly made against Benjamin Lapp and Leah Beiler. You will apologize immediately or face harsh punishment. You know better than to think these two have done anything wrong. I will give you one week to think about the wrong you have caused here. At that time, you will either make the apology or suffer the consequences."

Elmo Glick lowered his head. He had no idea his dochder was in love with someone else when she had married Benjamin Lapp. And they had always seemed happy together. His Annie had always praised her ehemann for being so helpful with the kinner all the time. He supposed she did have a wunderbaar gut life with him. She had been different after the death of their buwe. Annie became depressed and sometimes talked about the buwe as though he was still alive. Her death could have happened the way Benjamin said it did. And he did come to them after the fire asking for a place to stay.

After a few minutes of silence, he looked at the bishop. "I do not need a week. Please forgive me for being ever so high-handed, Bishop Miller." With a remorseful look, he then spoke to Benjamin. "I am ever so sorry I have accused you of such horrible acts. Please forgive me, Benjamin Lapp. Forgive me for blaming you and for blaming the kinner too. I do hope you will permit us to visit with the kinner now and again."

Benjamin tried to speak as calmly as he could. He knew he had to accept Elmo Glick's apology. However, he was still somewhat angry for Elmo lashing out at Leah the way he did.

"I forgive you. However, it will take some time for me to get past the anger I have for you treating my new fraa with such disrespect. The kinner do need to get reacquainted with you."

Elmo nodded his head. "I understand your anger, I would be angry too if you treated my fraa the way I treated Leah." He then looked at Leah. "I truly am sorry, Leah Lapp. It was never about you. I only wished to punish Benjamin and the kinner for my Annie's death. I felt I needed to blame someone, and I was afraid to blame Gott. You will forgive me, jah?"

Leah's face was red with embarrassment. She kept her head lowered and softly said. "Jah, I forgive you."

It was now Greta's turn to speak. "Leah Lapp, please forgive me. I am ever so glad my grandchildren have a mudder to raise them. You have been ever so kind as to take them in and love them. You were right when you said it was my grief talking. I shocked myself at the way I spoke to you. I know you understand the pain I feel over losing my Annie. I am sure it is the same pain you have felt yourself over the loss of your ehemann. I am ever so sorry I permitted the pain I felt to bring such disrespect to you." When Leah smiled at the woman, Greta Glick reached out and hugged Leah.

The bishop left, and the four of them continued to talk for a while. Benjamin convinced Leah the kinner would be gut with her parents for the night. If she was still worried about being away from them, they could pick them up in the morning.

Leah thought about the events of the day. Elmo and Greta Glick were no different from anyone else. They dealt with death in much the same way Benjamin and Leah had. They had all forgotten their Amish instruction. Their teachings included being quick to forgive and slow to anger. The Bible teaches about forgiving others and about letting go of anger. And yet, not one of them acted in a way that was pleasing to God. Nevertheless, anger and hatred are most definitely emotions each person has felt at some point in their lifetime. She supposed even with the strict ways of the People, they were merely human and bound to make mistakes, sin, and displease God at times. She was thankful Jesus came and paid the debt for their sins. The thought of living with Him throughout eternity left Leah awestruck.

"What is my fraa so deep in thought about this night?"

"Ach, I was thinking about our day, and how each of us handles tragedy when it comes into our lives. You know Benjamin; Elmo and Greta Glick really didn't react any different to their Annie's death than you or I did when we lost our spouses. I wish they would have come to you sooner. Beth may remember them, but I am sure the twins have no idea they are their grandparents. They have lost so much precious time with the kinner over the hate and anger they felt. It puzzles me how they could blame the bopplin for the death of their dochder, though."

"Leah, can we please not discuss this anymore tonight? It is our wedding night, and I had hoped to make it special for you. On second thought, if it is bothering you, then we should talk about it."

Leah snuggled closer to him. "We do not need to discuss it. I was letting my thoughts run wild." She looked up at him and smiled. "Can you make the horse go faster?"

Benjamin slapped the reins and clicked his tongue. The horse responded and started to trot.

Soon they were back at the barn again. Leah insisted if she helped with the horse and buggy, they could finish the chore much quicker.

As they were walking up to the house, Benjamin's stomach growled loudly. They both giggled at the loud noise. "Ach, I guess I had better feed you, my ehemann, or you will think I am a terrible fraa."

"I would never think such a thought. Gott has blessed me abundantly, Leah. I have thanked him for the many wunderbaar gut gifts He has given me. I am ever so happy." He took her into his arms and kissed her.

"We best get inside. Do we wish to have someone see us behaving in such a way out in the open?"

"Jah, I suppose it would not be a gut thing to get caught a second time today."

Once they had finished eating, Benjamin leaned back in his chair. "Why don't you leave the dishes until morning?"

Teasingly, she replied. "Ach, it is not a gut way to start our marriage, by leaving a dirty haus."

He stood to his feet and pulled Leah to hers. He looked down into her eyes so lovingly. He kissed her. When he pulled away, she begged for another kiss. "So this means you will leave the dishes, jah?"

"Jah, that is what it means, for sure and for certain."

The following morning, as they held each other, they decided not to go to the beach as they had planned. Staying close to home felt right. The bed and breakfast over in Bird in Hand sounded like a better plan. It would still give them time alone, but they wouldn't be far from the children. They would make the trip to the beach, but it would be a trip they would take as a family.

CHAPTER 17
ళ్మిళ్

*"These things I have spoken unto you, that in me ye
might have peace. In the world ye shall have
tribulation: but be of good cheer; I have overcome the
world."*
John 16:33

Several months had passed when Leah began
to think she was with child. She had floated
on a cloud all day, thinking about a child growing
inside her body. The children were all tucked into
their beds for the night. And Leah had finished
the chores for the day. She thought it was the
perfect night to watch the stars.

She stood at the edge of the porch, looking
out into the night. The full moon illuminated the
evening sky. She watched the stars twinkling as if
they were winking at her. She was in awe as a
meteor streaked across the universe. The cool
breeze threatened to pull her prayer kapp loose

from her hair. She repositioned her hairpins. Benjamin startled her when he came up from behind and wrapped his arms around her waist.

"Ach, vergeef me, my fraa, I didn't intend to scare you. I only wished to hold you. Being close to you brings me the greatest joy."

Leah put her hands on Benjamin's and leaned her head back, resting it on his chest. He reached down and kissed her neck. "Look at this sky, Benjamin. It is magnificent, jah?"

"Jah, it is a beautiful night indeed." He held her a little tighter.

"I watched a shooting star as it raced across the sky. Have you ever seen such a sight?"

"Nee, my fraa, I have never had the pleasure of seeing such a great wonder. But then again, until recently, I never paid the evening sky much attention. You have given me an appreciation for it. I have never *stargazed* as you put it. I used to think it was such a waste of precious time, but now I find it ever so relaxing. Especially when you permit me to hold you while we watch the stars."

After a few moments of silence, Benjamin cleared his throat and asked, "You are going to share with me what has occupied your thoughts all day, jah?"

"What do you mean?"

"Come now, Leah, you have had a look of pure joy on your face as you walked around here today. It is as if you were expecting something—." Benjamin abruptly stopped speaking.

"Go ahead, as if I were expecting what?"

"Leah, are you expecting a boppli?"

"I'm not sure. Would it make you happy if I was expecting?"

"If it makes you happy, then it would make me happy too. Do you wish to come and sit for a time and rock with me?"

"Jah, I would like that."

Benjamin held his arm around Leah as they rocked together until they both dozed off.

The following afternoon, during their lunch date, Leah confided in Lyddie of her suspicion. Lyddie suggested Leah take a pregnancy test. Leah was uncomfortable with the idea but promised to think about it. Lyddie assured her she would get the test for Leah and explain how the test worked if she decided to try it.

Leah spent the next few days thinking about the pregnancy test. She had never heard of such a thing. Surely the Lord would not be against such a test, or Lyddie would never have suggested Leah purchase one. The bishop would, without a doubt, disapprove of it. Benjamin would most likely frown on it as well. Leah made up her mind to tell Lyddie she felt uncomfortable going against what she knew the bishop would oppose. Lyddie had, after all, been Amish at one time; surely she would understand Leah's position on the matter.

The women had made plans for lunch the following afternoon. Lyddie no longer taught in the one-room Amish schoolhouse, so she had free time these days to enjoy their lunches together.

Leah woke earlier than usual with cramping in her abdomen. She was confident her body was telling her she was not pregnant. Lyddie's test wouldn't be necessary now. She was happy she wouldn't have to tell Lyddie she would not go against the bishop's wishes and use the test.

Leah shared the disheartening news with Lyddie as they sipped their lemonade. The server finished taking their lunch orders and left them to continue their conversation.

"Ach, Lyddie, maybe I'm not meant to have bopplin. I mean, I never got pregnant with Adam. And now, it looks as though Benjamin and I won't have a boppli together either. I'm not angry with the thought. I am ever so grateful Gott has blessed me with my Benjamin, Beth, Katie, and Caleb. I am genuinely happy, and if I never have a boppli, I can accept that. I'm ever so glad Benjamin already has a son. I feel it will help him overcome the grief of me not being able to give him anymore kinner."

Lyddie smiled at her friend, "Oh Leah, what a wonderful attitude you have. I am so happy you have peace in God to accept whatever His will is for you and your Benjamin. You have grown so deep in your faith. I know you will lean on Him for whatever life throws at you." She took a drink from her glass. "Have you told Benjamin you're not pregnant?" Leah shook her head, telling Lyddie she had not told her husband. "So you haven't discussed any of this with your Benjamin? Did you tell him you thought you were pregnant?"

Again Leah shook her head no. "Not really. When he asked, I told him I wasn't sure."

"Leah, you need to talk to him and tell him about your concerns. I know pregnancy issues are not something Amish women normally talk about with the men. Nevertheless, I know Benjamin Lapp, and I believe you and he can discuss it openly."

"I believe you are right." She reached and touched Lyddie's arm. "I have been able to freely talk to my Benjamin about anything. I will discuss it all with him tonight, for sure, and for certain."

The two finished their food, hugged, and said their farewells. Leah was left alone with her thoughts. She steered the horse toward home. It concerned Leah how Benjamin might react to the possibility that she may never give birth to his babies. They had never talked about having more children, but then again, it wasn't something the Amish discussed. It was a known fact that the Amish produce babies.

Nearly all Amish families consisted of eight to ten children. Large families were what kept the district growing. The Amish culture's survival depended on each woman producing many babies. In earlier times, the other women would have looked down on Leah if she was not able to give her husband many children. Times had somewhat changed, however. Being looked down on, by the People, didn't bother Leah in the least. It was her husband's opinion of her that mattered. She would know his feelings soon enough. She only hoped Benjamin could get beyond the disappointment if she could never give him a child.

Leah kept herself busy the rest of the afternoon, scrubbing her floors. Once Beth, Katie, and Caleb woke from their naps, she didn't have time to think about anything. She gladly took the time to play with them out in the warm sun.

After the evening meal was over, and she finished the chores, Leah sunk into her rocking chair, exhausted. She was thankful Benjamin was entertaining the children. Leah watched as they built a house with their blocks. They were having fun as their blockhouse grew taller. Benjamin had been adding to his son's block collection for some time now. It had kept him busy during the winter months, making different shapes for Caleb. He would have to stop making them, though. They were running out of places to store them.

When Leah announced it was time for bed, the kids begged to leave the house standing. She agreed it could stay and they could finish it the following evening.

Together, Benjamin and Leah got the three ready for bed and tucked them in tight. It was the twins turn to hear a story from Leah, while Benjamin read a bedtime story to Beth.

As Leah got ready for bed, Benjamin approached her. "Ach, my fraa, are you not feeling gut tonight? You have seemed so tired today, and you didn't join in with the kinner's playtime."

"I am gut. I do, however, have something weighing heavy on my mind, and I need to talk to you about it."

Benjamin went to his wife, hugged her, and encouraged her to tell him whatever it was that was bothering her. "Leah, you know you can talk with me about anything, no matter what the subject is, jah?"

"Jah, Benjamin, I do, and for that, I am ever so thankful." She took a deep breath and continued. "I'm so sorry, my ehemann, I am not pregnant. I thought I might be, but I wanted to make sure before I told you. I wasn't trying to hold the truth from you."

He held his wife close. "You were truthful. You said you weren't sure if you were going to have a boppli." He sympathized with his wife. Even though it didn't matter to him if they had any more children, he thought it was agony for Leah.

"Ach, my fraa, I do not mean to make light of your suffering, I don't know what to say."

"Benjamin, there's more than me not being pregnant. And trust me; it is not my emotions talking. I truly fear I will never give you a boppli. After all this time, I haven't gotten pregnant. When Adam was alive, I thought it was because we were always so busy, and we wished to hold off until we got the farm in order. But now, I'm not so sure that was the problem."

"I wish you wouldn't have carried this worry for so long. Leah, it's all in Gott's hands. I know every woman wishes to have a boppli of her own, and if you become pregnant, I will be happy for you to have that experience."

"Do you not wish for more kinner?"

Ach, Leah, I watch you around here each day. You are ever so busy with the three we now have. I feel somewhat selfish for thinking another boppli will take much more energy. I have come to enjoy our quiet evenings spent together. I, for sure, do not wish to give them up."

"I will always make time for you, my ehemann."

"It truly isn't only about me and my selfish wishes. More bopplin means you will have to do so much more work around here. I wish for you to have time with your pups, your chickens, and I know you enjoy selling your goods to the bakery.

It will take much more energy from you if we have many more bopplin. I know it's our way to have many kinner, but I remember watching it drain the life from my Mamm. I watched her get sick and lose the will to live. I do not wish for you to have so many kinner that you have no time to take care of yourself. I do wish for you to experience what the women call *the joy of childbirth* if it is what you want." He kissed his wife's neck again and continued to hold her tightly.

When Leah didn't add anything more, Benjamin asked, "Leah, will you be any less content with our life if we do not have any more bopplin?"

Smiling up at him, she replied. "Nee, as long as you are gut with us not having more bopplin, then I am gut with it too. We have been so blessed. So as you have said, *it is in Gott's hands*, and we will leave it in Gott's hands and wait to see what He has in store for us."

Leah and Benjamin celebrated their first wedding anniversary. Benjamin arranged for them to go out for a nice meal. Lyddie and Blake came and drove them to their favorite restaurant in Bird in Hand. Then they dropped them off at the bed and breakfast there, while they kept the kids for the night. It has been a *wunderbaar gut* year for Leah and her family. There were times when Leah struggled, and times of confusion as well, but Leah did her best to keep focused on the Lord and the goal at hand. Whenever a dark cloud arose in their lives, she reminded herself of the saying Delia Daniels had hanging on the wall in her bakery. "The darkest hour comes before the dawn." It had taken Leah time to realize what the quote meant. Now she understood it was similar to the Bible's teaching. We may have to cry through some things in life, but joy will come after all the crying. Lyddie told Leah, "To me, this quote is saying, *when we are at our lowest point, God shows up.*" And Leah believes this with her whole heart.

THE END

GLOSSARY

Ach—Oh
Aenti—Aunt
Aldi—girlfriend
Boppli/bopplin—Baby/Babies
Bruder—Brother
Buwe—Boy
Daed—Dad
Danki—Thank you
Dochder—Daughter
Dumm Kopp—Dunce
Ehemann—Husband
Englisher—Anyone not Amish
Fraa—Wife/Woman
Gott—God
Grossdaadi—Grandfather
Grossmudder—Grandmother
Gut—Good
Haus—House
Ich liebe dich—I love you
Jah—Yes
Kinner—Children
Liebchen—My love
Maedel—Girl
Mamm/Mudder—Mom/Mother
Meidung/Shun—Harsh punishment/to ignore
Narrish—Crazy
Nee—No
Ordnung—Written and unwritten rules
Pacifist—One who believes violence is unjustifiable
Plain/People—Amish
Published—Engaged
Rumspringa—Time of freedom/Running around years
Schweschder—Sister
Telling—Story
Vergeef—Forgive
Verhuddelt—Confused
Waar kom je?—Where are you?
Wunderbaar—wonderful

ABOUT THE AUTHOR

Amy Case (born Nellis) hails from the small country town of Emporium, Pennsylvania. Her journey in life took its start in rural Pennsylvania. However, she has lived in several states and has traveled over much of the United States. Amy and her husband, Jackie, make their home in Middle Tennessee, near the Ethridge Amish communities. The peaceful countryside of the area seemingly brings inspiration for more stories. The passion for writing has remained with Amy since her childhood. Amy is the author of two previously released novels, The Journey of Lyddie Fisher and Enduring Strength.

Made in the USA
Monee, IL
02 August 2020